THE TRUTH ABOUT THE ACCIDENT

BOOKS BY NICOLE TROPE

My Daughter's Secret

The Boy in the Photo

The Nowhere Girl

The Life She Left Behind

The Girl Who Never Came Home

Bring Him Home

The Family Across the Street

The Mother's Fault

The Stepchild

His Other Wife

The Foster Family

The Stay-at-Home Mother

NICOLE TROPE

THE TRUTH ABOUT THE ACCIDENT

GRAND
CENTRAL

NEW YORK   BOSTON

Grand Central Publishing
Hachette Book Group
1290 Avenue of the Americas, New York, NY 10104
grandcentralpublishing.com
twitter.com/grandcentralpub

Originally published in trade paperback and ebook in June 2023
by Bookouture, an imprint of StoryFire Ltd., Carmelite House,
50 Victoria Embankment, London EC4Y 0DZ

First Grand Central Trade Paperback Edition: December 2023

Grand Central Publishing is a division of Hachette Book Group, Inc. The Grand Central Publishing name and logo is a trademark of Hachette Book Group, Inc.

The publisher is not responsible for websites (or their content)
that are not owned by the publisher.

The Hachette Speakers Bureau provides a wide range of authors for speaking events. To find out more, go to hachettespeakersbureau.com or email HachetteSpeakers@hbgusa.com.

Grand Central Publishing books may be purchased in bulk for business, educational, or promotional use. For information, please contact your local bookseller or the Hachette Book Group Special Markets Department at special.markets@hbgusa.com.

Library of Congress Cataloging-in-Publication Data has been applied for.

ISBN: 978-1-5387-6716-0 (trade paperback)

Printed in the United States of America

LSC-C

Printing 1, 2023

For Christina Demosthenous, editor extraordinaire and friend.
Thank you.

PROLOGUE

The first time I saw him, I finally felt the fluttering of butterflies inside me that romance novels talk about.

I had never felt that before. Truthfully, I didn't believe it existed.

Beautiful women flower everywhere, but a beautiful man is a rare find. Lots of men are good-looking. Few are truly beautiful. But he is.

He is a Greek god made flesh, someone who could have been carved from marble, Narcissus come to life, from his large hands with neat fingernails to his broad shoulders under a tight black shirt. And his eyes... green jewels in his face. I wanted to giggle when I looked at him. That was the only reaction I could muster, as I bit my lip and walked past him with a nod of my head.

"It's a lovely day, isn't it?" he said, his voice a low rumble that proclaimed the perfect maleness of its owner.

The sun was shining although it was the middle of winter and there was an icy chill in the air, so I agreed with him, stifling my giggle when he smiled. There was nothing about him that wasn't perfection and so what happened between us was inevitable really.

And I suppose, when the truth of who he was came out, what happened then was inevitable as well.

I've never felt such instant attraction or love for a man. I wanted him to be mine, all mine all the time.

I still want him to be mine.

And I'm going to make that happen.

I'm going to take back what was taken from me.

ONE

Wednesday, 11:30 a.m.

"Police, fire, or ambulance?"

"Hi, yes, I don't know. I'm not sure really. I don't know who I need. There's no fire, I mean. Obviously there's no fire because of the rain."

"Can you tell me why you've called emergency services today, sir?

"There was an accident, I mean. . . a pedestrian was hit. I saw him get hit."

"Right, and what is your location?"

"I was in Park Hills, but I'm closer to Campton Grove now."

"So, to confirm, you're still driving?"

"Yeah."

"And were you involved in the accident?"

"No, God no, of course not. I would have pulled over if I hit him, but I didn't hit him. I don't know who did. I was waiting to turn right and this guy just ran across the road in front of all the other cars and I saw him get hit by one of them. The light had turned green, so everyone was already moving. I don't know

why he did it. I really think I saw him get hit, but the rain is so
heavy it's hard to see anything at all. But I definitely heard the
sound of it, I mean, the sound of his body hitting the car, but
there was. . . there was a thunderclap at the same time. I'm just
not sure, but I had to phone just in case."

"Do you have any information on the car that hit him?
Make, model, color?"

"I don't know. I think it was the car that was in the lane next
to mine. But honestly, it was at the front or nearly the front of
the queue and I was three cars away from the traffic light so. . . it
wasn't really easy to see. It um. . . it was definitely blue—not
dark blue but more sky blue. That's why I noticed it—it's odd to
see a light blue car and it was a sedan of some sort, I think. But
like I say, I'm not entirely sure. I just didn't want him to be left
there in case no one else saw."

"And can you give me the name of the street where the accident happened and the nearest cross street if possible?"

"I was on Williamsburg Road; you know the road with four
lanes? Near um. . . Cook Avenue."

"And the car that hit him didn't stop?"

"I don't think so. To be honest I didn't actually see.
Everyone was moving slowly and I was concentrating on the car
in front of me. . . because of the rain."

"So just to clarify, you're not sure someone did get hit."

"I'm not entirely sure but I'm fairly sure."

"Did you see who was driving the car that you think hit the
pedestrian?"

"There was a woman driving. I mean, I assume it was a
woman—it looked like a woman from behind, but. . . Shit, I
missed my turnoff. I have to go."

"Can I have your name, sir?"

"Sir?"

"Hello?"

Wednesday, 11:31 a.m.

"Police, fire, or ambulance?"

"Yes, I believe it would be the police and I'm quite sure that an ambulance is needed as well. I'm in the traffic heading toward the big pub in Park Hills and. . . Turn left here, Gerald."

"Sorry, did you say you need an ambulance?"

"Not me, dear, the man who got hit by a car at the intersection of Williamsburg Road and Cook Avenue. I saw it happen, saw the whole thing, and I'm not sure what happened after he got hit because the light changed and everyone moved and I told Gerald to wait but then the person behind us beeped. Everyone is always in a tearing hurry and they should slow down in the rain. Anyway, we couldn't see much because of the rain so we just went and. . ."

"Okay, so you saw a man get hit by a car, and where is he now?"

"Well, I don't know, dear. Gerald and I are nearly at the pub now. I just thought I should let someone know in case no one else had called. It was at that intersection by the fruit shop, the big one. A little expensive for my taste, but each to his own, I say."

"Did you see the car that hit him? Do you have any information on that?"

"Oh, yes, we were directly behind it and it was a gold Audi, although Gerald thinks it was closer to bronze in color, and a very pretty woman was driving it. I made sure to look even though it was very hard to see through the rain but I'm pretty certain. Well, I wasn't wearing my glasses, but I've got them on now. She turned after she hit him, turned around to see who was behind her, and I thought maybe she was going to reverse. That's why I told Gerald to wait, but the man behind us was obviously in some sort of rush and. . . well, we didn't want to miss lunch. And then she went, so we went as well."

"Right, can you tell me a cross street closest to where he was hit?"

"I already told you, dear, Cook Avenue. You're trained to listen, aren't you? Now, my name is Beverly Stonestreet. That's like the words *stone* and *street* put together. And my number is 0413929811 and I will be happy to speak to the police if they need me to, but I have to go now. Gerald, don't open the umbrella in the car. Are you mad?"

Wednesday, 11:35 a.m.

"Police, fire, ambulance?"

"Yes, this is Detective Sergeant Jackson with the Park Hills police. I'm off duty but... can you hear me? The rain is really bad."

"I can hear you, sir, go ahead."

"I'm on the side of Williamsburg Road with a man who's been hit by a car. I need an ambulance at the corner of Williamsburg Road and Cook Avenue. I'm here with him. I can't feel a heartbeat, but maybe that's because of the rain, and my daughter who's here with me is not entirely sure she can feel one either but... he's definitely unconscious. He's in a pretty bad way."

"Ambulance is on the way, sir. Did you see what happened?"

"Look, I can't be sure because I'm with my kids, and when we stopped at the light, I turned to say something to my son who was sitting in the back seat, so I missed him getting hit, but I heard it happen and then I saw him land on the pavement. I think the car that hit him was a black Mercedes, an SUV, but a small one. The light changed color and the traffic moved off. I don't know if anyone noticed because of the rain. It's really coming down out here. But no one stopped except me. They all just kept going."

"The ambulance should be there soon, sir. There have been another couple of calls about the same accident."

"Wait, I can hear them, but the traffic is all backed up. I don't know how they're going to get through and I can tell you— this guy doesn't have long. My daughter is a trainee nurse and she's doing CPR. Keep going, Steph, the ambulance is nearly here. Get out of the way, you idiots!"

"I can hear them, sir, so I'll leave you with them."

"Yes, thanks, okay, great... Yes, here, here, over here."

TWO

MARLA

Wednesday, 1:00 p.m.

Marla fills her glass of wine again, taking a deep sip and savoring the dark cherry flavors of the Merlot.

Outside, the rain soaks the lawn, forming puddles of mud where the grass is patchy because Rocky has dug up enthusiastic holes everywhere.

"Your dog needs to stop digging up the garden if you want the grass to grow properly," her gardener, Alex, tells her each time he comes over. Alex has been caring for her garden for years and complaining about Rocky for just as long. Marla knows she should try and encourage Rocky to find another activity, but the little dog gets such joy from digging she hates to stop him.

"He's a Jack Russell and that's what they like to do," Marla always replies, usually with Rocky sitting in front of her, his brown triangle ears perking up at his name. Now Rocky is lying on the floor by the glass double doors that lead from the kitchen to the patio and the garden. He has his little head on his paws as he watches the pounding rain. "It will stop soon, puppy," she says, and he lifts his head and turns to look at her, and then drops his head back onto his paws again with a heavy sigh. He doesn't believe her.

From her seat at the granite kitchen breakfast bar, she can barely see the garden, with its new spring flowers, through all the rain. Alex will no doubt have a lot of head-shaking and tutting to do at the damage done by the downpour.

Only a few days ago, the whole garden was beautifully in bloom, and she remembers taking pleasure in all the vibrant pinks and purples as she sipped her morning coffee. The air had been filled with the light warmth that signified an end to the biting Sydney winter and summer felt just around the corner.

But everything is different today. The spring sunshine is gone and in its place is a heavy gray sky and incessant rain.

Things change from one day to the next, between one breath and another. One day you're in your garden drinking coffee, filled with a sense of well-being, and the next you're slumped on a kitchen stool, staring out at the rain and getting drunk on a Wednesday afternoon. "To life," says Marla, lifting her glass for another sip.

"Where's Dad?" asks Bianca, coming into the kitchen. Marla takes another sip of wine and looks at her daughter, who is dressed in the ridiculous sparkly pink oversized hoodie she has worn all through winter and into spring. It's made for a much bigger person and so it accentuates her daughter's fragile beauty. Bianca looks like Marla did at seventeen, with enormous light green eyes and a small pointed chin. But she gets her slightly olive-colored skin from her father, which contrasts beautifully with her burnished red hair. Marla used to have the same red hair until she started bleaching it in search of a new look, a different face... something. In search of a way to stay beautiful and young forever. Now her hair is brittle and dry and yellow-blond, her forehead smooth and unmoving, and her eyes slightly tilted up. She is still beautiful and she knows this. She still draws the eyes of people when she walks into a room, but in her bathroom magnifying mirror, she can see that nothing has stopped time from leaving its marks all over her face and body.

There is nothing left of seventeen-year-old Marla—in more ways than one. She can only look at her daughter with envy. "Why do you need to keep doing that to yourself?" Damon asked her after she came home with a frozen face from her latest Botox appointment. Marla didn't answer the question. Visiting the clinic is always a torturous experience—not because of the pain, she's used to that—but because the nurses in charge of injecting the poison into her face are all stunningly beautiful. As soon as she walks into the hushed pink-marbled interior of the clinic, Marla feels herself to be old and dried up, as she's greeted by the receptionist, who wears her youth with confidence, and then is escorted into a room where she lies on a bed and looks up at another beautiful woman named Nina. Nina is one of the most stunning women Marla has ever seen, but she works with a certain malevolence that makes Marla question why she keeps returning to that particular clinic. "Take that, father time," Nina mutters under her breath as she stabs at Marla's face with a needle. Marla goes to the clinic to feel better about herself but inevitably ends up feeling worse. And yet she cannot stop going.

Damon questioning why she needs to visit the clinic frustrated Marla because he knew exactly why. He's aware of the neighborhood they live in, the school community they're part of, the people they mix with. Not using Botox, not working out obsessively, not watching every carb she eats would be frowned upon by everyone. She is socially obliged to maintain herself, just like she was socially obliged to spend years ferrying her children from one expensive activity to another. Violin lessons from a former member of the Sydney Orchestra for a child who had zero interest in the violin—yes, please. French tutoring for a child who had no desire to ever visit France—absolutely. Math tutoring, English tutoring, gym memberships, soccer practice, and a myriad of other after-school activities had dominated Marla's life for years. She has a list in her phone of the best instructors for every single hobby a child could have, and Sean and Bianca have tried most of them. Other mothers in her circle whose children were younger would often call asking for numbers and advice on which activity their child should be directed into. "Don't do it. Don't waste your time or money," she wanted to tell them, but never did.

Instead, she maintained her role in the status quo as she bought T-shirts for two hundred dollars that looked remarkably similar to the T-shirts she glanced at in the discount stores, worked out with the same trainer everyone else did, went to the same restaurants and vacationed where everyone else did. She fit in. To not fit in would be awful, to want the two-hundred-dollar T-shirt and not be able to afford it, unimaginable.

Now that Sean is nineteen and Bianca seventeen, she is floundering a little, as she suspects that her life is living her rather than the other way around. Social media Marla feels more real than she does, and she often scrolls through her own Instagram posts and envies the life the woman she is looking at is living, because she seems to feel such joy in every picture, whether it's with her children at a restaurant, out to dinner with girlfriends, or sharing a smoothie with her trainer. Social media Marla has nothing to do with real Marla at all. The children don't even need to be ferried around anymore since Bianca got her license two weeks ago and Sean has had his for two years already. Social media Marla was delighted to share that her baby now had the fabulous red P of a provisional driver that gave every parent more freedom, but real Marla is quietly devastated that she is no longer necessary to Bianca the same way she was only months ago.

"Where's Sean?" asks Marla, answering Bianca's question with one of her own.

Bianca opens the fridge and grabs a yogurt, tearing off the foil lid and grabbing a spoon. "Well," she says, slumping down onto a stool next to Marla, "after you and Dad left, he got up and got himself some breakfast and then went to his room to go back to sleep. He's been totally depressed ever since Julia left to study overseas for a semester. He needs to get his act together and just get on with things. He can't sleep until she comes back."

"He's been with Julia for three years, Bianca, so obviously he's upset. When university goes back, he will get up and get on with things, and he's going to visit her anyway in a couple of months. They're in love." She smiles as she thinks of her steadfast son, who has his father's black curls but her pale shade of green eyes. He is also taller than his father, long and lean rather than muscled and compact like Damon is. Their looks are not the only way father and son differ. Sean is committed and loyal and believes he has found the woman he will be with for life. He has never even contemplated being with anyone else since his first date with Julia. Marla has watched him on the rare occasions mother and son are out together, his eyes always focused forward and his interest in whatever they are talking about. Beautiful girls float past her son all the time, offering shy smiles and tossing their hair, but he doesn't even seem to register them. When Marla is out with Damon, he glances at himself in store windows and smiles at every woman who smiles at him, and a lot of women smile at him. He is not just good-looking, but beautiful in the way that few men are. Sean is good-looking as well, but he doesn't have the boisterous charisma his father does. At university he is studying veterinary science, having had a passion for animals since he was a small boy, just like Marla always has.

Most men, Marla knows, look at beautiful women. Some do more than look. A lot more. There is something different about Sean and she loves him all the more for it. He will make a wonderful husband one day. Marla knows that marriage is something he and Julia have already talked about despite their youth.

"Whatever," says Bianca, scraping the spoon around the yogurt tub.

"You sleep almost as much as he does. How are you going to manage to get up when next term starts? This is the final year of school and you need to really concentrate to get the grades you want."

"Please don't ask stupid questions. I always manage to get to school. And spare me the lecture. I've only just finished year eleven exams. I deserve a break. Where is Dad? I thought he was working from home today. Where did you two go?"

Marla shrugs her shoulders. "I don't know where he is. We just went for a drive to talk without being interrupted. He. . ." She stops speaking, unsure what to say to her daughter, not wanting to offer an outright lie.

"That means you were fighting. You always leave the house when you fight, as though we don't understand what you're doing. What were you fighting about?" Bianca scrapes the last of the yogurt out of the tub and drops it into the recycling bin. She flings the spoon into the sink, ignoring the open dishwasher. The fridge door is opened again and she takes out half a chocolate bar she left there last night. Last night Marla opened and closed the fridge at least five times, staring at the chocolate and talking herself out of taking a bite. She had been able to close her eyes and imagine the gooey caramel sticking to her teeth as she crunched through the nuts, but she had contented herself with a cup of chocolate-scented tea instead. If she had to add up all the time she had spent thinking about calories, denying herself treats and obsessing over every pound, she's sure she could have used the time to write a novel or paint a gallery of pictures or something. Instead, she has fought her own body to remain her perfect weight, even though she knows—and has known for months, for years really—that there is simply no point in any of it. But she can't think how else to live her life. Or at least she couldn't think of any other way to live her life until recently, when the possibility of continuing on as before became untenable. And today was meant to change everything.

Today was going to be a day of confrontation and discussion with her husband and his need to do a lot more than look at a beautiful woman. Today she was finally going to speak to Damon, calmly and rationally, and get him to admit what he had done.

She has been holding in her words as they churned through her body, disturbing every night, holding them in and waiting for a day that she was ready. She had it all planned, and today the opportunity to put that plan into place presented itself. She was ready, but nothing has gone the way it should have done.

Bianca grabs some chips out of the pantry to take with her to her room where she will slouch in bed scrolling through Instagram and TikTok all day long. In a corner of her room her guitar and ice skates and ballet shoes are tumbled together in a pile until she's ready to throw them out. In Marla's circles every child is Serena Williams or Keith Urban in the making. They are all concert pianists and Hollywood movie stars until they abandon whatever activity they have been encouraged into and prove themselves ordinary children. With her children now grown, Marla can watch the younger women she knows treading the same path she has already walked and view them as faintly ridiculous, but mostly she views her past self as faintly ridiculous.

In Marla's circles every marriage is a match made in heaven until the lawyers are called in and terrible secrets come tumbling out. Everyone she knew pretended until they couldn't possibly pretend anymore. Marla cannot pretend anymore, but she's not willing to give up everything either.

Today was meant to be a first step on the road to some form

of authenticity in her own life. She had visions of fulfilling her fantasy of a cabin in the Blue Mountains where she collected animals without fear of mess and eventually became known as some kind of mad hermit. She also fantasized about an apartment near the ocean for her and Damon and long walks along the beach with Rocky. Her fantasies seesawed back and forth depending on her mood, but today she had been going to put her foot down with Damon, force him into a proper discussion and then see where her life took her.

Today went horribly wrong. Authenticity has a price and today she realized that she might not be willing to pay it.

"That's not exactly a healthy snack," says Marla to Bianca as her daughter goes to leave the kitchen, remembering when she used to eat exactly the same way before age caught up with her.

"I agree, Mum, wine would be so much healthier," her daughter says, stopping and turning back to confront her mother. "What were you fighting about?" Bianca asks again. She is sharp and quick and doesn't give up easily. Marla feels her shoulders round slightly. Her head is fuzzy and she is no match for her intelligent daughter.

"It really has nothing to do with you," snaps Marla, pouring another glass of wine. She would love to tell her daughter the truth, to let this daddy's girl know exactly what her perfect father has been up to, but she knows her love for Bianca will always trump her hate for Damon, regardless of what he has done or what he does in the future. Damon will have to explain this one himself if... if what?

Bianca flounces out of the kitchen, breaking off chocolate to put in her mouth. Marla is grateful to be left in silence again but she knows she needs to get up and do something, something, but she has no idea what.

Marla doesn't know what happens from here.

THREE
SONYA

Irritation thrums through her body and she sighs. Sitting behind her desk, she uses her feet to spin her white leather office chair around and around as she focuses on the white ceiling—like she used to do as a child visiting her father's office in the city. The fact that he had his own office and his own desk, where he kept a photograph of her, her mother and brother, seemed to six-year-old Sonya to be something almost magical. Those who worked with him called him "sir" and seemed worried every time he got up from his desk, leaping to attention in case he might need something. He kept his office door open, "so they know I'm watching," he told Sonya. To Sonya he was just her dad, who always pretended to fall asleep while reading her bedtime stories, but at the insurance firm he was respected and feared. He's a wonderful grandfather to Jasper, understanding that he needs to be the constant male in her son's life.

Round and around she goes, enjoying the disorienting feeling of spinning as she waits for Jessica to buzz her and let her know her patient has arrived. There is work she could be getting on with, but the energy required to log in to her computer and begin making notes feels like too much. She has raced to get here and now he is late, which is more than a little annoying. She wasn't even supposed to come in today since Wednesday is her day off from work, the day when she gets all those bothersome little tasks completed so that the weekend is free to spend with Jasper. Her twelve-year-old son will not want to spend many more weekends with her. She can already feel some reluctance coming from him when she suggests a movie or a walk. He wants to be with his friends at the skate park or at the shopping center or anywhere at all but with her. She can see a time ahead when she is alone all weekend after dropping Jasper off wherever he wants to go.

Outside, the rain continues, but she supposes it's needed in Sydney after the dry weeks at the beginning of spring. She is looking forward to a hot summer, but right now there are some October days that are just perfect with blue skies and enough warmth so that she can remember why she loves being outside so much. She and Jasper spent a couple of hours in the wild-flower garden near where they live last weekend, and she loved every minute of it. Jasper, not so much. He was on his phone a lot, smiling at memes and laughing at a text he received from "never mind, Mum, stop being so nosy."

What will she do with herself when Jasper really is off with friends all the time? She only has a handful of girlfriends and they are all married and usually busy with their own families on the weekend. When she and Lee first got divorced, Jasper was only three, and she remembers her intense resentment of her ex-husband when he took a job in the U.S., leaving her to care for Jasper alone. But now Jasper is older and FaceTimes his father nearly every day. Lee wants him to come and spend a month with him and his new wife and daughter—something Jasper is keen to do. Sonya can feel her son is on the verge of not needing her at all, and it scares her.

It had been a conscious decision to stay away from a relationship of any kind while Jasper was still young. It's not that she's been celibate, just that she's never brought anyone into her home. And it's not that she hasn't made some questionable choices in her desire for intimacy—she has, but she has always made certain that Jasper didn't know so he could never be affected.

Pushing her feet in her sensible wedge heels down onto the plush blue carpet, she stops the chair spinning and hits the intercom button on the phone console on her minimalist glass desk. "Anything?" she asks.

"I said I would let you know," sighs Jessica, and Sonya can hear a slight edge of exasperation in her assistant's voice. Jessica is used to Sonya being away from the office on Wednesdays and she catches up on all the paperwork for Sonya, even as she manages clients for Romy, who uses the office next door. Romy's specialty is child psychology and she never takes a day off during the week, but then Romy has a boyfriend but no children and arrives every Monday morning with tales of divine restaurants, new cocktails, and lazy Sunday brunches.

For something to do while she waits, Sonya stands and goes to the small round mirror fixed on the wall so she can check her chestnut hair. It's just because she's bored, not because she wants to check her appearance for the tenth time today. The fringe she had cut yesterday feels strange after years of wearing her hair off her face, but it makes her look younger than her forty-four years and the new copper-colored highlights emphasize her hazel eyes. She had it cut to just below her shoulders and she is enjoying the feeling of it swishing around her neck, but she also knows that it will soon be back in its sensible ponytail, pulled out of the way.

"Just beautiful," her hairdresser Jason had said when he was done, making her feel the word as he said it.

Lately she has begun to wonder if she has put off real dating for too long. She has no idea how she will ever get back out there and meet someone who can become part of her life and her son's life. Sex is easy—relationships are not.

Returning to her chair, the digital clock on her desk tells her the client is now over half an hour late and she picks up her bag to leave. He will still be charged for the session. She should never have agreed to come in today, but he had sounded so desperate when he called. "I need to see you. I just have to," he said and she had given in. She thought that maybe he. . . She shakes her head. "Don't think about it," she scolds herself aloud. Maybe he nothing. Any thoughts she has had of him becoming another kind of person have been ridiculous. She is often guilty of this as a therapist, of wanting change for her patients so much that she believes it's happening even when it's not.

The meeting was supposed to be at 1.00 p.m. and she cancelled a dentist appointment to make it. Her exasperation with his rudeness flares as she glances out of the window at the still falling rain. It shouldn't surprise her that he has simply not turned up. He would have been here if he wanted to. His arrogance is one of his most dominant personality traits. He's also a classic narcissist and she has been trying to find a way to get him to come around to that realization himself, but he doesn't like her to interrupt him when he's speaking, preferring that she simply sit there and write down his words. He came to her saying he wanted help with a hideously complicated situation, but all he was looking for was dispensation to continue, not help to change things. He will always be the narcissist he is, but she's not going to stop accepting his money if he actually turns up again.

She really doesn't want to have to drive back in this weather, but she has no choice. Driving in the rain always makes her feel a little out of control and when she got here her neck was stiff from hunching her body over the steering wheel as she tried to see the road through a fogged-up windshield.

Picking up her phone in its silver case, she glances down at the screen. He has her private phone number if he wants to contact her but he hasn't done so. She usually makes it a policy to never give out her private number, but in the last few months she has done a lot of things she would never do.

She won't let his no-show affect her. She will simply file this away to discuss the next time he comes in—if he comes in. He apparently had needed to see her but then avoided seeing her. Why? Well, she knows why. "No one is better at hiding the truth from themselves than a psychologist," Romy told her last week as they shared lunch in the office. They were discussing a colleague who had just found out about an affair her husband was having. The woman had confided to Romy that she knew all along, but at the same time didn't want to know. Sonya is adept at not thinking about things, at explaining behaviors away, at simply ignoring the truth about her situation. When her marriage to Lee was faltering, she ignored it until Lee told her he didn't want to just be a co-parent with her in their marriage. He wanted more or he wanted out. The whole messy tiring experience of divorce was not something she wanted, but Lee knew what was best for both of them.

She's trained in human behavior and she knows exactly what she's hiding from herself. Particularly in this situation and definitely today. Today was going to be an extraordinary day but now it's just. . . She's not sure how to think about it.

"I'm leaving," she tells Jessica as she opens her office door.

"And if Mr. Kennedy turns up?" asks Jessica.

"He won't," says Sonya and she sweeps past her receptionist without another word.

FOUR

ATHENA

Wednesday, 3:00 p.m.

Her eyes keep straying to the door, imagining him walking through, rushed and apologetic; "So sorry, darling." It's cold in the examining room, even though they have, as she requested, draped a blanket over her legs. The clinical smell of disinfectant hangs in the air and the bright light bounces off the shiny metal equipment. She nearly didn't make it here on time herself, the slightly worn tires on her old car struggling with the rain-slick roads. "Let me buy you a new car," he said last month, but she refused. Now she wonders why she'd refused when she had the chance. Stubbornness, she supposes. If felt like too big a gift. Bigger than the chocolates and flowers and the delicate white-gold bracelet threaded with diamonds and amethysts and tiny woven goldfish—symbols of her star sign and birth month. The bracelet had taken her breath away, not just because of its beauty and obvious expense, but because it had so perfectly captured things that meant a lot to her. It proved he listened when she talked about her work and the ideas that guided her life. He didn't believe in astrology or the healing power of crystals, and when she had tried to do a tarot reading for him, he had laughed off everything she had told him, had found the tower card—the harbinger of doom in every reading—funny rather than frightening. But he understood that it was her life and her work and he supported her pursuing her passion. The presents were nice, but she would have returned them all if it meant she had more time with him.

Athena closes her eyes, tries to ground herself with a deep breath, but she feels exposed with her belly on display and her body about to be scanned. She would not invade the private space inside her if it weren't for her age. It seems wrong and terribly intrusive on the soul coming into being, but here she is anyway—worry forcing her to turn to medicine against her instincts.

"I know you prefer everything to be natural, but you must have the tests, sweetheart," her father told her a month ago. She wanted to refuse, but there is a lot of fear crumpled up inside her—perhaps because she feels so alone.

"Shall we get started, or are you waiting for someone?" the young woman in pale pink scrubs asks.

"Yes, yes," says Athena. "I'm not waiting for anyone. It's just me."

Meeting the young woman's gaze, Athena catches a brief glance of sympathy and she takes a deep breath, struggling to avoid saying anything. Plenty of women have babies alone these days, but perhaps the fact that she is not accompanied by a mother or a friend is what has drawn the woman's sympathy. *No mother, no real friends to speak of, and a boyfriend who has no interest in this child.* Her father would have been here for her, would have come back to Sydney if she'd asked him to. But she had believed with everything she had that he would come, that, after today, he would be here with her and stay with her forever.

She has no right to self-pity. She got herself into this situation. Walked right into it with her eyes open, so she should not be surprised at all that she is alone. Mentioning the sonogram while they were in bed last week was probably a mistake, but she hadn't deserved his reaction. The blissful moments after sex as she lay with her head on his chest seemed like the perfect time. But it was not the perfect time, because no time was perfect for something he did not want.

"I told you," he had hissed, shoving her away from him and standing up, grabbing his pants from the floor. "I specifically explained that I have no desire for a baby in my life."

"But I'm pregnant and keeping this child," she replied, her voice softly repeating what she had been saying for weeks already. "You said that you loved me."

"Don't whine, Athena," he snorted and then he grabbed his shirt from the floor and picked up his jacket and tie from the soft purple velvet armchair in her bedroom, shoving bare feet into his shoes. She found his navy-blue socks under the bed this morning and had put them in the washing machine, seeing herself handing them to him, clean and neatly bundled, the next time he came over. It was pathetic. She was pathetic.

The sonographer spreads the gel across her stomach slowly. It's warm and sticky and Athena swallows to keep the nausea at bay. It's mostly gone now, but sometimes it rears its churning head. Watching the screen closely, she waits while the ultrasound wand moves across her stomach, holding her breath until she sees the flickering of her baby's heart, strong and quick.

"There's your baby now," says the young woman, who has her hair wound around her head in an intricate plait.

Athena smiles, because there he is—the little boy she knows she's been waiting for. Small hands seem to be waving as a little foot kicks out and he dances around inside her.

"Do you want to know the gender?" the woman asks.

Athena nods but she knows it's a boy. She can feel his energy, has felt it from the moment she knew he existed. She has named him Caleb, a name that means "faithful and brave," because she knows he will be both these things.

"It's a boy," says the sonographer and Athena nods, swipes away a stray tear. She had almost given up hope. She's thirty-nine and, from everything she's read, she had nearly missed the biological boat. Caleb had not been planned, despite what *he* seemed to think. The baby is not here to trap him or make him do something he doesn't want to do. Although she did imagine that when she told him, when she explained that her vague nausea in the morning had a cause, he would share her joy even if he could not exactly feel it himself yet. Instead, his first reaction was anger. She had expected surprise and then maybe even a little excitement. His "I love you, you're the most beautiful woman I've ever seen, I can't imagine life without you" statements were on a never-ending loop when they were together. He showered her with attention and care. Surely, he could love the child they had created together?

She had been entirely and thoroughly mistaken.

"What? How could you do this to me? You know my situation. You agreed, you said, you. . ." Accusations and fury poured out of him. She just stood there, taking it, allowing it.

And then she agreed to a termination. And he took her in his arms and told her he loved her. And everything was good and wonderful again. It was addictive—his approval, his love. It made her feel high sometimes, as though she were floating just a few inches above the ground as she moved. She had basked in his approval for the rest of the night.

When he was gone, when the intoxicating scent of his skin from the honey and spice aftershave he wore was out of her apartment and she was cleaning up in the kitchen, loading the dishes from the pasta meal she had diligently chopped vegetables and browned meat for, she watched her hands tremble as she rinsed dishes in the sink. It was not fear she was feeling but shame. She was ashamed of herself for allowing him to speak to her that way, ashamed that she let his anger frighten her into agreeing to do something she would never do, ashamed that she had taken him into her life and been fooled by his smile and his charm and the gifts and words of love. The child inside her had chosen her and she could already feel his spirit, even as he took shape, developing from cells to a little being. Leaving the rest of the dishes in the sink, she sat down on her sofa, covered with a colorful blanket of crocheted squares, and sent him a text. *I'm keeping the baby.* At first, she typed up an explanation, citing her age and that she absolved him of responsibility and her belief that their love for each other could conquer anything, but all those words were quickly deleted. *I'm keeping the baby.* That's all he needed to know. He didn't reply, but he did come back. She assumed that meant he understood and would support her, although she had noticed that anytime she tried to bring up her plans for the future he managed to change the direction of the conversation or he would suddenly need to go.

"I'm just going to do some measurements now," says the woman, and she moves the wand back and forth as she records the size of the baby and examines him carefully.

It's not his fault. He was very clear. But she had been clear as well and he had returned, flowers in his arms and a sheepish smile. She had permitted this ignoring of the truth until last week. Last week she had wanted assurances and support. "I want you to come with to the ultrasound," she said. "I want you to see our son."

"Nearly done now," says the woman, and Athena knows the fact that it has been quick means that everything is probably fine, that she has a healthy baby boy on the way, but she cannot celebrate the feeling. She is angry. Not just angry but furious, heat simmering in her body, making the baby kick and squirm. He should have been here, should have chosen her, and yet she is alone. Today was supposed to end with them together but instead... She won't think about what has happened instead.

"Angelic Athena," he calls her because her hair is long and golden and her eyes are sky blue, her lips soft and full. But she's not angelic. In Greek mythology Athena is the goddess of war, but he's never had much interest in what she knows of Greek mythology. "I'm more of a math person," he told her when she talked about the origin of her name.

He should have paid more attention to the old myths and legends. Numbers can't help him now.

FIVE

MARLA

Wednesday, 6:00 p.m.

Marla clicks on the television in the kitchen so she can watch the news while she cooks. She needs something to concentrate on because her head is fuzzy with wine. *You're a bad mother and obviously a bad wife,* she admonishes herself. *How bad a wife am I? How bad a human being?*

She should not drink wine in the afternoon. Alcohol makes her nasty, or so Damon says, but according to Damon, just about everything makes her nasty. Having her period, being on a constant diet, needing a picture for Instagram, having to cook. . . The list can be extended to include anything that comes to Damon's mind in the moment.

That wasn't always the case. When they were in their early twenties, alcohol made her funny, her dark sense of humor emerging, and it made her flirty and easy to talk to. She had been raised to always be a lady in every situation and sometimes that meant that she came off as prissy when she didn't really want to. Alcohol allowed her to drop some of her inhibitions and just enjoy herself. Damon would stand at gatherings and watch other men try to charm and impress her and revel in the knowledge that he was the one going home with her. She had been able to literally feel his pride in her beauty from across the room. Twenty-three-year-old Marla walked into every room sure that someone would want to speak to her, helped by a glass or two of whatever she had downed before she left home. Growing up beautiful made everything just a little easier for her, and she knows that. But beauty fades regardless of how hard you try to hold on to it. In her forties she often pictures herself with a rough blanket in her hands beating back the flames of time. Now a pizza eaten at midnight makes her feel sick and bloated, and alcohol makes her acerbic and sarcastic. The change happened gradually, so she didn't notice, or perhaps Damon is the one who has changed—not that he would ever admit it. Attack first and defend later is Damon's motto. "You're the most beautiful woman I've ever seen" has given way to "it's possible to be too skinny sometimes" and "what have you done to your hair?" Bianca is finding her a chore to even be in the same room with, and Sean is lovely but very much busy with his own life and Julia. And Damon cannot seem to look her in the eye anymore. Perhaps out of guilt, but she can sense boredom from him as well.

Today she attacked first, but instead of defending himself or accepting his wrongdoing, he flared up and attacked back, and now he is not here and she is too drunk to be cooking.

In addition to the alcohol, she has consumed nearly a whole family-sized bag of potato chips, desperate for the salt and the crunch in her mouth, not even savoring the tangy flavor of the vinegar, which she can still taste on her slightly burning lips. She feels like she's gained ten pounds already, as her pants bite into her waist, even though she knows it's not really possible. But, so what? Everything she has done to stay slim and toned and attractive has been for nothing. Everything she has done with her life, every choice she has made has been for nothing. Alcohol also always makes her maudlin.

She has done everything she was taught to do. She did well at school, got a nice degree—that's what her mother called her degree in psychology. A nice degree for a young woman to have, but obviously not to practice. Marla can barely remember anything she learned at university or in the few years she did actually work in a practice, as she got her hours in so she would be awarded her degree. Marriage to a good man had always been the ultimate goal. Her mother holds a degree in accounting but still lets her father—a doctor with little interest in bills—handle the finances. It's completely mad when you think about it, but her parents are very happy. That's what she had been hoping for, the easy happy friendship of a long marriage. Her parents spend a lot of their time on cruises now, traveling the world, coming home with new friends every time. They are in Sydney now but leave in a week for a cruise around the Middle East. Marla would like to call her mother and talk about what happened today, what has happened to her life, but she fears being accused of dropping the wife ball. And she hasn't just dropped it but has well and truly kicked it away from her.

Marla had been raised to succeed at marriage and she has completely and spectacularly failed at it. She would have liked to have studied veterinary science, like Sean is doing, but her mother had said, "What kind of a man would marry a vet, darling? All that nasty mess. You'll be single forever."

So, Marla studied psychology while she waited to find the one. And she *had* found the perfect man—or so she thought. Damon was from a good family, meaning rich, and he had worked for his father until he had enough business experience to open his own firm specializing in IT. Everything had gone exactly according to plan, including the births of their two beautiful children. She loved Damon, but more than that, she thought they were friends. He could discuss his work with her and she made sure she understood enough to ask questions and remain interested by taking classes online. She had been kidding herself, obviously.

Now she has no idea where he is, no idea at all, and she wants so badly not to care. She has an app on her phone that lets her see where the children are at any given time, but Damon refused to join the family group. "I'm not a child, Marla. You don't need to know where I am every minute of the day," he had sneered when she asked him to add his number.

Even if he were on the app, it would make no difference. His phone is here. His locked phone that she cannot get into because he has never deigned to share his password. That's a secret she has kept from everyone in her circle, just smiling and nodding as friends complain about having to remember their husband's passwords for them.

"I deal with sensitive issues and I can't allow just anyone access to my phone—you know that" was Damon's explanation for why she didn't need to know his password.

"But what if something happens to you and I need to get into it?" she asked, feeling the sting of his words. *Just anyone.*

"What would happen to me?" he replied.

"What would happen to you," mutters Marla as she concentrates while she chops vegetables for a salad, worried about cutting herself as she imagines having to ask Bianca to drive her to the emergency room.

She has left the phone upstairs, wrapped in a T-shirt and hidden away, not willing to listen to the light hum of it vibrating anymore. Damon keeps it on vibration only most of the time so only he knows when he gets a call. On its screen are missed calls and messages from numbers she doesn't recognize, names she doesn't know. So many she can't answer, can't read. She doesn't want to know anymore, not now.

As the news begins, she looks up at the television to see a

scene of a road in the pouring rain. Outside it's still coming down, heavy and loud. This morning the overly excited weatherman promised sunshine for the rest of the week.

She recognizes the road that's being filmed and she stops what she's doing so she can listen. There's an ambulance and police cars on the screen. The road is four lanes and it looks to be in complete chaos, traffic backed up and cars attempting to change lanes. There is a man in jeans and a T-shirt holding up a blanket, which means someone is dead. They only do that to hide a body, don't they? Even though the sound is loud enough, she turns it up.

"Police are appealing for help identifying a man who was hit by a car on Williamsburg Road this morning. The accident was called in by numerous sources and a constable present at the scene got out to help the pedestrian. The man is believed to be of Caucasian appearance and in his forties. He has dark hair and was wearing a blue shirt and black pants. He also had a black and gold wedding band and gold watch. Police are also asking for any witnesses to come forward so that they can identify the car that hit the pedestrian. At this time, no one has claimed responsibility."

She stares at the TV, watching as a hand falls from the side of the covered stretcher that is now being shown onscreen, and at the same time she notices a pain in her thumb and she looks down. Her thumb is on the blade of the large steel chopping knife and she has pressed down, cutting into the skin at the top.

She steps back a little and puts the knife down on the kitchen counter, grabs a tea towel and holds it over her thumb. There is not a lot of blood but there is a stinging pain that lets her know some of the acidic juice from the tomato she just sliced has already found its way into the cut. The news anchor is back on the screen, her blue eyes wide with concern, her hair a perfect blond helmet, but Marla stares, still seeing the hand, as though the image is still on the screen.

A bottle of wine has allowed her to temporarily forget exactly why she started drinking the wine in the first place, exactly why today happened at all.

As the news reporter moves on to a story about the high price of gas, Marla is taken back two weeks, and she sees herself coming in from a walk with Rocky, buoyed by the early-spring sunshine and the beautiful gardens she had passed as they walked.

It was only 5:00 p.m. but she had found Damon in the kitchen, grabbing ice from a drawer in the freezer.

"Hello," she said, going up to kiss him, "you're home early today."

He had offered his cheek instead of his lips, but she had thought nothing of it at first. His brow was furrowed with worry. "What's up?" she asked as he poured himself a whisky from the bottle on the counter.

"Shitty day, whole systems went down, and it looks like someone has managed to hack into a government department we just installed software for."

"I'm so sorry," she said, brushing his shoulder lightly and trying not to be offended at how quickly he moved away to take a seat at the breakfast bar.

"Is there anything I can do?" she asked, going to the fridge to get ingredients so she could begin preparing dinner.

"Have an IT degree, do you?" he snarled.

"Damon," she said, shocked, "what on earth is going on?" Whatever his failings, it was very unusual for Damon to be outright rude to her. He was a master of keeping his emotions in check.

"Nothing," he sighed. "I'm sorry, I just need some space. I may just give Ivan a call and maybe go for a drink with him. He's always good with perspective." Ivan was Damon's brother and was older by two years and also a finance lawyer.

"Okay," she said lightly, trying not to be hurt that Damon

wanted to speak to his brother about whatever was bothering him and not to her.

"I'll just go get changed," he said and he left his drink sitting on the kitchen counter as he went upstairs. He left his phone sitting next to his drink, and when it rang, Marla was unsure what to do. If Damon had left the sound on, he was obviously waiting for a call and didn't want to miss it. Glancing at the unidentified number, she debated over just leaving it but imagined that it might be a client and it might be urgent based on Damon's mood, so she swiped her finger across the screen before it could lock and said, "Hello, Damon Kennedy's phone, Marla speaking."

"Marla?" asked a woman's voice.

"Yes, I'm Damon's wife. He's just changing. Can I help you with anything, or can I get him to call you back?"

She grabbed a pen from a jar she kept near the microwave and pulled a sheet of paper off a lined pad that always sat next to that.

"No," said the woman. "No, thank you," and she hung up as Damon appeared in the kitchen.

"What are you doing on my phone?" he yelled, startling her, so that she stepped back, dropping the phone onto the counter with a clatter.

"It rang and I thought. . . I'm sorry. . ." she said as he grabbed the phone and looked at the number. "Who was it?"

He shook his head. "A client, she's a real pain, always complaining. She calls so much I recognize her number, but she's brought a lot of business to us, so I don't want to block her. Sorry, Marla, sorry, I'm not fit for company. I'll see you in a couple of hours." Nodding mutely, Marla went back to preparing dinner.

It was odd that the woman who called wasn't saved under a business name. It was odd that she had not wanted to leave a message. But the voice she heard was not odd, not odd but familiar, and it told her that everything she had tried to do to keep her marriage together had failed. She was no longer beautiful enough or clever enough or funny enough. Marla was no longer enough, and even though she was aware that she never really had been, the woman's voice on the phone sliced through her.

This morning just how badly she had failed was made crystal clear.

She closes her eyes and sees the hand falling from the stretcher in the pouring rain.

Holding the tea towel tightly over her cut thumb, she finds her cell phone. She wishes she hadn't started drinking because now she feels hideously sick and she's going to have to concentrate hard not to slur her words.

They didn't say he was dead, just in a coma. That's what she needs to hold on to now. He's not dead.

Before she shouts for her daughter, she types a quick message awkwardly, her cut thumb hampering the typing of the two words she needs to send to a contact saved as "Gardener-Peter" in her phone. But he is not a gardener, and he is not named Peter.

Everyone has secrets in a marriage. Damon certainly has his, but he has never given a thought to the secrets she might have. The message sends, and she knows the instruction will be followed.

Delete everything.

SIX

SONYA

Sonya checks on the lasagna in the oven. It's nearly ready. Walking from her kitchen through the living room, cluttered with framed photographs of Jasper from babyhood to now and filled with turtle ornaments of every different kind and material that she has collected for years, she goes to the bottom of the narrow staircase and calls, "Dinner in fifteen minutes!"

"Okay," Jasper yells back through his closed bedroom door. He is doing his science project, which is due at the beginning of the next school term, or at least he is supposed to be doing his project, but occasionally she has heard the words "on your left, no, go back" drift down the stairs, so she knows that he's probably doing a fair bit of gaming as well. His group of friends play online together. Sonya should have put a stop to it when she noticed that it was taking up more and more time, but she left it too late and now Jasper has argued that a) all his friends do it so it's essentially a social activity; b) the games are improving his hand–eye coordination and one day will help him be a better driver; c) they are actually helping him to do better at school because he knows that if his grades drop she will take away his gaming computer and leave him with the laptop that is good for nothing except schoolwork. When Jasper started on the letter d, Sonya knew she was done arguing. "Fine," she yelled, "but know this, if those grades drop even a tiny bit. . ."

"Yes, yes, Mum. . . the lecture is imprinted on my brain," he had laughed. Jasper is intelligent and mature beyond his years, partly because he is an only child and partly, she knows, because he was witness to some of her emotional distress after the divorce, before he could even really understand it. At three he would find her crying in the kitchen and gently pat her arm until she hiccupped herself to a stop. The world had felt overwhelming in the weeks after her divorce, as she questioned how she would ever work and raise a child all alone. Her parents were both gone, and she had no one she could turn to for help. Nightmarish scenarios of her falling and hitting her head and Jasper being alone for days as she lay comatose filled her dreams for a long time. Jasper knew how to dial 911 by the time he was three and a half. If he couldn't wake Mummy, then he knew to call emergency services—something that had once led to an embarrassing visit from the ambulance service when she forgot about the rule and pretended to be asleep as he prodded her to get up and make him breakfast on a Sunday.

Today she feels very far away from that desperate woman and so grateful that she managed to leave her behind.

Jasper is, as every teacher tells her, incredibly clever and a lovely boy to have around, which is always a comfort to hear when she wonders how much of her distress he really understood. He is not good at many sports but excels at cricket and is always at the top or near the top of every class, and he's kind to everyone he meets. She cannot complain about her hazel-eyed son, whose face is a miniature but more masculine version of her own face, although she can see his father's square jaw emerging as he matures. He is still in that knobbly-kneed skinny phase that boys go through and she's sure that one day he will be much taller than her, with his father's broad shoulders. Sonya has no doubt that soon enough there will be a girlfriend or two, and she tries to see that as a good thing. *Get a grip, Sonya. No one likes a clingy mother.* She just wants to protect him from everything.

Walking back through the living room, she sighs at the mess. Jasper has left his school laptop on the floor where it could be stepped on. She hasn't vacuumed in here for a couple of weeks and the floor has a smattering of crumbs from when Jasper eats in front of the television, and everything could use a dust. She should throw away the jade turtles and glass turtles and wood turtles that she has gathered over the years and which cover all the surfaces, but ever since she praised the first one Jasper handmade for her in preschool—despite it not actually being identifiable as a turtle—turtles have been his go-to gift for every birthday and Mother's Day. The turtle is a symbol of steadfastness, loyalty, and protection. Jasper wrote that interesting fact on a birthday card a couple of years ago. *I will always protect you and be there for you,* he had written carefully as well, and her heart had melted. So of course, she's never going to throw away the turtles. She could use a bit of loyalty and protectiveness, even if it's just from her twelve-year-old son.

Returning to the kitchen, she sits down at the table and switches on the television, hoping to catch the news. In the first story, the camera pans across Williamsburg Road, the rain a solid sheet of water. She drives that road every day to and from work. She drove it today, her windshield wipers going faster and faster but still not managing to keep her view completely clear. It was so hard to see that she was barely aware of anything else other than the car in front of her she was trying to follow.

That's not quite true, is it?

She shakes off the thought and concentrates on the news reporter's voice accompanying the film.

"Police are appealing for help identifying a man who was hit by a car on Williamsburg Road this morning. The accident was called in by numerous sources and a constable present at the scene got out to help the pedestrian. The man is believed to be of Caucasian appearance and in his forties. He has dark hair and was wearing a blue shirt and black pants. He also had a gold and black wedding band and gold watch. He was not carrying a wallet or a phone. Police are also asking for any witnesses to come forward so that they can identify the car that hit the pedestrian. At this time, no one has claimed responsibility. The man is in an induced coma at North Vale Hospital."

Another shot, obviously taken by a mobile phone, jerky and unclear at first and then zooming in, appears, and she sees a person being loaded onto a stretcher in the pouring rain, while a man dressed in jeans and a T-shirt holds up a blanket to protect the identity of the victim from whoever is filming. Sonya wonders what kind of a person films an accident? As they move the stretcher, the man holding the blanket steps aside and a hand belonging to the man on the stretcher falls to the side and Sonya catches a glimpse of a wedding band. It's inlaid with black stone, distinctive on the film even through the rain, because of its unique smooth black onyx inlay surrounded by thick yellow gold. She has only ever seen such a ring once. How close is the person filming? It's gratuitous and awful, but she can't look away.

It is suddenly difficult to swallow.

Sonya sits frozen in the chair, wanting to mute the next story on gas prices but unable to move. She recognizes that hand and that wedding band, zoomed in on with absolute precision by the person filming.

That's why the narcissist didn't make it to therapy.

SEVEN

ATHENA

Wednesday, 6:00 p.m.

Athena puts a pot of water on to boil for pasta. She hadn't planned on cooking dinner because she'd assumed the two of them would be out celebrating a healthy baby and finding out the gender of their child. In her mind she had played out a scene where he came to the ultrasound at the last minute, just walked in dusting the rain that was falling outside off his shirt and, upon seeing the screen showing their son moving inside her, was profoundly changed and suddenly completely in love with the idea of having a child with her. She even pictured him thanking her for refusing to terminate the pregnancy.

"Flights of fancy won't take you anywhere," her mother used to say. Athena had always connected more with her slightly dreamy father, who was open to new ideas and ways of thinking. Her mother was practical, pragmatic and short on patience for her daughter's beliefs in astrology, and the existence of fairies, although Athena had never questioned her mother's devotion to her only daughter.

For as long as she can remember, Athena has known that there is more to the universe than just what can be seen. In her darkest moments she comforts herself with the idea that her mother is looking down on her, even though Jackie had never believed that you were anything except dead and gone after you died.

Today there was no last-minute arrival and no gratitude to her for not terminating the pregnancy. Regardless of everything she now knew about him, everything she had been told, she still held out hope that he would become someone else, that he would turn up to the sonogram and somehow be a different kind of person entirely. Yesterday she'd even booked a table for two at her favorite Italian restaurant tucked down a suburban side street, with its tables covered in cheesy red checked tablecloths. It had taken every ounce of self-control she had not to cry when she called to cancel the reservation. And now it is Athena who is profoundly changed.

She is alone with only a sonogram picture on the fridge for company. Perhaps her anger is unfair, because he told her the truth and yet she has managed to keep deluding herself. Perhaps her anger is exactly what she needs now.

Last night he stayed at his place in the city to be close to work for a morning meeting. "I hope you sell that one day and move in with me," she told him a few months ago, joyful at the idea of him being with her all the time. He had laughed when she said that, she now remembers, and not in a nice way.

He had laughed but he hadn't said they would never be together in one home, living their lives, because then it seemed that sometime in the future—it could happen. That was before the baby got in the way, before everything got in the way, when she was still hoping that, somehow, she would be the woman he would be with forever.

She would never have believed when they met that she could find herself in this situation. On their second date he opened up to her so completely, made himself so vulnerable that she knew she had found the man she wanted to be with for life.

"I was really hurt by my last girlfriend. She got clingy and when I told her we needed to slow things down, she cheated on me. It's hard for me to be close to anyone because I never learned that from my parents. I've never really connected with a woman the way I connect with you." She had savored those words, repeated them to herself when she was alone and missing him. But that was at the beginning when she was wrapped in blissful ignorance about the truth of who he really was.

There was no last girlfriend. But there was something infinitely more complicated.

She still loves him, that's the worst part. Maybe that's where the anger comes from—it is directed at herself as well as him. His rejection of their child cannot make her stop loving him. His complicated life didn't make her stop loving him, so why should this? Taking the pasta from the cupboard, she sets it down on the counter, trying not to hear the word *doormat* repeat in her head. She is not a doormat. She is kind and loving and open and understanding. Everyone makes mistakes. Sometimes it takes years for a person to realize that the person they have chosen to be with is not their soul mate. Athena had imagined that he was her soul mate and that he felt the same way. It had just taken them a little longer to find each other in the first place.

Lately, since she told him she was pregnant, he has been spending more and more time at his apartment in the city. The apartment is necessary because he is so important, because he has to work late as the CEO of his company, but mostly because he needs a place to hide from all the complications in his life. Athena is now just one more of those complications.

It wasn't supposed to be like this. Even after she found out the truth about him and the hideous confrontation that followed, she was still his respite from the world, his peace. Not anymore.

Athena adds salt to the pasta water and then picks up her phone again, in case she has somehow not heard the musical tinkle of an incoming text message or the melodious voice of Enya letting her know she has an incoming call, but there is nothing.

"We'll be all right, won't we, baby," she murmurs, rubbing the tiny mound of her belly. At eighteen weeks she is barely showing at all.

After the ultrasound, all she wanted to do was go home and sleep off the stress of going through the whole thing alone, but she knew that she couldn't leave Gail alone in the store for the rest of the afternoon. Wednesdays are always busy because it seems to be a favorite day for large groups of people having lunch, almost like a midweek break. Inevitably, people from the four surrounding cafés wandered into the store after lunch, and they usually bought something.

"So?" Gail had asked as soon as she saw her. Gail has been working for Athena since the store opened, first on a part-time basis while she finished school, and then permanently for the last few years while she studied nutrition and naturopathy at night. As usual, Athena's assistant had a pair of glasses buried in her thick curly black hair and another set hanging around her neck. Athena thought of her as an old soul and it was true that Gail did manage to quickly connect with older customers, especially those who were skeptical about the collections of crystals and stones and the racks of books on magic.

Athena hoped that upon entering her incense-scented store, where the lighting was a warm yellow and feathered dream catchers hung from the ceiling, she would feel at peace as she usually did, but today, even surrounded by the healing crystals, she couldn't hide her devastation.

Instead of explaining that she had been right about the baby being a boy, Athena burst into tears and Gail had pulled her into the back office while a customer stared, open curiosity on his face, a chunk of brilliant purple amethyst clutched in his hand.

"He didn't come," Athena had sobbed, and Gail had clucked and soothed and then made her a cup of ginger and cinnamon tea. "You rest," she had instructed, as Athena lay on the overstuffed blue velvet chaise longue in her small back office. Athena had sipped the tea and placed the cup on an octagonal-shaped mosaic stool next to the sofa, closing her eyes and allowing herself to get angry again, not an emotion she liked at all. But it was better than the sadness. Angry people rarely became doormats. Instead, they stomped all over everyone else and lived their lives as they wanted. She felt anger's ugly heat right through her body and at the same time fear coursed through her veins at what she had done, intentionally or unintentionally. Opening her eyes, she picked up her phone and texted him once again, but this time she had expressed her anger. *I don't know where you are or why you've done this. It doesn't matter because nothing could explain your callous disregard for me and my child. You are not the man I thought you were.*

She needed the text to be there, to be something that could be seen. Just in case.

She had dropped off to sleep as soon as she sent the text, waking half an hour later to the beeping of the cash machine. Struggling off the sofa, she had glanced in the mirror and tried to smooth her blond hair. Her blue eyes were puffy from sleep and tears and her skin pale. She did the best she could with a dab of lipstick and some blush from her bag, and then she squared her shoulders and went out to serve customers. She would take care of herself and her son and she didn't need anyone else. Athena has spent her life looking for a savior, a protector, someone who would make her feel as safe as her father always did—and she thought she had found him. But as she smiled at two women giggling over some racy tarot cards, she admitted to herself that she had known, almost from the beginning, that he was too good to be true. The extent of what he was hiding was beyond what she imagined, but she had always known he was hiding something.

Placing the tarot cards in a decorative purple bag covered in black swirls, she took money from the women, who were blushing slightly at what they had bought. "I'm sure you'll have a lot of fun," she said and one of the women replied, "we're going to terrify our husbands with them," and they both burst into hysterical giggles, making Athena smile. She had tried to put him out of her mind for the rest of the day as she concentrated on enjoying her customers and her store.

But there is nothing to distract her here at home.

Grabbing some cherry tomatoes from the fridge, she takes a sharp knife and slices through each one on a wooden chopping board.

As the hand holding the knife slices cleanly through the small tomatoes, she watches the juice burst out when she presses a little too hard. Like blood.

While she waits for the water for the pasta to come to a boil, she turns on the television to take her mind off her swirling thoughts. The news is on, and while she usually doesn't like the news—knowing that the negative energy it creates is bad for the baby—she needs something to distract herself from looking at her phone every two minutes. She closes her eyes briefly and surrounds her son with a white light of protection from anything she may see or hear as the tragedies of the day are explained by an attractive blond woman wearing a tight red dress.

The first story is about an accident in the pouring rain that even now is still battering the windows of her apartment.

She recognizes the road—she travels it every day. Today the rain had been so intense she had worried about her old car remaining stable on the road. She will have to invest in a new one before the baby comes. She is still driving the first car her parents bought for her at eighteen. It's time for a change.

Her father will be delighted to learn the baby is a boy. She will call him in the morning to let him know. He's in Queensland right now on a camper van tour of Australia with a group of friends, all of whom are either widows or widowers. They are a great comfort for each other. Her mother died ten years ago, and the sadness of that loss is constant, but she is glad that he will be able to experience the joy of a grandchild.

The remote control for the television is on a side table next to the sofa and she grabs it to turn up the sound.

"Police are appealing for help identifying a man who was hit by a car on Williamsburg Road this morning. The accident was called in by numerous sources and a constable present at the scene got out to help the pedestrian. The man is believed to be of Caucasian appearance and in his forties. He has dark hair and was wearing a blue shirt and black pants. He also had a black and gold wedding band and gold watch. Police are also asking for any witnesses to come forward so that they can identify the car that hit the pedestrian. At this time, no one has claimed responsibility."

Athena is standing behind the sofa, but she leans forward, peering at the scene on the television. In the kitchen she can hear the water begin to bubble but she cannot move.

The paramedics are standing in the sheeting rain, wiping their hands across their faces as they work, and there is someone else, a man holding up a blanket that's not doing much good because it is saturated and sagging with water. Athena stares hard at the screen and then gasps as the man holding the blanket moves and the person filming the scene zooms in, making sure to get every distressing detail and allowing her a glimpse of the watch on the hand of the man on the stretcher. It is gold with a chunky metal strap. She recognizes that watch instantly. She knows what's engraved on the back.

"It was the only gift my mother ever gave me that let me know she had any love for me," he told her one night as she ran her fingers over the small engraved letters at the back. A lie. A nice sentiment but a lie all the same.

The urge to cry clogs her throat, and she has no idea what to do. What is she supposed to do?

In the kitchen the pot of water bubbles furiously, the lid jumping and water cascading down the sides of the pot, sizzling onto the stovetop.

Athena darts for the kitchen and switches off the stove, touching the pot by mistake and burning her hand.

"Ow," she cries and runs the cold tap as her heart races. She needs to call someone—the police or the hospital, someone—but she doesn't know what to do first as her skin turns red and the sting of the burn spreads.

Her cell phone is on the kitchen counter, and she stares at it, remembering the last text she sent him, remembering the terrible things she said, remembering what she has done. Self-loathing creeps up from her toes as she stands with her hand in the water. "Oh, Caleb," she moans, "what kind of a mother have you got for yourself?"

Her mind takes her back to the road as she made her way from her store to the doctor's office for her ultrasound. She wanted to be there early in case he turned up, though she hadn't gone directly from her store. There was another stop first, another question that she needed answered, something else that was supposed to happen. There was so much traffic on the road and everywhere there was a sense of chaos caused by the rain and then suddenly there was... She shakes her head as she watches the water run over her hand, cooling the burn.

She cannot think about what she saw on that road today, what she realized and what she did after that. She cannot think about it at all.

EIGHT

The truth about beautiful people is that our road through life is more easily traveled. No one wants that to be the truth or to believe it. "Beauty is in the eye of the beholder" is one of those famous quotes that everyone seems to know. It means beauty is subjective and what one person finds beautiful another may not—but that's rubbish really. Everyone, even a baby, recognizes beauty in a person. Babies respond better to people with symmetrical faces, will coo and smile more readily at wide eyes and a pretty smile. I read that somewhere.

Beauty is hard to maintain but I've done the work, made the sacrifices, given up what I needed to in order to hold on to it. Sometimes I stand in front of a mirror and take myself apart, trying to determine exactly what part of me makes me this pleasing to look at. Is it the shape and color of my eyes or perhaps the shine on my thick hair? Is it my slightly too generous lips or my perfect white-toothed smile? I can't quite work it out. All I know is that I have rarely had to buy myself a drink and I have never wanted for company and I have always gotten most of what I desired. Most, but not all.

I want it all. I want loyalty and love and friendship and sex and admiration. I want the happy ending, the romantic-novel perfection that everyone is searching for. I thought I had it. I really thought I had it, but it has been snatched away from me even as I have tried so desperately to hold on. I don't like it when things are taken away from me. It's not what I deserve. Because I have worked very hard to maintain my beauty as I age. I deserve to be rewarded for that with loyalty and love.

I'm sure I never meant to be this kind of person. I have spent years seeking a kind of spiritual peace that will allow me to view myself as connected to everyone else in the world, to see everyone as having their own pain and problems and to try for nonjudgment, but I have never quite managed to find that space. And then I met him, and the ugly parts of me, the jealous, angry, fearful, vengeful parts of me, rose up in a wave and drowned everything else. His fault. My fault as well. I knew what I was doing.

I keep going back to that first dinner, to the first night we spent together when everything was new and the future was a bright spot on the horizon, a time just for him and me and everything we could possibly want.

The restaurant was far away from where I lived. I didn't know him well enough to get into a car with him, but my heart knew him. My body already yearned for his. It was hard to enjoy the charred crust of the perfectly made pizza as he stared at me, the food lodging in my throat.

"You're making me uncomfortable." I smiled. "I can't eat while you're watching me."

"I'm sorry"—he flushed slightly—"it's just that you are so beautiful I almost can't believe you're sitting here with me."

I have heard those words from a man before and I have never worked out the correct way to respond. Should I say "thank you," or perhaps, "you're not so bad looking yourself"? Usually, hearing them irritates me because it means they are not listening to a thing I'm saying. But it felt different with him, as if the words were touching my soul, and as if he was not just seeing my shell but inside me as well.

I didn't say anything, not wanting to spoil the mood by saying something stupid. Instead, I picked up my piece of pizza again. The cheese had bubbled brown and the salty artichokes paired perfectly with the basil leaves. I took a bite, chewing as he watched.

"I love that you eat, that you really eat," he said. "My wife lives on air and anger."

I was in my late thirties. I had been dating for decades. There was very little a man could say that would shock me, and I was grateful for that because it allowed me to pick up my glass of blood-red wine and take a deep sip, enjoying the heavy plum taste and the slight acid kick as I swallowed.

There it was. The catch.

"Perhaps if you brought her here, she might try the pizza," I said lightly.

He waited a beat before replying, his hand playing with the stem of his wineglass, which I noticed was already empty. He had needed some liquid strength to tell the truth.

"I didn't want to lie to you," he said softly. "I never want to lie to you. It's not a happy marriage, hasn't been for a long time, and I know a lot of men say that because... well, it's a great excuse, but it's completely true for me. My daughter, my youngest daughter, will get her driver's license soon and then it's over. My wife and I are done and she knows that. I've made sure she knows that. And I shouldn't have started dating. It's wrong, but you..." He opened his arms wide. "Who could resist you?"

Oh how I preened and giggled. Who could resist me indeed. I let him take me to bed. I let him promise me the world. I didn't ask to see a picture of his wife or his children. I didn't ask the reasons his marriage was over. I reveled in his body and his words and the way he looked at me. I didn't ask if he was lying, and I should have asked.

And then I let him go home to his wife because I was in my late thirties and nothing is ever perfect. I saved my guilt and shame over what we were doing for when I was alone so that I could chew on it, let it burn me, allow it to hurt. Mostly I allowed it to turn into something else.

I knew what the catch was and, at some point, I knew there was more to it than that, but I kept going back for more.

I betrayed myself first. And yes, perhaps I also betrayed his wife—the sisterhood and all that—but screw the sisterhood. I wanted him to be mine.

In the time we were together I lost weight, despite always making sure to eat when we were together. Anxiety and hate burn up a lot of calories. I tried looking at other men, even dating a few, but no one came close to him and he knew that. You could see he knew that by the way he spoke to other women. It didn't matter who the woman was or what she did. If he turned his attention to her, she would instantly fall under his spell. It's his size, his looks, his charm, his broad shoulders. It's everything. People talk about charisma, but few people could actually explain what exactly it is. He has charisma. When he walks into a room, the energy changes and then he draws you in and holds you there and you cannot help but desire his attention forever.

I told him I didn't want to see a photo of his wife, but I looked at her pictures online. Her Instagram is perfectly curated, every shot more beautiful than the last, all painting a picture of extreme happiness.

"Liar, liar," I whispered to her as I scrolled.

I found a shot of the whole family, a restaurant dinner with the caption: Our baby boy is a man. Happy nineteenth birthday, Sean!! *It was a Japanese restaurant, sake in a jug, crispy tempura vegetables and a bubbling pot of something on the table.*

Jealousy surged through me and I printed the picture out. Slowly, I cut around her head and, with great care, I inserted a photo of my own head on her body. My body is better, but I did like the black silk top she was wearing.

I stuck it on the fridge and took it down only when he came over.

It gives me great comfort to look at that picture every morning, to imagine my future, to know that one day she will be gone. And it will just be me and him.

That time can't come soon enough.

NINE
MARLA

Wednesday, 8:00 p.m.

Marla sits next to the bed where Damon lies, the soft sound of his heart being monitored driving her stir crazy. Nurses pad in and out on silent feet and check the drips going into his arm as a machine breathes for him. His face is a mess of deep purple bruises, and one arm is bandaged and splinted as they wait for the swelling to go down before setting it.

As soon as she saw the news, she knew; recognized the watch, the watch she gave him for their eighteenth wedding anniversary three years ago, recognized the ring she placed on his finger twenty-one years ago. The ring that slid so easily on and off his finger.

That's him. It's him. It really happened, she had thought, as she stood in the kitchen pressing the tea towel hard against her sliced thumb. The ringing in her ears drowned out all other sound as the thought repeated. *It really happened, it really happened*. And then she became aware of her surroundings, of where she was and what she needed to do. Too drunk to drive, she had to yell for Bianca, who didn't understand at first, as

Marla kept pointing at the television, her words slurring, her thoughts garbled.

Bianca had yelled, "Can you just stop shouting and tell me what's wrong?"

Marla had taken a deep breath and felt her head clear a little. "There was an accident on Williamsburg Road. Your father was hit by a car—at least I think it's him. They are asking for help in identifying him, and we need to go to the hospital so I can tell them it's him. You need to drive me to the hospital." She would have much preferred it to be Sean. Her son would sympathize and reserve judgment, but he was out with friends and she didn't want to call him back just yet, not yet. What if she was wrong? There wasn't time anyway. He was in the city at a hip new Cajun restaurant, at least forty minutes from where she was.

Bianca folded her arms, skepticism on her face. "Why do you think it's him? You said you don't know where he went."

"I... don't, but I saw... Look," she said, trying to slow her heart with some deep breaths, "I think the man who got hit by a car is your father. I need to get to the hospital so I can see if that's the case. Please drive me there, okay? My car is at the mechanic's."

"And you'd be way over the limit," snapped her daughter, causing Marla to hang her head as her cheeks burned.

Having achieved the reaction she was looking for, Bianca softened. "It's probably not him. You always worry too much. You guys had a fight and he's probably just having a drink in a pub or something or he's gone to see Uncle Ivan," and Marla realized that she could be right. The image on the screen had been taken by a mobile phone through the rain. It could have been anyone and she'd jumped to conclusions.

What she couldn't say to her daughter was that she knew it was her husband, knew it without a shadow of a doubt. Marla bit down on the words, suddenly conscious that she was talking to her little girl, no matter how old she was, to Damon's little girl, who adored her father and would be devastated that he had been hurt.

"If it was him, they would know already. Wasn't he carrying his phone or his wallet or both?" asked her daughter.

"No. . ." Marla hesitated, thinking of the phone hidden upstairs. It had been in her car, in the car that was now parked at the mechanic's. He rarely carried a wallet anymore. "I don't know. . . maybe he had his phone but lost it or something or it's broken. I'll get his wallet from the bedroom because I'm sure I saw it there."

"Okay," Bianca finally agreed, and Marla was grateful that her daughter chose not to dwell on the irony of a seventeen-year-old having to drive her over-the-limit mother around.

Marla grabbed a Band-Aid from a basket on top of the microwave and they headed out to the car. As Bianca drove, Marla called Damon's brother Ivan. They were close, friends as well as brothers, and they spent a lot of time together, but Ivan didn't answer. She would have called Ivan's wife, Paula, but she and Paula rarely spoke to each other. Sean and his cousin Gem were the same age, and when they were babies, a competition had sprung up between the two women that ended any possibility of friendship. Gem was the perfect child, clever, sporty, polite, perfect. . . Marla knew there were not enough positive adjectives in the English language to describe the brilliance of Gem, but Sean was just a regular child, according to Paula. No, Marla would not be calling her sister-in-law, whom she hadn't spoken to properly for years. They air-kissed at every Christmas and at every Christmas Paula remarked that Marla was looking really tired, by which she meant old. Paula was a year younger than Marla and a lawyer, who always asked Marla if she wasn't bored doing nothing all day long. Paula was the last person she would call.

Finally, they were at the hospital and Marla's stress had dissipated any alcohol in her blood, leaving her with nothing more than a thumping headache and acid churning in her stomach.

The receptionist was patient and kind as Bianca and Marla explained, but it was still a half hour wait until a doctor came to find them and pepper them with questions about the man who was in the accident.

"Does he have any birthmarks? Was he carrying anything or wearing anything that you can tell us about? Where did you think he was? When last did you hear from him?" the young man asked, his eyes straying to Bianca even as he spoke. Marla thought he didn't look much older than her daughter.

"No," said Marla firmly, so the dark-haired young man looked back at her. "He doesn't have any birthmarks, but he does have a scar on his chest from falling out of a tree when he was eight," she said as she searched her mind for identifying characteristics. "Also his watch is engraved with the words *with love*. It's from me and his name is Damon Kennedy and I'm his wife. I recognize his wedding ring as well. It's him." She had taken the wallet out of her bag and clumsily removed Damon's physical copy of his driver's license, her bandaged thumb getting in the way and causing her more pain than such a small cut should.

The doctor had peered at the picture on the license for a long time. "You can see it's him," she snapped, irritated at still having to wait.

"Um. . . well," he said, flushing slightly, "if you could just give me a moment, please. Do you mind if I take this? I'll just get some of my colleagues to take a look."

Marla had shrugged and handed over the license and it was only when she and Bianca were sitting on a fake leather couch in the waiting area that she realized that the reason it might not be clear that the person they were trying to identify was Damon was because his face was damaged. His beautiful face with his perfect smile. The face that most people found themselves drawn to, men and women, the face he used to get whatever he wanted in the world. The face he used to take what he wanted from the world, regardless of who he hurt or what the consequences were.

And then the full horror of the situation hit her and she burst into tears.

"Please, Mum," Bianca had whispered, "please stop crying. I'm sure it's not him. I'm sure." But Marla knew it was. Bianca seemed to be struggling with what to do, never having seen her mother so out of control before, and an instinct to protect her kicked in, so that when the young doctor came back and said only Marla would be allowed in to see the patient, Marla told Bianca she should go home.

"I need to see my father," she had protested.

"We can only allow one person in the room," the young doctor explained.

"Then I'll just wait here," snapped Bianca. "Maybe it's not him, maybe you're wrong." Her voice was hopeful and she sounded so much younger than she was.

"Please, sweetheart, just go home and wait for Sean. I'll call you as soon as I know anything," Marla begged, desperate to have her daughter safely at home so she didn't have to worry about her.

Finally, Bianca acquiesced and left. "Call me as soon as you've seen him," she said.

When the young doctor led her into the room, there was still a question of his identity, even though Marla had identified his watch and his ring. The man in the bed looked smaller than he had this morning, but Marla was in no doubt that it was him. She had walked over to him, looking down at his hands that she knew so well, at the body that she had traced every inch of, at the dark curls she had run her hands through so many times, and nodded. "It's him," she said, pinpricks of shock covering her body as she looked at how damaged he was.

The name Damon means to overpower, to tame, subdue

and conquer. In his hospital bed, with a tube in his throat, it is Damon who has been conquered and overpowered. Damon who has been subdued by what has happened to him.

Now Marla is sitting next to her husband and what she wants to do, or what she thinks she wants to do, is reach out and touch some part of him to offer some comfort, even though he is unconscious. She wants to tell him everything will be fine and not to worry, but the part of her that wants to touch her husband's hand is being held back by the part of her that is marinating in humiliated fury, a place she's been for some time now. Not just since this morning but for many months already.

This morning she was looking for a full confession and an apology. Perhaps she had even pictured contrite tears. But that's not what she got at all. She had hoped that all his lies festering under the surface would burst out when he was properly confronted, and then the two of them could be free of deceit once and for all. It had even been possible to picture their marriage moving forward with honesty, just the two of them. What a ridiculous notion that had proved to be. It wasn't that she hadn't considered and accepted the alternative, which was Marla continuing on alone and Damon being free to continue doing what he liked. She was prepared for that as well, imagining that if that was where the conversation led them, he would be filled with guilt and shame and willing to do whatever she wanted to make her happy. She had a lifestyle to maintain. But even after nearly twenty-two years of knowing him, she apparently had little idea of just how nasty Damon could get.

In the same way that social media Marla seems to have little to do with real Marla, the man Damon pretends to be is far removed from who he really is, and even though he is lying in a bed, damaged so badly that she understands why they couldn't identify him with his license photo, she's not going to forget that. Who has she been married to all this time? What has she allowed him to become by willingly looking away for so long?

The image had been more important than the reality. That was just the truth. The truth for both of them.

Did you hear about Sandra? She and her husband are divorcing and she'll be left with absolutely nothing. It's so humiliating for her, she can barely hold her head up at bridge club and she'll have to get a job after forty-five years of not working. Her mother's words emerge from the air around her, reminding her of the necessary choices she has always needed to make. But the truth is that her parents would have understood if she had left Damon, understood and been supportive.

She cannot blame her mother for the choices she has made, cannot blame anyone. She has enjoyed the privileges of her life, from the large house to the fillers and Botox that are supposed to keep her looking young and fresh. Right now, the outfit she is wearing cost close to three thousand dollars and it's just a casual outfit, just something she wears every day. Tomorrow her cleaner will spend the day doing washing and cleaning the house as she did on Tuesday. Last year she and Damon took the children and Julia on a cruise around the Mediterranean, taking in the sights and shopping at every designer store they could find. The compromises she has had to make to hold on to this life felt acceptable, until they didn't. All along what she has been compromising is herself and her own needs, her true need to be loved and respected and have someone by her side who is a partner in everything. She left it too long to make a stand, she allowed too much, and now she is here and she cannot even touch his hand and whisper words of love.

Instead, she leans forward in her chair and whispers, "I know what you did. I know everything you did," acid filling her throat as she says the words. Damon's chest rises and falls and the machines keep his heart pumping and his eyes remain closed. Marla sits back in the chair and places her hand on her chest where her heart is. There is no relief in saying the words, not now.

She shivers a little because the room is cold and her coffee-colored cashmere sweater is still a little damp from the brief moment they were in the rain as they walked from the parking lot into the hospital.

The door opens and she doesn't take her eyes from her husband's bruised face, sure that it is just another nurse. But then someone, a man, clears his throat and she looks up.

There are two people, a man and a woman. They are both dressed in pants suits of a distinctive dark blue and wear tags around their necks, and Marla can tell immediately that these are the police.

"Excuse me, Mrs. Kennedy," says the man who has dark hair and a neat black beard, "my name is Detective Sergeant Rahim and this is Detective Constable Stevens and we just wanted to talk to you about what happened to your husband."

The female detective is as tall as her partner, with large powerful shoulders, and Marla immediately imagines her in a gym, squatting under an enormous weight, her slightly ruddy face straining with effort.

"Um, okay," she says, suddenly unsure what to do with her hands, which she finally sits on.

"Do you have any idea why your husband was on Williamsburg Road this morning?"

Marla hesitates. "No," she says because she's not going to explain anything to these people. It has nothing to do with them. "Do you know who hit him?" she asks. "I mean, did the cameras catch what happened?"

"How do you know there are cameras at the intersection?" asks Detective Stevens, her pale eyebrows lifting.

Marla stares at her, unsure if she's being made fun of. "It says so," she replies. "There are speed cameras, but I assume they catch everything, don't they?"

"Well," says Detective Rahim, "the thing is that because of the rain and. . ."

"And the fact that they weren't working," adds Detective Stevens.

"Yes, and the fact that they weren't working," sighs Detective Rahim, and Marla has a feeling that Detective Stevens has had a lot to say about the state of the traffic cameras. "We haven't actually been able to clearly see the car that hit him. We have some dashcam footage and cell phone footage and we are going through that now to get a sense of what happened, but it's possible that we will not be able to identify the car that hit him."

"Oh," says Marla, and she takes her hands out from underneath her legs and rubs her arms, feeling her blood warm a little with the relief flowing through her veins.

"Do you know why he was there in the middle of the day?" says Detective Stevens, pushing for her answer.

"It's near where we live," says Marla. "Well, not that near but..."

"Yes, we are aware of that," says Detective Stevens, "but from the footage we have got we can see that he ran across the road in front of all the cars. He didn't have a jacket or an umbrella and it's an unusual road to be out on for no reason. It's a four-lane highway, so not somewhere people usually take a walk. He also wasn't carrying his wallet or phone, as you know. The light had already changed but it was obvious there was a person on the road, so whoever hit him needs to be interviewed by police. Leaving the scene of an accident is illegal."

Marla bites down on her lip, suppressing a ridiculous giggle at how serious Detective Stevens sounds, and then her eyes fill with tears.

"Any help you can give us would be appreciated," says Detective Rahim.

"I don't know anything," she answers, rubbing a hand across her cheek, more tears appearing.

"When last did you see your husband?" ask Detective Stevens, oblivious to Marla's tears.

Marla looks down at her husband in his hospital bed as she works through what she should say. They will keep asking the question, so she needs to have an answer. "This morning," she says.

"About what time?" asks the detective.

"Around ten or so," says Marla, her gaze fixed on Damon. "We went for a drive and then he told me he wanted to get out and walk for a bit. He was having some issue at work." She looks up and waves her hand. "He wouldn't tell me what. He got out and I told him he was being ridiculous because it had already started raining but walking helped him think."

"Right," says Detective Stevens, and Marla watches her write down what she has said, feels a shiver run through her at the permanence of the words on paper, at words that cannot now be taken back.

"And where did you let him out of the car, Mrs. Kennedy?" asks Detective Rahim softly.

Marla takes a deep breath and wipes her hand across her face, using it to cool the skin on her cheeks. "About a ten-minute walk from where he got hit," she says slowly. "But there's a pub near there and I thought he might just go and get a drink." She looks at Detective Rahim as she speaks. He seems to have some sympathy for her, unlike his partner.

"At ten in the morning?" asks Detective Stevens, not even attempting to disguise the skepticism in her voice.

Marla is reminded of a confrontation she had with one of Sean's teachers when he was accused of cheating in an exam in his final year of school. The man had been full of bluster and threats until he realized that Marla would not be pushed into accepting her son was guilty. He wasn't; he simply worked harder than he had before. Marla can see that Detective Stevens is an expert in bluster and probably threats as well, but Marla knows just how careful she has to be. She won't let fear force her into saying something she'll regret.

She raises her head and stares straight at the detective. "I'm not sure what he did," she says firmly. "Once he got out of the car, I drove away. He's a forty-six-year-old man and he wanted time to walk and think, even in the rain. And I'm sure he wouldn't be the first person in the world to have a drink early in the day." She holds the detective's gaze, narrowing her eyes slightly until the woman looks down at her writing pad and makes some more notes.

"All right," says Detective Rahim, and he walks over to her, taking a card out of his wallet and handing it to her. "If you can think of anything else or if anyone gives you any information, can you please pass it on to us?"

Marla nods, silently taking the card and clutching it tightly enough to bend the cardboard.

"Thank you," says the detective. "I hope that he recovers quickly," he adds softly and then there is a swish of the door and they are gone, leaving Marla with the card and her broken husband.

Grabbing a tissue from the box next to Damon's bed, Marla blows her nose, and then she crumples up the card and throws it away with the used tissue.

TEN

SONYA

Wednesday, 8:00 p.m.

Get it together. Keep it together, she repeats to herself as she approaches the information desk at the hospital. Her breathing is shallow, her lungs refusing to properly inflate. How is she going to say this? What is she going to say, and how is she going to keep from being the focus of anyone's attention? No one deserved to die alone and unnamed. That's what she's told herself all the way here. This is simply a good deed. This is just her trying to tip the scales of karma back in her favor.

"Just ducking out to get some milk," she told Jasper after they had shared a dinner of lasagna that tasted like glue in Sonya's mouth. Fortunately, they were watching the television show *Stranger Things* together while they ate, so there didn't need to be any conversation. Sonya thought Jasper was a little young for the horror series, but he seemed to find the dramatic effects funny rather than scary. "Do you know that the guys who directed this wanted it to be kind of like an old-fashioned horror movie, so the Demogorgon is actually a guy in a suit... It's not just VFX," he told her, and she nodded as though she were paying attention to the horrifying apparition on screen. Her mind was twisting in on itself as she tried to work out what to do. If she went to the police, would she have to tell them everything? Surely not. All she needed to say was that he was a patient of hers. Would they ask how she recognized him? Maybe, and she didn't want to have that conversation. She was not obligated to give out any information unless she had a reasonable belief that a patient was in imminent danger, or in imminent danger of hurting someone else, and that was not the case here. Damon Kennedy was already hurt, hit by a car, a car the police were looking for.

"Mum, Mum, Mum," her son repeated and she had started out of her thoughts.

"Sorry, love, I was miles away," she said.

"Yeah, I could see that. I asked if you want to watch another episode."

"Um no. . ." she said and his face fell. "I mean I'm not going to watch it with you, but you can."

"But then you'll miss something," he protested.

"You can catch me up tomorrow, but now I just need to get some milk," she said, standing up and picking up her half-full plate to take to the kitchen.

"Okay, cool," he said, excited at the midweek treat of another episode.

Sonya had quickly cleaned up the kitchen as she debated over the right thing to do, her hands moving over the familiar stone surface of the countertop as her mind worked the problem. After her divorce she had never imagined feeling in control of her life again, but long hard hours of work, including night-time work with Lifeline for extra money, had eventually allowed her to take the money she got after she and Lee sold their place and put a deposit on this small inner-city terrace. Her garage is barely big enough for her car and there's never parking on the street and on the weekends the noise from the pub just up the road drives her crazy, but she loves her little home and the life she has created with Jasper. She is safe here and her son is safe here. The house is theirs and no landlord can make her move out.

Then why did you do something that could mess it all up?

She cleaned harder, scrubbing the sink and making sure Jasper's lunch was made and in the fridge for the next day at coding camp.

"I thought you were going to get milk," Jasper called from the living room. "Can you get me a Maxibon ice cream if you still are?"

"There's ice cream in the freezer," she said, "and I'm leaving now." The decision had been made for her, she felt, even as her hands trembled as she unlocked her car.

There was no way she could get into any trouble, was there? It wasn't like they were going to ask where she was when the accident happened. She was in her office, waiting for him. She got there just in time. She needed to identify him. It was the right thing to do and she had done so many wrong things lately.

Why hadn't his wife identified him already? Had she not seen the news? Did she not want to know?

And now she is here at the hospital, her heart in her mouth, and all she wants is to be told that they have identified him. She has her phone in her hand and she keeps refreshing the news screen, hoping for an update.

At a desk behind the stark white counter is a large woman in a white uniform, her hair tightly bound in a low bun. She is wearing a headpiece and directing calls, her hands dancing across her computer keyboard, long deep purple nails clicking and clacking against the keys.

Sonya steps up to the counter and waits, wanting to be and yet not wanting to be noticed.

"Putting you through to room 333 now, love," says the woman, and then she looks expectantly up at Sonya, who shoves her phone in her worn handbag and clenches her fists, bracing herself against the desire to turn and run.

"What can I help you with, my love?" says the woman, whose plump lip color matches her nails perfectly.

"Um," says Sonya, and then she hesitates as a woman with glorious blond curls hanging to her waist approaches the desk breathlessly, her pale blue embroidered dress swirling around her ankles, the hem touched with mud. "Yes, I'm sorry," the woman says quickly, "but I need to talk to someone about a man brought in today. He was in an accident." She glances at Sonya and then immediately looks away again.

Sonya takes a moment to study the woman, who is ethereally beautiful, delicate and free all at once.

"I'll just talk to this lady, love, you just hang on there. I won't be a moment," the woman behind the desk says. Sonya can see her nametag as she gestures. Doreen, someone who is obviously adept at dealing with panicked, worried, scared people as part of her daily routine. Her smile remains and she exudes an air of calm efficiency.

"No, it's fine," says Sonya, backing away from the counter as she watches the woman whose hand strays to her stomach. She doesn't need to be here now.

"I left my... my gift in the car. I'll just get it," she says, the idea the first thing that comes to mind.

Sonya's nails dig into her palms. She steps back again and looks at the woman, but she is staring at the receptionist and does not look back at Sonya. They are strangers to each other.

She thinks about Marla, Damon's wife, and how different she looks from this woman. He once showed her a picture of the whole family that he carries in his wallet. In it all four of them are arranged artfully on the grass, all dressed in black jeans and white T-shirts. His son looks like him, with the same jawline, but his eyes are pale green like his mother's. His daughter looks more like Marla, although she has gorgeous burnished red hair.

Marla's hair was probably the same color when she was younger but now it's a bright yellow blond that must come from a lot of bleaching, and it's dead straight. Sonya remembers wondering how long the woman spent at the hairdresser to get that fake, overdone look, but she assumed it was as much time as she spent getting her face seen to. Sonya could spot a Botox junkie from a mile away. A secret she was keeping from herself was the streak of jealousy that ran through her when she looked at the picture-perfect family. At the time she had smiled and said, "lovely," and Damon had agreed.

She had tried to create a picture-perfect family for herself many years ago, but it was not meant to be. And now Lee has managed to do it with another woman. Her ex-husband's picture is complete, and her picture is nothing like she imagined as a young woman.

Sonya suddenly feels sick, especially as the blond woman standing at the desk pointedly ignores her. This is the complication in Damon's life, the reason he was seeing her, the reason he needed help to sort through his guilt and his worry. Sonya becomes aware that her new bangs have parted strangely in the wet weather and that she is dressed in the old pair of jeans she changes into when she gets home, worn at the knee, baggy and stretched. Her makeup from this morning has worn off. Even though she would like to touch the woman on the shoulder and say something, she backs away farther.

She turns around and leaves the hospital with quick steps and a racing heart.

At some point today, she convinced herself that this morning was this morning and there would be no repercussions from that. But that's not the case.

He will be identified, so it's not her problem. Not anymore.

ELEVEN

ATHENA

Wednesday, 8:00 p.m.

Athena watches the woman leave. The woman is a stranger in a hospital, just a stranger, and nothing to do with her, so she's not going to worry about her or what she wanted to say to the receptionist. A couple of weeks ago, when everything was different, Athena would have stepped back and allowed the woman to speak first. Athena prides herself on being polite, on seeing the vulnerability in every person she meets so that she is always aware that other people are fighting battles she may know nothing about. But that's not how the rest of the world works. She has been pushed aside, had her heart broken, and now knows for sure that everything she had ever imagined about her life with Damon was just some ridiculous flight of fantasy she had taken a ride on by herself.

In truth Athena was done being nice a couple of weeks ago, done accepting explanations that sounded false and pretending to understand everyone else's point of view. Now it was just about her point of view, her and her baby's. But old habits die hard, and she was shocked to learn on the news they hadn't identified him. She couldn't let him lie in a hospital bed in a coma without anyone there to help him.

Even after everything she had done, she would not do that.

A tiny flutter inside her reminds her that this child has a father. Whatever kind of man he may be, he is this child's father. And still, some part of her that she doesn't want to acknowledge hopes for an outcome where Damon is hers and they raise their son together. She is embarrassed for herself and her foolish dreams.

"Not sure what that was about," says the woman. "Now, what can I do for you, love?"

"Um, it's about someone who was... There was an accident and he... I saw it on television, they were asking about his identity... I just saw it on the news," she says, speaking quickly. She hasn't just seen it on the news. She saw it on the news two hours ago, but as soon as she recognized his hand, or thought she did, she began throwing up. He doesn't usually wear his ring, but she always knows it's there in a pocket or in his car, somewhere close so that it can be slipped on again when needed.

The vomiting was awful. It felt like she had some sort of bug, but eventually it stopped and she managed to get herself into a shower and over here. The rain has not stopped and she felt her shoes squelch through mud as she cut across some grass next to the parking lot at the hospital. She was going to just call the hospital but then... she just couldn't. She didn't want it to be real. And if it was real, she needed to be here, needed to be taken to him so she could hold his hand and tell him how sorry she was.

Are you sorry? Her stomach twists, and for a moment she feels like she might need to throw up again, although there is precious little left inside her.

"Are you all right, love? You look a bit flushed? Do you want to sit down?" The woman, whose red and white nametag identifies her as Doreen, begins to rise from her chair.

"No, no," says Athena, taking a deep breath so she can compose herself and say what she needs to say. "A man was brought in today. He was hit by a car and they were asking for help identifying him on the news and I think I know who he is. I mean I do know who he is," she says firmly. She'll say he was a customer in her shop, not entirely untrue, say that he was there recently and paid with a credit card and she recognized the watch on his hand. She can say she recognized the ring as well because as a customer there would be no need for him to remove his ring, no need to pretend there was no wife attached to that ring. A whole story unfurls in her mind, and she sees herself clearly commenting on the ring he is wearing, hears herself saying to him, "Onyx is a stone of protection and perseverance." No one could doubt the explanation.

"Oh, right... right," says Doreen, and she taps away at her keyboard. "I know who you're talking about. It was a bit all over the place this afternoon what with the rain. There were quite a few accidents but only one where someone wasn't known. But it's fine now. He's been identified and he's with his wife, so it's all good. Do you know him?" She smiles as if delighted to be able to let Athena off the hook from having to get involved.

Athena's hand goes to her mouth. She cannot throw up here. With his wife? She supposes Marla still is his wife and of course she would come. But as she drove over here, once again peering through the rain, she had imagined that he would be alone, that somehow she would find a way to see him and to sit with him. She wanted to tell him that the child was a boy and that she was sorry, deeply, deeply sorry.

She had imagined that she would cope with the idea of a wife, of a family, when she first found out. She had tried, she really had, but the fact that he had lied to her had devastated her and the warrior goddess had reared her head to protect Athena's broken heart. She should have left him then, but as she has realized over the past months, it's harder to leave someone than people think it is. If he were awful or mean, that would have made it easier for Athena, but he was generous and kind and loving and so, so beautiful to look at, so wonderful to touch.

"No, I thought. . ." she stutters. "I thought I did." And then she turns swiftly and leaves the hospital, but not swiftly enough that she doesn't hear Doreen mutter, "The rain always makes everyone crazy," before she answers the phone again. "North Vale Hospital, can I help you?"

Athena walks slowly, letting the cold rain dampen her curls and drench her clothing. She wants to feel cold, wants to stop all other thought except physical sensation.

His wife is with him.

Unlocking her car with trembling hands, she slides in and turns her key in the ignition, turning up the heat. Instead of reversing, she remains where she is, her mind crowded, thoughts jumbled. She imagines Marla with her perfectly straight hair and her manicured nails holding Damon's hand, and drops her head onto her steering wheel. As she closes her eyes, she goes back to the day they met, that wonderful, glorious day when her whole world changed. That dreadful, terrible day when her whole world changed but she just didn't know it then.

It was only seven months and three days ago. Athena laughs and then sits up straight, covers her face with her hands, taking a deep breath. She will not allow tears because once she starts, she will never be able to stop. She can still count the time she has been with Damon in days, sometimes she can still work it out to the hour, and she knows that for seven months, three days, and twenty hours, she has been lied to.

Damon came into the store at 12:00 p.m. on a Thursday. Athena noticed him immediately because he was dressed in a pinstripe suit, because he had thick dark hair lightly threaded with gray and stubble on his face, and because he was so physically attractive. She didn't get a lot of men in her store because of its suburban location, and those that did come in were often elderly. She assumed he was waiting for a lunch order from one of the cafés, but he seemed to be looking around quite seriously, so she went up and asked if she could help. As she got closer, the spicy musk smell of his aftershave enveloped her and she focused for a moment on looking down at his large hands with neat fingernails. "Oh, yes," he said, offering her a generous smile when she glanced up, "I'm looking for a birthday gift for my... colleague and she's very into this kind of stuff."

"And what kind of stuff is that?" Athena asked, matching his smile, held by the vivid brilliant green of his eyes. She was used to the things she sold being dismissed by most people as airy-fairy and having no real value.

"Well, this," laughed Damon, gesturing around the store. Athena didn't even care that he didn't seem to be taking the things she sold seriously. She helped him choose a scented candle and a book of spells for success, and then after she had wrapped everything and placed it all in a carry bag decorated with flowers and swirls, he said, "I don't want you to think I'm making fun of the things you sell; I just don't understand much about it."

"Well, you should ask then," said Athena, her heart fluttering like it had when she was a teenager talking to a boy she liked.

"All right, can you tell me about your crystals," he said, "maybe over a drink?"

"It's only just after lunch," said Athena, her cheeks flushing.

"So?" Damon smiled and shrugged, and Athena felt a nudge from behind her where Gail was standing. "I can watch the store," she said.

"See, even your assistant wants you to educate me about what you do," he laughed. "I'm Damon," he said.

Athena knew right then, right there, that her life was shifting and she would never be the same.

And today it shifted again.

And she will never be the same.

TWELVE
MARLA

Thursday, 9:00 a.m.

What is the protocol for sitting beside the bed of your husband who is in a coma? Marla is unsure. Every now and again she gets her phone out and scrolls through her social media and the news before guiltily putting it away again. She supposes she should be speaking to Damon all the time so that even in his state he is aware that she's here and that he is not alone. But anything she starts to say feels silly and wrong, and she is always hyperaware of the nurses who seem to be in and out of the room every few minutes. When she speaks it sounds rehearsed, as though she is someone playing a part, rather than someone trying to communicate with the man she loves.

Last night she had only left the hospital after midnight so that she could get some sleep. Sean and Bianca were waiting up for her, drinking hot chocolate in the kitchen and sharing a packet of Oreos. For a moment, as she looked at them, she was reminded of them at eight and six on a Christmas Eve when she allowed them both to stay up late, and the four of them had sat together in the kitchen with the door open to the garden, where the hot day was lingering in the air, drinking hot chocolate and eating Christmas cookies as they each tried to guess what their presents would be. Can memories be a way to trap yourself, to keep yourself in a situation longer than you should stay, as you gaze, misty-eyed, into the past? Marla thinks so.

"Mum," Sean said, jumping up and then leaning down to offer her a long hug. "How is he?"

Marla had wanted more than anything to be alone under a hot shower so that she could wash off the clingy astringent smell of the hospital, but she owed it to her children to let them know what was happening.

"He has some swelling on the brain and they are hoping it goes down so they don't have to operate. He has a broken arm and they are waiting for that to stop swelling as well. His face is very bruised and he seems to have chipped a couple of teeth, but they won't know for sure until they wake him from the coma and a dentist takes a proper look." She tried to recite the words without emotion, to remain very clear and factual, but even as she did, she felt the words land like punches on her children, saw their shocked faces and wished they were too young to have all this information, wished she could keep it to herself and keep them away from the pain of this. "But there's not much more to say. It's mostly a waiting game," she finished, stepping toward Bianca and holding her daughter tightly around her shoulders, feeling the girl's visible shaking ripple through her own body.

"Can I get you anything, Mum?" asked Bianca. "You must be starving." She stepped away, running her hand over her face to rid herself of tears. Marla knew that Bianca would save her tears for later when she was alone. Even as a child she had done that.

"No, thank you, sweetheart. I may just get some rest before I go back in a few hours." She had turned away, unable to look at her children's ashen faces. Damon was a good, if slightly absent, father and they both loved him, Bianca especially.

"When can we see him?" Bianca asked.

Marla held back a sigh, found the strength to turn back. "Not for a bit. They're allowing only one visitor in at the moment." She shook her head, feeling the whole day settle on her shoulders. She wasn't sure how she was even going to make it up the stairs to her bedroom, how she was going to look at Damon's aftershave in its distinctive white bottle, standing on the marble countertop in their bathroom. How she was going to lie in their bed and close her eyes without guilt strangling her so that she couldn't breathe.

"But, Mum. . ." Bianca said as she left the kitchen and she heard Sean shush his sister as she dragged her heavy legs up the stairs. In the bathroom she threw all her clothes into the hamper as she avoided Damon's side of the vanity, avoided her own face in the mirror, avoided thinking about what she had done.

She had crashed after her shower, dropped into a thick black sleep only to wake four hours later with her heart racing and her mouth dry. It seemed easiest then to simply get up and come to the hospital.

A nurse comes into the room and smiles at Marla, who tries to lift the sides of her mouth in greeting but fails. Damon hasn't even been in the hospital for twenty-four hours, but she is already starting to recognize the staff.

Downstairs there is a small café where she goes virtually every hour for a cup of coffee or something sweet to eat, and the woman behind the counter told her an hour ago that she was praying for her.

"But you don't know why I'm here," she said because she could be visiting for a happy reason, a brand-new grandchild perhaps, although she had been at the hospital since 5:00 a.m.

"Oh, love," said the woman, who was older than her with gray hair in a low ponytail and lined eyes of pale blue, "I can always tell and I hope it gets better."

"Thank you," Marla managed as she felt her eyes fill with tears. Genuine sympathy from strangers was always so hard to bear and she had no idea why. Perhaps it was the guilt. She was not deserving of sympathy because, as she sat at her husband's bedside, all she could think about was getting away.

"How are you feeling, Mr. Kennedy?" says the nurse, who is a young man with bright red hair and braces on his teeth. He moves around checking things and then updating a chart as Marla wonders whether she is supposed to reply for Damon or not. What is the proper behavior for the wife of a car accident victim?

"All right, I'll be back in a bit. You rest, Mr. Kennedy," he says with a gentle squeeze of Damon's arm and he leaves.

Marla gets up from her chair, feeling stiff and sore from all the sitting. She stands at the window of the private room and looks out and down onto the hospital parking lot, where she can see an older couple with a giant bunch of balloons festooned with the words IT'S A BOY. The woman is talking nonstop, practically jumping with excitement, and Marla feels a small smile on her face. Grandchildren are still far away for her, but she looks forward to loving a child without having to actually raise them, all the fun and none of the responsibility. Will Damon be around to meet his grandchildren? How bizarre to be here today when at the same time yesterday she would have found the question absurd. Yesterday she didn't know if she and Damon would be together for the rest of their lives. Today she doesn't know if Damon has reached the end of his life.

She feels her eyes grow hot and she shakes her head.

Her phone vibrates in her hand and she looks down to see a message from Ivan.

Any news?

No change, she replies, glad that her brother in law doesn't require a whole explanation or a text conversation. She texted him last night, explaining the same way she had explained to her children everything that had happened to Damon. He had wanted to come to the hospital immediately but there were rules in place for visiting and so he would have to wait just as the children would have to wait.

Let me know if you want me to come and sit with him. Give you a break.

Thanks so much. I'm fine, she replies. Ivan is a good man, and someone Marla has always enjoyed speaking to. He has a measured way of looking at the world and never says anything without taking the time to think it through. It makes the advice he does give or the opinions he expresses seem to have the weight of authority behind them.

"Do you want to know a secret?" she asks her silent husband as she continues to look out of the window at the parking lot, watching a red Porsche try to maneuver into a small parking spot. "Ivan asked me if I knew what I was doing marrying you on the day of our wedding." She shakes her head as she remembers that day, remembers walking out of the reception and onto the patio of the beautiful old house they had hired for the day to get some air. They had been married in the garden of the castle-style home surrounded by a canopy of white roses and baby's breath set among the manicured greenery. The reception in the large ballroom had been going for hours and she felt she wouldn't be able to thank or smile at one more person, so she had gathered her soft silk dress in her hands to keep it from trailing on the floor and walked onto the patio and around to the side for a moment of peace and quiet as she inhaled the gardenia smell of the night air.

"Needed some space, did you?" someone asked and she gasped, startled, and then laughed when she saw it was Ivan smoking a cigarette.

"I know," he said, raising his eyebrows, "filthy habit and I am giving up."

"It's fine." She smiled. "I don't actually mind the smell so much. My dad used to smoke, so it vaguely reminds me of my childhood."

"You look beautiful, Marla," he said suddenly. "I know people have been telling you all day, but you really do—you're radiant." She had been truly beautiful then, with thick burnished red hair and full lips. He smiled at her and she shivered, even in the summer heat. He had the same perfect smile his brother did and he even shared his green eyes, but he didn't have Damon's square jaw and full lips and he was shorter, less physically fit.

"Are you sure you know what you're doing?" he asked.

"I'm just having a few minutes outside, Ivan," she giggled. The cool night air and the Champagne mingled to make her feel slightly dizzy.

"No," he said, his voice serious as he pulled at his bow tie, loosening it so that it hung open around his neck, "do you know what you're doing by marrying him?"

She had laughed again but more uncertainly. "It's a bit late now, isn't it?"

Ivan sighed and dropped the cigarette butt on the floor, grinding it out with his heel and then picking it up to throw away. "I know you love him and I love him too, but you're fabulous and you should be made to feel that way every day of your life. The one thing I know about my brother is that he thinks he's fabulous and he always has." In the year that Marla had been dating Damon, she had never spent more than a few minutes alone with Ivan. Usually, she and Damon met him for dinner with whoever he was dating at the time, and Marla always felt slightly resentful at having to entertain someone new as the brothers inevitably spent all their time speaking to each other. It was odd for Ivan to say something so clearly from his heart, especially something that cast Damon in a less than golden light. She hadn't known what to say so she had retreated into silence, biting down on her lip and looking out over the garden where fairy lights twinkled in the bushes. "Listen to me going on. I've had way, way too much to drink. I'll see you inside," he said, and he left, leaving her standing in the light breeze, her fist crushing the silk handful she was holding.

She knew even then what Ivan was talking about. Damon was a flame to every pretty moth around, and sometimes at parties she had found herself drinking way too much so that she would not erupt in a jealous rage as he flirted and laughed with another woman. "It doesn't mean anything" was his favorite line, and she had taught herself to accept that as the truth, until suddenly, it began to mean something.

The first time she caught him cheating, actually cheating, was when the children were small. Sean had been only four and Bianca two, and she was consumed by the never-ending needs of small children, even as she kept up an exercise routine and never missed a beautician's appointment so that no one would ever say she had let herself go. The visceral slap of shock she had felt seeing her husband with another woman on a casual Tuesday afternoon has never left her. She had been trying out a new beautician, who was being lauded in their circles for the best facial, and she was half an hour away from home in an unfamiliar suburb when she stopped for a coffee and saw them at the back of the coffee shop, huddled together, his arm around her, her pretty face tilted up to his. In an instant she was boiling hot and then cold as she stared at her husband and another woman.

Without thinking she had walked over to where they sat, knowing that if she waited to confront him that night, he would deny everything. She had understood her marriage to be on the precipice of something. She was balanced between what she would and would not accept. Damon held all the power because she was still looking after young children and leaving was an impossible thing to imagine. All she had was the element of surprise. It was more important in that moment that he know she knew.

"Damon," she said.

"Marla, God. . . I. . ." he said, leaping to his feet.

Marla watched the pretty young woman color.

"Perhaps he forgot to mention his wife?" she said, and the woman nodded, her face beetroot red. And then she'd turned and left. A wave of pride had flowed through her because she had managed to maintain control, because she had not burst into tears or screamed in an undignified way. She had conducted herself like a lady, but a lady who would not be fooled.

That night he had stumbled through an explanation, made excuses: *she's just a friend, we only had sex once, it never meant anything, it was a mistake, I can't help myself.* The next week he bought her a diamond bracelet and booked a family vacation where the children would be tended by nannies the whole day so they could reconnect as a couple. Marla had two young children and no job. She forgave him and they moved on. She accepted it. A tiny piece of her heart was destroyed but she moved on, even as Ivan's words to her at her wedding came back to haunt her in the middle of sleepless nights.

But there is only so much accepting and moving on a person can do before they cannot do it any longer, only so many pieces of a heart that can be destroyed before there's nothing left.

That's where Marla was two weeks ago, and yesterday and today. She cannot move on.

"He tried to warn me about you," she says now, and then she turns back to look at him, still and bruised. "Maybe you should have been the one he warned," she murmurs, and then she picks up her bag. She'll get a chocolate bar this time, something thick and chunky with nuts, something she should never, ever eat. It's just one more thing she shouldn't do

THIRTEEN

SONYA

Thursday, 9:30 a.m.

"And it's not like I don't host Christmas every year. I do host it and I don't complain and I don't mind when people bring friends or anything. All I do is just keep cooking, so when I said to Lisa that she should host lunch for Boxing Day, and she told me she was too busy with work and I don't work. . . but it's the day after Christmas and who works on Christmas? So I said. . ."

Sonya's pen moves in a spiral as she completes one doodle after another, her mind not on her session with Ellie, who is once again complaining that she feels her family doesn't take her seriously because she doesn't work. This morning at 7:00 a.m. she had briefly flirted with the idea of cancelling her day because she couldn't bear to be stuck inside her office listening to people talk about the same things they talked about last week and the week before that. Yesterday's rain has disappeared, leaving only mud-soaked fields and gardens under a bright blue sky. The idea of a day spent at home in her small garden with her hands in the earth warmed her whole body, but Jasper had a whole day at coding camp booked and it was being held at a local school close to her office, and by the time she had dropped him at the school vacation activity she was sure she would regret making Jessica reschedule all her appointments for the day. And if she didn't see her patients, she didn't get paid. Her car insurance was due and the coding camp wasn't cheap either, but Jasper was loving every minute of it and so it was money well spent.

For a moment when she woke up this morning, she had imagined that yesterday was some sort of surreal nightmare, but the news on her phone quickly told her the truth. Sonya always read the news headlines on waking, waiting until the last possible second to slide out of her sleigh bed and get on with her day. The sleigh bed was her first purchase after the divorce because she needed to get rid of the place where she and Lee had been together—read together, laughed together, slept together. She imagined the new bed would one day be shared with a new partner, but nine years later she can admit to herself that the only way a new partner would enter her life was if she actually wanted it and until now, she hasn't wanted it.

Yesterday's accident was the second headline on her news app, just below a story about a football player who had hit someone outside a nightclub.

ACCIDENT VICTIM IDENTIFIED

Sonya felt herself growing cold, even under her warm duvet, as she read about Damon Kennedy, who had been hit by a car in the pouring rain yesterday morning. He was, according to the article, in a serious but stable condition. Police were investigating and were appealing for witnesses to come forward. The cameras at the intersection where he was hit hadn't been working. Sonya was glad to know that but less glad to read that the police were going through cell phone and dashcam footage. She tried to imagine Damon in a hospital bed with his wife, Marla, next to him, perhaps wiping away a stray tear. Would she hold his hand?

Damon had come into her practice four months ago, and from their first session, Sonya understood that he was in a crisis. He hated his work, even though he was the CEO of his company, and he no longer knew if his marriage was viable. He was depressed but also aware of his privileged situation. And he was cheating on his wife with another woman. A woman he thought he might love but wasn't sure of.

"I don't want to be some sort of middle-aged cliché," he told Sonya. Sonya was always interested in a new client, always hopeful that she would find herself using her skills to help someone make a breakthrough. "I got your number from the internet," Damon said and then he had laughed and blushed. "To be honest I looked at images more than anything else. I thought that I would know the right person for me when I saw him or her and I was right. I saw you and I just knew that we would be a good fit and then I read all your reviews, so I was absolutely certain I made the right choice." That should have been a giant red flag for Sonya, but sometimes a red flag waves right in your face and you simply refuse to see it. Damon had obviously only been looking at pictures of women therapists. Even with her degree and her learned and experienced understanding of human beings, she couldn't help her biological reaction to Damon. It wasn't just that he was so good-looking. It was the aura of confidence, of ownership of the room, that he brought with him. He was so obviously a man who had everything he could desire and who had been raised to simply expect that life would go his way, and yet he was miserable and that made him seem vulnerable and sad and Sonya wanted to be the woman who helped him feel better. Her therapist self shook her head at this. Any woman who believes she can rescue a man from himself is inevitably disappointed. No one can actually be rescued from themselves, especially a man like Damon. Especially a liar like Damon.

He saw her picture and liked what she looked like. It wasn't the first time in her life that Damon Kennedy had liked what she looked like. But he had come into her office and introduced himself with a smile and offered to shake her hand with not even a glint of recognition in his gorgeous eyes.

Had she changed so dramatically? Is that what marriage, divorce, and motherhood did to a woman? He was different too. Much, much better looking, the few lines on his face adding to his appeal.

She remembers smiling and nodding as he spoke at that first session and trying not to find him attractive. She watched the way he twirled his wedding band as he talked about his wife and children and then she asked for a picture so that she could visualize them, which she always felt helped her.

"How long have you been married?" she asked, shocked at how old the children were.

"Twenty-one years, and as they say, you get less for murder."

"Who says that?" she asked quietly, and she was gratified to see him suitably chastened as he dropped his head before looking at her again, the irresistible smile back on his face before he sighed and continued with his thoughts.

"I am thinking about asking Marla for a divorce, but I'm not sure if I would be happier with someone else. I have. . ." He had stopped speaking, growing suddenly silent after having talked almost nonstop for twenty minutes.

"Whatever you have or have not done, you can talk to me about it," Sonya told him. "It's not my job to judge you. It's my job to help you find the best way forward so that you can live a fulfilling life."

Damon had nodded. "I have. . . been with other women," he said, and then he had looked up at her and in his deep green eyes she could read such hurt, such devastation at his own behavior that she knew she had to save him. *"Come into my parlor,"* said the spider to the fly, and she had followed him willingly, beguiled by his depth of emotion, by his need to be a better person. "I'm worried I might have some sort of sex addiction," he told her. He played her so deftly that she didn't even register the manipulation. Her senses were off, captivated by a man she was attracted to—was attracted to again.

"I think we would need to talk a lot more before I could make that assessment," she said.

As a therapist, the first thing she should have done when she felt her attraction to him was refer him to someone else. But she didn't. The first thing she should have done when she recognized him was remind him they had met. But she didn't.

And the things she didn't do piled up over the months they saw each other, until the one thing that she did do.

Although she never turned away a client who came to her asking for help, she was aware that some people did not want to change anything about their lives at all. They merely wanted to be able to complain uninterrupted for an hour. Damon wanted to change, he said. He wanted to fall back in love with his wife and to enjoy his work again. Just because someone had money and a picture-perfect family didn't mean it was the case. He was lying, to himself and to her, but she wanted to get him to see the truth. She really felt like she and Damon were getting somewhere before this. He claimed he was feeling a lot more positive about his future. It wasn't with Marla, and he told Sonya that he understood that, but he was working on a way to move forward that would lead to the best outcome for everyone. He and his wife had long grown apart. "She never asks me about my day, and if I try and tell her something, she tells me she has no interest or understanding of my work. All she wants to discuss is her latest diet or the kids. I married someone I thought was intelligent, but she seems more vacuous as the years go by. Her looks are the only thing she concentrates on, and she's too skinny, too frozen in place with Botox."

Sonya had felt ashamed as she warmed when he told her his wife was too skinny. She's not exactly overweight, but she's definitely a few sizes up on her twenty-something self. Her feelings should never enter a session and yet, with Damon Kennedy, they were right there, thrumming below the surface, reminding her that she was a woman who needed someone to touch her and be with her and share her life. She forgave him quietly for not remembering her. Damon Kennedy was not the answer, but he was a beautiful fantasy.

"Sonya. . . Sonya, what should I do?" asks Ellie, startling Sonya from her thoughts. She feels herself flush at having been so unprofessional and focuses on the question.

"I think you need to simply put your foot down and refuse to host," says Sonya, "and it may be a good thing to look into finding some work. I'm sensing you're bored at home now that"—she consults her notes briefly—"James and Jenna are both at university." As soon as the words hit the air, Sonya realizes her mistake. She is not supposed to make concrete suggestions to her clients. She is supposed to listen and patiently encourage them to come to their own realizations. She presses down harder on her writing pad, her face flushing.

"I'm not bored," says Ellie indignantly, and Sonya lifts her eyes from her writing pad to see Ellie's furious red face. Ellie is very overweight and originally came to see Sonya for help with her binge eating, but whatever direction Sonya tries to steer her in always leads back to how unappreciated she is by her mother and sister. Sonya has helped Ellie connect her binge eating to her feelings of inadequacy around her mother and sister, both of whom are university professors, but any connection is immediately forgotten from one week to the next. Ellie wants someone to tell her that she is badly treated by her family, so she can tell them that a professional agrees with her. And she wants to remain mystified about her eating habits instead of confronting them.

The musical chimes of the timer on her desk prevent Sonya from having to say anything else, and she offers Ellie a bright smile. "We can pick this up again next week, Ellie."

She stands and offers Ellie a hand to help her off the sofa, but Ellie bats her hand away. "I'm perfectly capable," she snaps. It is obvious that Sonya has failed to make Ellie feel any better this session and she wants to apologize, but she cannot do that without risking Ellie losing faith in her abilities. She closes the door behind her patient with a fixed smile and takes a deep breath.

Glancing at her schedule for the day, Sonya sees that her next patient, due in fifteen minutes, is Nina. Sonya hopes to do better with her than she has with Ellie.

Her intercom buzzes. "Just letting you know that Nina just cancelled. I told her that she'll have to pay for the session, but she said that's fine. She has a family emergency. She also wants to move to a Monday, so I've slotted her in at one p.m. next week."

"Did she say what the emergency was?" asks Sonya, wanting to add it to Nina's file for the next time they meet.

"No and I wasn't going to ask."

"Thanks," says Sonya, and she sinks into her desk chair, spinning it around so she can look out of her office window at the street below and the blue sky above, deeply grateful for the unexpected free hour.

It amazes her that after seeing Damon every two weeks for four months, she still knew so little about him. What she did know—what she was absolutely sure of—was that she should never have made the terrible mistake of forming a bond with him again, of really liking him again. Of having sex with him.

Again.

FOURTEEN

ATHENA

Thursday, 10:00 a.m.

Athena lies listlessly on the sofa, the remote control in her hand, clicking between news channels, listening to different news reporters giving her exactly the same information she came home with last night.

The news comes on with a dark-haired reporter standing outside the hospital in a shiny blue coat tightly belted against the morning wind, and Athena turns up the sound, aching for another tiny piece of information, although she's not sure what she wants to hear, what she expects to hear.

"Last night a pedestrian brought here after being hit by a car on Wednesday morning was identified as Damon Kennedy. No one is sure why the forty-six-year-old CEO of Crisis IT was on the road yesterday afternoon, but doctors have said he is still critical and in an induced coma. His wife is by his bedside. Mr. Kennedy has two children and his company provides IT support to some of Australia's biggest corporations. The car that hit Mr. Kennedy has not been identified due to the traffic cameras being non-operational. A detective from the major collision investigation unit, Detective Idris Rahim, has stated that police are looking at dashcam and cell phone footage in an attempt to identify the car that hit Mr. Kennedy."

A picture flashes up on the screen of Damon, just a head-shot of him in what looks like a suit, his eyes a perfect startling green and his smile wide.

"Police are appealing for information from the public. Please call Crime Stoppers on 1800 333 000 or report online."

He is not separated from his wife, but very much with her—but she knew that, of course. Despite everything he has been saying, she knew that.

She has known that since May, so for nearly six months. In May she was blissfully in love with a man she had only just met, every day filled with the fizzing joy of early infatuation. In May she was patiently waiting for Damon to leave his terrible wife and move in with her. In May—she met Marla.

The days leading up to Mother's Day, to the second Sunday in May, are good for turnover in her store as people looking for something different swarm through her doors. She and Gail usually don't even get a chance to sit down for five minutes on the day before Mother's Day and it's the frantic nature of things that meant Athena wasn't concentrating. If she were, perhaps she would have understood that the thin, immaculately dressed bleached-blond woman was in her store not to search for a gift for her mother but to blow up Athena's life by forcing her to face the consequences of her actions.

Gail had been busy wrapping gifts at the counter, so Athena had been walking around the store, making sure everyone who was thinking of buying something was encouraged to get out their credit card and actually make the purchase. Athena loved talking to customers, loved finding out what they were thinking and what they were hoping to find in her treasure trove of a store, and she was good at putting together person and object so that some kind of harmony was achieved. After helping a confused-looking teenage boy with some beautiful scented oils and a burner for his mother, she went over to a woman standing by the display of stones. The woman was holding a labradorite stone in her hand, the beautiful blue-green melding of the colors on the stone matching the large designer handbag in a deep blue that the woman was holding. Athena felt her hand stray to her tumble of curls as she smoothed them down. She felt messy compared to the woman, who had dead-straight hair, a perfectly made-up face. She was wearing a tight pair of white pants teamed with a gray and white silk top. Everything about the woman screamed money, right down to the ring encrusted with diamonds on her left hand.

"Labradorite is the stone of psychic abilities," she said to the woman, who put the stone down carefully and then folded her arms.

"Perhaps you should have been holding it then," said the woman, her voice low, her tone slightly menacing.

"Is there... anything I can help you with?" asked Athena, unable to understand the tension she could immediately feel.

"Well, I think you've already helped enough, but I am here to meet my husband's girlfriend and I suppose that's you. The woman at the counter is too young, and say what you like about Damon, but he prefers women closer to his age." Her tone was matter-of-fact, not even a hint of emotion. She could have been discussing the mild autumn day outside, where clouds drifted across the sky in the breeze.

Athena felt her whole body grow fiercely hot and she knew that her ears were a bright burning red. She had never wanted to know about his wife, the wife he was going to leave because he no longer loved her. But she hadn't been able to resist googling her—needing to know what her rival looked like, searching for clues as to why Damon no longer loved her. It had been a while since she looked at the woman's pictures on the internet, but she still should have recognized her—although in real life, the angles on her face were sharper, her lips thinner, and in place of the usual perfect smile was a deep frown.

"Is there somewhere we can talk?" asked Marla. Athena knew her name was Marla. She had looked the name up after Damon told her about his wife, searching for a sign of some sort, and found one of the meanings of the name to be "sea of bitterness," something she took to be a sign from the universe that Damon's wife was as terrible as he made her out to be. There was evidence of bitterness on the woman's face, evidence of anger and distaste. Athena felt compelled to obey her directive.

She had led Marla silently to the back office even as Gail raised her eyebrows at her because the shop was teeming with people.

The office felt smaller with Marla inside it. For a small, skinny woman, her karmic energy took up an enormous amount of space, and Athena had found herself standing behind her ash-gray timber desk, needing to put something between her and the other woman.

"I just wanted to meet you," said Marla as she looked around, wrinkling her nose slightly at the smell of the sage-, chamomile- and lavender-scented candle that was burning on Athena's desk, supposedly filling the air with calm vibes, "just wanted to see you so that I knew exactly who he was sleeping with this time." The words *this time* ricocheted around inside Athena.

"You're separated," Athena said, her voice just above a whisper. She was feeling sick, horrified, scared. Her body was a rabbit with a racing heart being chased by a lioness with one aim in mind.

Marla waved her hand, perfect glossy nails flashing in the light. "No, no. . . he just tells them—and by *them* I mean *you* right now—he just tells them that, but I will spare you the questions and tell you that we are still together, still having sex, still happy in our own way. You've lasted a bit longer than the others, so I wanted to meet you and let you know that whatever he's told you is a lie. And I wanted you to meet me. We have two children, we are a family, we have a life together. Do with that what you will."

Athena dropped her head for a moment, overwhelmed by the confrontation, and when she looked up, Marla's lips were pursed together, her pale green eyes burning right through Athena. She did not utter another word, just opened the door to the office and started to walk out, leaving Athena stunned and near tears.

"He'll break your heart," said Marla, turning back once. "He always does." Athena wasn't sure if that meant Damon always broke Marla's heart or the hearts of the other women he slept with, but even as she stood in her office waiting for the wind chimes moving by the front door of the store that would tell her that Marla had left her space, she felt a pain inside her chest, so large it took her breath away.

She had been unable to explain to Gail what had happened and had gone on through the rest of the day with a robotic smile on her face, mechanically speaking to customers. They were still having sex, not "she won't let me touch her anymore and quite frankly I don't want to." They were still happy and a family, not "we barely spend time in the same room and the kids don't care if I'm there or not." They were still together and not separated. Fury rose inside her only to be quelled by guilt and self-loathing. Was she really that stupid? Really that easy to deceive? She wanted to leave the store and find him, find him and scream that he was a liar, but she stayed, working, smiling, helping customers as her heart slowly crumbled.

"Do you want to talk about it?" Gail asked after they had closed and tidied the store.

"Not yet," she said, and Gail nodded, understanding.

That's when she should have ended things with Damon. But she didn't. Instead, she called him.

"I was just thinking about you," he said when he answered the call, his voice low and filled with desire.

"You weren't the only one," she began, squeezing one hand into a fist so that she would not cry. "Your wife, the wife you are still very much married to, was here, in my store—my store," she said as her resolve not to cry abandoned her and tears appeared. Inside the despair was a fury deep and dark that the woman had come into her space, her beautiful safe space, and made it ugly and unsafe, made it dirty. She wanted to scratch Marla's eyes out, wanted to kill Damon, and no matter how many deep breaths she took, how much she tried to meditate herself to a place of peace, she couldn't do it.

"Oh," he breathed, "Athena, angel, I'm sorry, but whatever she said, it's not true. We're not together."

"You're lying," she screamed, "lying and you're an awful human being. How could you have done this, how could you?" All her self-control disappeared as she sobbed on the phone.

"I'm coming over tonight," he said, without any other explanation, and then he ended the call.

It had been her plan to tell Damon she never wanted to see him again. It was her plan from the moment Marla left until that night when he turned up at her apartment clutching two tickets to Melbourne. "I've cleared it with Gail. You have two days off and it will just be the two of us. I know that it's hard being the other woman right now, but I want to tell you that it's not forever and I am nearly sorted on my end. Soon it will just be us forever. Marla is lying when she says we're happy or that we're still married in anything except name only. She's jealous and lying because she can tell that I'm in love with someone else. I love you, Athena. I love you with everything I have and I will do anything, anything to make this right. I'll leave her tonight. Leave my kids and not explain anything to them at all. They'll cope. I think they'll cope." Now she understands how clever he was. What kind of a woman asked a man to leave his children? He knew she would never ask such a thing of him.

"We need to stop seeing each other," she said.

He dropped his eyes to the floor. "I'll die," he whispered. "I can't live without you. You're my soul mate. I know that now." When he looked up, his eyes were glass green with tears, and then he touched her cheek with such beautiful gentleness that Athena could not help leaning into his hand.

Standing in her doorway, surrounded by his smell, looking into his beautiful eyes, Athena gave in to the yearning of her body and her heart.

"She cannot come near me again," she said feebly, wanting to still hold on to some of her anger.

"I'll make sure she understands," he said firmly.

She went to Melbourne, let herself get swept up in him, in everything about him, and she stayed with him and got pregnant. And she somehow expected the pregnancy to speed things along, to bring him into her home and life permanently.

But that's not what happened at all. And now she is here, alone, pregnant, and sure that the man she loves will never be hers.

At least the traffic cameras were broken. That's one good thing, she supposes.

FIFTEEN

The shock of finding out he was in the hospital has dissipated a little. At first I was frantic, needing to get to him, to be with him, but of course, the wife is there. It's easier to think of her as the wife rather than by her name. My heart aches for him and for myself, for what I may lose. This is not how things should have turned out. It's all over the news, people professing their shock at something like this happening. Who hits someone with their car and drives off? Someone aiming for someone else, perhaps? Someone who had a plan that went awry? Someone who definitely can't get caught.

He is in the hospital, in a coma, drifting between this life and the next. And now they are trying to find out what happened. By they I mean the police, the press, interested vultures. Let them look. Let them see what they can find.

I want to see him, need to see him, even though I know I should stay away.

In the mirror I stare at my face and know that this is not the face I can take to the hospital.

I need to be someone else, someone different so that I can pass unnoticed, so that I will not be recognized by her—by the *wife—by anyone. I slip a wig onto my head, mousey brown, fine and cut into a bob—dull. It washes out my skin and makes me look older. I've done this before, for amusement, mostly. It's good to be someone else sometimes, to be the person who looks at others rather than the person looked at. Beauty makes you stand out, and I need to be invisible.*

I would add a fake nose if I thought that would work, but it always looks exactly that, fake. Instead, I shade my face, using makeup to make lines appear where there are no lines, gray under my eyes to make me look tired. And then I add a pair of glasses, the lenses thick but containing no prescription. My eyes seem to bulge slightly.

It's a busy hospital, filled with nurses, and I put on a dark blue scrub set, easily obtained on the internet, but this is mine and it's been used in a hospital. I complete my outfit with a clipboard because no one questions a clipboard. A badge on backward, to look as though it has just turned around as I moved, helps as well. I will go after dark, when things may be quieter and, perhaps, I may go unnoticed.

Later, my heart is in my throat as I walk through the doors and go to find the Intensive Care Unit. That's where he would be, I'm sure, and I imagine he will be in a private room. The wife will make sure of that. Once I am on the right floor, I am left with a conundrum. How will I find his room? I cannot simply ask or questions would be asked of me. Who are you? Why do you want to know? What are you doing here? No, I cannot answer any questions.

I dither near the elevator for a moment with my heart drumming in my chest, waiting, hoping for something. Sweat gathers under my arms and I want to run, but I have to see him. And then luck smiles on me because the elevator doors open, and out she comes. The wife.

The one with all the status, the one with a ring on her finger—a diamond-encrusted deep blue sapphire. I squeeze my fingers around the clipboard, expecting the hard plastic to bend with the force of my hate for her.

Out she comes with her shoulders rounded and her head bowed, and she walks along the corridor. I notice her pants are creased and her face is pale. I notice she is not as perfectly put together as she usually is. I notice everything about her and I do not feel even an ounce of sympathy for her. She walks past me, not looking at anything but her own moving feet, and then she opens a door and slips inside a room. I stare hard at the door, letting the number thirteen burn into my brain.

I watch quietly and then a nurse walks past me and stops. "Hi, are you...?" she begins and I shake my head. "Sorry, wrong floor," I say with a light laugh. And I turn and walk quickly toward the elevator, escaping, my heart thumping, my cheeks burning.

I leave the hospital, as anger rises up inside me. She should not be there. She should not be the one sitting by his bedside. That should be me. He should not be the one in the coma. That should be her. I hate her with a visceral fury for everything she has that I want and deserve.

I drive out of the parking lot with the anger bouncing inside of me with nowhere to go. I don't know how I have let this happen to me, how I have allowed myself to get here. I should not have had to want a man who I cannot have. My beauty should have served me better. He should have wanted me enough to leave her and never go back. Perhaps that is why he is hurt... Perhaps that is why he is lying in a hospital bed.

I drive without thinking until I find myself outside his house, a house I have driven past many times. I don't seem to be able to stop myself from doing it. The first time I drove past was two weeks after that first wonderful dinner. He had come over nearly every night, and that made his story about their marriage being at its end seem plausible. He always left by nine, but I didn't let that worry me. He explained that he needed his sleep and couldn't get *it at my place. My apartment is not large and it's on a busy road. I had become used to the sound of truck compression brakes squealing through the night, but it took me some time to adjust. It's all I could afford, but after I met him, I comforted myself that it would not be long until I left that apartment behind. I drove past the house just to look, to see, and I was stunned by the wide road, by the absence of traffic, by the beautiful decorative black metal gates that partially hid the large home. The home worthy of a beautiful woman.*

I didn't let myself seethe over the wife's good fortune. Instead, I imagined myself in that house. I kept going back as I go back tonight. Over the last months, I have caught glimpses of the wife and the children, seen them going in and out, seen her—Marla, the wife—out walking her dog, and I have thought how easily I would slot right into that kind of life. I'm sure the dog would love me.

I pull up outside and turn off the engine, taking a moment to relish the silence of their tree-lined road. But, as it is doing more and more, the churning anger over her place in his life returns, especially now, when he is in a hospital bed and needs me to be with him.

The house is quiet, the blinds in the front down and every-thing cloaked in darkness. But upstairs, there is a light on in a bedroom that faces the street. I wonder who is in the room, where the curtains have a silver-gray sheen. I watch for a few minutes, waiting to see if a face will peer out the window at the road, but no one comes. What is there to look at in this street? What is there to watch out for? Those inside don't know about me. They have no idea at all.

I urge myself to drive away but I can't, and instead I open my car door and climb out and walk slowly over to their mailbox.

It is part of the sandstone wall that surrounds their beauti-ful house, just a silver rectangle in the stone, a dull gleam under the streetlight. I poke my fingers through, reaching for something, anything, but I can feel nothing. Mail only comes on certain days in this age of emails and parcels. I am frustrated and still furious, and I have to do something—anything.

Growing in front of the wall is some hedging, dark in color with a slightly lemony scent and trimmed to square perfection.

I reach down and tug at one of the bushes, tug harder until it starts to give and then I pull it out of the soil and drop it on the ground, only looking around me when I am done, the effort making me pant a little.

I am alone on this suburban street, alone with no one watching, so I reach down and tug at the next section of hedge, pulling hard and feeling a nail break as a stick catches my skin. I pull out the next section and throw it down and then I stand up.

"Excuse me," I hear and I turn. An elderly lady is coming toward me. She is wrapped up against the spring night air in a coat and wearing a beanie. She waves at me to get my attention, to get me to stop.

In a moment I am in my car, my foot on the brake as I turn the key once, twice, blood racing around my body as I hiss with frustration at the old car. The engine turns over and, in seconds, I have roared away, some of the anger left behind with the damaged hedge.

Some, but not all.

SIXTEEN

MARLA

Friday, 10:00 a.m.

Lifting her face to the hot water, she stands with her eyes closed, letting nothing fill her mind but the drumming of the droplets on her face. She has told Bianca and Sean that they will visit the hospital once she is out of the shower. There are strict rules around visiting patients in ICU so they will only be able to go in one at a time, but at least the children will have seen their father. She worries about Bianca's reaction. Marla has spent many hours sitting by Damon's bed now, and she has become acclimatized to the tubes running in and out of his body, to the noises the machines functioning for his body make, to the purple black bruising of his face. Before she left last night, she considered taking a picture of him so at least Bianca and Sean would be prepared before they saw him, but it felt hideously ghoulish and so she left it. It will be incredibly difficult for both children, but especially for Bianca, who cloaks herself in an outer layer of teenage sarcasm but is actually deeply sensitive and adores her father.

For fifteen minutes she has been standing under the hot water and she would like to stand here forever. She is not playing the wife of an accident victim very well. Going back to the hospital feels like an insurmountable task when all she wants to do is run away from everything and everyone.

Her phone is filled with texts from their friends and family all asking about Damon, all wishing him a speedy recovery and offering any assistance they can give. Every time a message comes in, Marla's heart sinks. She has no idea what to say to each *Sending love.*

Thinking of you.

Hope he's better soon.

Let me know if I can do anything.

You're in my prayers.

So she is just not responding at all and that is making her feel guilty because kindness deserves a response, but that guilt is nothing compared to the heavier, darker guilt she feels over everything that has happened. There are other texts as well, texts from those in her social group who are all dying to know the full story.

Let me know if you need to talk.

We're all here for you.

Can we bring you some food?

I'm here as a shoulder to lean on.

Those are more irritating than anything else. She also received an email from Jonathon, Damon's second in command at his company.

> Hi, Marla, just wanted to let you know we're all here for you. As you may or may not be aware, you have signing power on all the business accounts. I know this is the worst possible time, but I may need to have some documents couriered over for you to sign just to keep things going. I want the company to be in great shape when he returns. I apologize for bringing up business now, but I know Damon would want me to keep things running for him. I'll contact you before I send anything over just to let you know.

Jonathon is an eager young man, naturally gifted in all things technology, with a keen business sense. Damon was delighted when he hired him two years ago, and Marla thought that Damon would eventually grant him signing power for everything, including all bank accounts, but Damon was obviously not ready to trust Jonathon with everything. Ironic that he still trusted her, that he still had absolute faith that he could count on her when he had given her so many reasons to betray him. He wouldn't give her his phone password, but he was happy for her to have signing power on his business accounts, and she wishes she had known that on Wednesday before she began her planned conversation with him. Why wouldn't he have told her? *What would happen to me?* He never expected to need her to sign anything, and if he were not lying in a hospital bed, who knows who might have signing power now. He had never even thought to think of Marla as anything except the faithful wife who had dedicated her life to him. Each time he strayed, she confronted him and there were long emotional discussions and fighting, but every single time she has taken him back. Every single time, the women have been one-night stands, a few weeks at most. But Athena, blond goddess Athena, has lasted for many months, and Marla knew she was different. And if the affair with Athena was different, then Marla knew that she had to change as well. And now she is here in her marble-tiled shower, trying to wash off the guilt and the shame.

This morning when she took Rocky out for an early-morning walk, she saw that some of the hedging had been ripped from the ground outside their house. It was such a random senseless act that she almost laughed before looking around her to see if the person who had done the damage was still there. Alex will be here next week and he will fix it, but it's an odd thing to do and not something that has ever happened before. It's unnerving, as though it's been done as some form of punishment or violence against her.

A knock on her bathroom door lets her know that her time of reverie is over and she sighs. "Yes," she calls.

"Mum, there's someone here to see you," yells Bianca over the rushing noise of the water.

Marla turns off the shower and steps out, a cloud of steam filling the bathroom as she grabs a soft ocean-blue towel to wrap herself in. "Who?" she asks as she opens the bathroom door to find Bianca there, her face pale and her hands twisting.

"It's the police, Mum," she whispers, "the actual police. What are they doing here?"

Marla shakes her head. "I don't... I'm not... Did you let them in?"

"Yes, I mean aren't you supposed to? It's the police," whispers Bianca as though they can hear her despite being a whole level below her bedroom.

"Look, don't worry, just take them into the living room. I'll be down in a minute."

Bianca nods, fear in her eyes, "What if. . ." she begins, and Marla cuts her off before she can say anything else. "If it was to do with Dad, then the hospital would have called and they haven't, see." She picks up her cell phone from the corner of the vanity unit where she has left it while she showers.

"Okay, okay," says Bianca, nodding, and she leaves, closing the bedroom door behind her with a soft click. Marla takes a deep breath, touches her hands to her chest. "I can deal with this," she says, her voice barely above a whisper as though, as Bianca seems to believe, the members of the police force in her living room have supersonic hearing. She throws on some jeans and a light sweater and expertly applies enough makeup so that she does not look ghost pale.

Downstairs she finds the same two detectives that she met at the hospital. The woman, Detective Stevens, is perched awkwardly on the edge of the leather sofa, her back straight and her body stiff, and the man, Detective Rahim, is glancing at the huge collection of family photographs in matching rustic frames that Marla has placed on the sleek marble-topped buffet. Each photo is a family picture taken on a different vacation over the years, from one in Fiji with the deep blue ocean in the background when the children were very little to one taken last year when the whole family went skiing in Aspen over Christmas. In moments when she questions her life, Marla takes comfort in these photos that tell of a life of privilege, of a close family, and of joy, captured forever. The truth behind the pictures is that the children have found them cheesy and irritating as they have gotten older, and some of them are taken right after a fierce whispered argument between Damon and Marla after she caught him flirting with a pretty waitress, or a pretty nanny, or a pretty ski instructor. The truth behind the pictures taken over the last few years is that the children have had to be bribed and cajoled into going on vacation with their parents, whose fighting grew more intense without the buffer of days apart from each other. But no one will ever know the truth behind those pictures. And, watching the detective study them, Marla reminds herself that no one need ever know the truth about the accident either.

"Has something happened?" Marla blurts out, unable to deal with the social niceties.

Detective Stevens stands. "No, well, not exactly, but we just wanted to ask you a few things about Wednesday. Perhaps we could speak in private," she says, looking meaningfully at Bianca, who is standing in the doorway, her pink hoodie covering her clenched fists, and Sean, who is staring openly at the detective's hip, where Marla can see the outline of what must be a gun under her jacket. Both her children look tired and so much younger than they actually are. Marla understands—their world is out of kilter. Damon's confidence fills the house every time he walks through the door. He has raised each child to believe that there is nothing they cannot accomplish, no obstacle that can't be overcome. He has frowned at weakness and celebrated success at school and on the sporting field over everything. And now he is in a coma. If their invincible father can be so hurt, what might happen to them? Marla knows they both feel this way, but she cannot think how to reassure them.

"Um," begins Marla, wanting to tell the detectives that they can speak in front of her children but quickly deciding that it's better if they are not here. "Kids, can you just. . ." she says, waving a hand, and Bianca shoots her a nervous look before disappearing.

"Are you sure, Mum?" asks Sean and she nods and smiles and then he also leaves.

"Can I get you something to drink, some tea or something?" Marla asks them, hoping they both refuse, which they do. She gestures that they should sit and she does as well, dropping into an upright armchair with sueded sides that she runs her hands along, comforting herself with the familiar texture.

"We just wanted to check where you were when Mr. Kennedy was struck by the car yesterday," says Detective Stevens.

"Home," says Marla quickly, perhaps too quickly.

"And can anyone verify that?" asks Detective Rahim, his voice just pleasantly inquiring.

"Well," begins Marla, "the kids are on vacation, so they were both here. I mean, still asleep, but you know teenagers." She tries to make it sound amusing, even adding an eye roll, but Detective Stevens squares her shoulders and presses her thin lips together.

"The thing is," says Detective Rahim, clearing his throat, "there are cameras all over the city, so even though it was raining and some of them are admittedly not working, we do have some footage from those that were working and not affected by the rain. There is footage from the cameras at the previous intersection and the one after that."

"Yes," says Detective Stevens, her voice dropping a tone, "those cameras were working and they have given us a pretty good view of the cars that were along that road at the time of the accident."

Marla nods as both detectives study her. She knows what's coming next. Her hand goes to her chest again, pressing down a little to center herself.

"Knowing that," says Detective Stevens slowly, as she pulls a notebook and small pencil out of her pocket, "would you like to change you answer about where you were?" There is no threat behind the words, just inquiry, but Marla can feel the woman's frustrated patience as Marla stares at her.

There is a way she should answer, a truth she should tell but, instead, she simply repeats her assertion. "I was home. I told you we went for a drive and then he wanted to get out and walk a bit, so I went home."

"Right. Could you take us through that again," says Detective Stevens, "just so we're clear."

"It was around nine-thirty," she says, hoping she is remembering the story she told them in the hospital correctly. "He was worried about some software problem, and I said we should go for a drive because sometimes it helps to get away from an issue for a bit."

"So he didn't go to work that day?" interrupts Detective Stevens, and Marla grits her teeth.

"He's the owner of the company, and sometimes he works from home for the day. It's not unusual for him," she says, looking directly at Detective Stevens and making sure not to blink until the woman lowers her eyes to write in her little notebook again. Marla allows herself a momentary vision of tearing the notebook into pieces before she continues speaking. "I said we would go for coffee, but he didn't want that, and as we were driving he was getting more and more worried about the issue and eventually he asked me to let him out so he could just walk. I told him that it was raining and that was ridiculous, but he insisted." She shrugs.

"Before, you said it was around ten a.m.," says Detective Stevens, consulting her little black notebook.

"I didn't really take note of the time," says Marla, her hands cramping with the force she is applying to keep herself from crossing her arms and clenching her fists. It's important she look relaxed. "I thought it was around then."

"Okay and you weren't worried about him at all, like his mental health, if he was struggling with something at work?" It takes Marla a moment to realize that the detective is asking if Damon may have deliberately run right in front of moving cars, deliberately tried to hurt himself, and, despite hating herself, she doesn't want to point the detectives in any other direction.

"He was very worried," she says, "but he's the CEO. His life is one stressful situation after another. If software he installs doesn't ward off hackers, people get very angry."

The detective nods and then writes silently.

"And the issue he was worried about was something to do with someone hacking into a system or a system crashing?"

Marla blinks slowly. What had she said last time?

"Can you explain exactly what the issue was?" asks Detective Stevens.

"I'm sure I wouldn't even know where to begin," says Marla. "It was to do with a new system he had installed. He didn't explain everything to me. A lot of his work is secret, and he is not allowed to talk about it."

"So. . . you don't know who he installed the system for?" asks the detective, her eyes on her notepad and her pen resting on the paper.

"No," says Marla. She puts her hands on the arms of the chair, squeezes hard.

"Did he have his phone?" asks Detective Rahim, and Marla folds her arms, despite trying not to, sure they know the answer to this. They are trying to trick her, trap her, force her to slip up, but she's not going to do that.

"No," she says, "he left it behind. He wanted to be free of the incessant messages and emails for just a bit." As she says the words, she realizes they make sense.

"Can we take a look at it?" asks Detective Stevens, and Marla feels her arms tighten around her body. "Detective, as I'm sure you know, my husband deals with a lot of very important clients, many of whom are in government. I am very uncomfortable giving you his phone to look at in case there is sensitive information on there, and in fact, I don't think I can unless compelled to by a court order, so that I have no agency in handing over such information."

Detective Rahim raises his eyebrows, shocked at her words.

They have dismissed her as a housewife, but she has been listening to Damon talk for more than twenty years. If they come back with a court order, she will have no choice, but he's an accident victim and there would be no reason for a judge to grant such an order. If she were able to get into his phone, she would have erased the many messages that she's sure are there, messages that would throw up all sorts of questions, but for now the phone is in her bedside table, under an old romance novel. The battery has finally gone flat.

As Detective Stevens appears to read back through her notes, Marla wonders if it's possible that Damon has a second phone, something that she's wondered before. If he does, she has never seen it, and if he does, she hopes it is never found by anyone.

Martin Lawrence, she thinks, reminding herself of their lawyer's name. She won't need him. Of course she won't need him. Time slows down as she waits for the detectives' next question, and Marla takes a slow, quiet deep breath.

"Okay," says Detective Stevens. "Do you mind if we take a look at your car?"

Marla knows she cannot say no.

Swallowing quickly, she says, "My car is at the mechanic, some sort of. . . noise that they're trying to figure out."

"Oh," says Detective Stevens, her eyebrows rising almost to her tightly pulled back hairline, "and when did you take it to the. . . mechanic?"

"Wednesday afternoon." Marla's voice is low and croaky, as though her throat is sore, but it's not her throat that's the problem. It's everything else.

Detective Stevens shrugs her shoulders and looks at her partner, a slight shake of her head indicating how she feels about Marla's lie. But it's not a lie.

Detective Rahim takes out his phone and walks over to her, his finger swiping the screen. "Would you agree," he says, "that this is your black Mercedes GLA SUV on Williamsburg Road at 11:28 a.m. on Wednesday, one intersection before the one where Mr. Kennedy was hit by a car?" There is a tiny hint of smugness in the man's voice, something she hadn't expected from him, and Marla shifts uncomfortably. She had him down as the friendly one. She told them she went for a drive with Damon at around 9:30 or 10:00 a.m., and when he got out, she went home. There is no way she should have been on the road at 11:28 a.m. Marla's heart thumps in her chest and she struggles to remain still, to breathe evenly. *Martin's number is in a file in Damon's home office. Martin works in the city and he's always on call for Damon.*

He turns the phone toward her slowly, a picture of a car filling the screen. It is a black Mercedes GLA SUV, just like the one Marla has. But the picture has been taken of the front of the car in the rain, water spraying up from the street obscuring the plate number. Marla leans forward, studying the picture. It's not possible to see who is in the car. It could be one or two people, but everything is very unclear.

Her blood pounds in her ears as she sits back, her mind running at warp speed. *Careful, careful, think before you speak, think before you speak.* She forces herself to relax her arms at her side.

"That's not my car," she says and then she looks at Detective Rahim, and even as she feels her racing heart must be so loud they can hear it, she maintains a steady gaze, not dropping her eyes until the detective nods.

"But you do drive a black Mercedes GLA SUV?" he says.

"I imagine," says Marla slowly, making sure to stop herself from folding her arms again, "that you know that already. But as I say, that's not my car. There are thousands of those cars in Sydney. It's pretty much what every one of my friends drives. And I'm sure you know black is a very popular color." She runs her hands along her jeans as though smoothing the material, but it's just for something to do. The slightly rough feel of the material against her hands, the light whiff of floral perfume from Detective Stevens, the sound of a hedge trimmer being used across the road, and the taste of metal in her mouth all assault her at once, her entire being on high alert as she stares at the detective.

The detective holds her gaze for only a moment longer and then he nods. "Well, we are still checking all the other footage we have to see if we can get a better view of the car. Can you give us the name of the mechanic so that we can go over and take a look, just to rule your car out?"

"Sure," says Marla, and she stands and goes to get her phone from the buffet where she has set it down, scrolling through her contacts quickly until she finds Rudy the mechanic's website and shows it to the detective, who writes it down.

"Is there anything else?" she asks. "I really want to take my children to visit their father in the hospital."

"No, no, thank you," says the detective. "We'll be in touch if we have any more questions or information for you."

Marla nods, grateful that she is wearing jeans so that her trembling legs are concealed. She walks the detectives to the front door and shuts it behind them, but she doesn't breathe a sigh of relief until she is up in her bathroom with the door locked.

There she sinks onto the side of the large spa bath and deletes the text she sent to Rudy after she left the car with one of his juniors on Wednesday afternoon. She and Damon have been taking their cars to Rudy for more than a decade. She hadn't wanted to explain the situation to his junior apprentice, who looked bored as soon as she started speaking. "I'll text Rudy," she told him, and he responded with an indifferent nod.

Hi Rudy, the car is making some strange knocking noise when I start it. It may be my imagination but I just thought I would leave it with you for when you have time to check it out. Also, there is some sticky stuff on the front—can you use something to clean it off? I'm worried about the paint being damaged. Thanks, Marla Kennedy

She deletes his reply as well.

Hi Ms. Kennedy—got the residue off, paint is not damaged. Give me till Monday to see what the noise is.

The sticky stuff is residue from a sticker she scraped off just before she took the car in. She had stopped in a parking garage briefly to get it off, but she couldn't remove evidence of its existence entirely.

The sticker was mostly peeled away since it had been there for over a year already. A red bumper sticker with white writing that said: IF YOU'RE GOING TO HURT MY CAR, MAKE SURE YOU KILL ME.

Sean got it for her for Mother's Day the month after Damon came home with the brand-new car. She had been looking forward to a new car and immediately made rules about Bianca eating in it and leaving different pairs of shoes and bits of clothing piling up on the floor like it was her closet.

"Oh my God, Mum, you love that car more than you love us," Bianca had joked, and everyone had laughed at her for getting so attached. But she did love the new car. It was smaller than all her others had been and felt like a transition to a time when she would no longer be driving children around. The bittersweet feelings she had over that were helped by the new-car smell that lingered as she drove Bianca for the last months until she got her license.

She hated the sticker, but she let Sean affix it to the front, not the back, where she would always wonder if the person behind her was judging her. It had started to peel after a rainstorm and she had let it, going at it with her nails whenever she noticed it.

On Wednesday afternoon she had removed the last red corner before dropping the car off at Rudy.

The red corner that was obvious in the traffic camera photo despite the rain.

SEVENTEEN

SONYA

Friday, 1:00 p.m.

"Thank you both for coming," says Sonya to her clients as she ushers them to the door, her head thumping with each step she takes. Robert and Carol Winston both murmur their thanks and Sonya gratefully closes the door behind them. She is not doing a good job of helping people this week. Robert and Carol are fighting to stay married after the death of Carol's mother made her question everything, and while it is the therapist's job to remain neutral, today Sonya was barely involved in the conversation at all.

Her mind is elsewhere, her thoughts scattered. Last night she called the hospital in an attempt to get an update on Damon's condition, but of course they wouldn't give her any information. The news has whizzed past the story and is onto a thousand other things, and the only way she will be able to find out what's going on is if she calls his wife, and she absolutely cannot do that.

She should never have made contact with the woman in the first place. Contacting Marla has led to this, led to her being in a situation where the only way she can cope is by self-medicating with a lot of wine. Last night she only meant to have one glass, but that turned into two, which turned into three, each one allowing her to justify her actions, to distance herself from what she had done, to explain away her almost criminally unprofessional behavior. The wine drowned out her fear for her future and by extension Jasper's future. Losing her job would mean that she loses everything she has worked for since her divorce from Lee. She would be disgraced in her profession, would make herself a laughingstock. It wasn't a possibility she could allow herself to contemplate, and so she sipped a dry white wine, sipping away her fear until she was well and truly drunk.

"Marla has no idea I'm having therapy. It would break her heart and I don't want to do that. I still love her as a person, just not as a life partner," Damon confessed at their first session. But Damon's having therapy would never have hurt Marla, everything else he was doing hurt her, and Sonya feels the prickle of thorns under her skin at the role she has played in all this. Despite her headache, she wishes for more alcohol to stop the hamster wheel of worry circling in her mind. She would like to tear her thoughts out of her brain.

If he dies, it will be on the news, just by virtue of it being a hit-and-run. That's what the articles she has read have called it. Someone hit Damon with their car and then just kept on driving. It could have been a terrible accident because of the rain and the chaos on the road that always accompanies the level of rain they had on Wednesday, or it could have been on purpose.

Sonya sinks gratefully into her leather desk chair, slipping off the black stiletto heels that had looked so good in the store but made her regret them every time she wore them. She rubs her feet on the carpet, feeling her toes uncramp.

When the intercom on her desk buzzes, she sighs and

touches the button to answer. "I have an hour before Emily gets here, don't I?"

Emily is thirty-five and pregnant with her first child via sperm donation. She is determined to be the best mother she can be and so is working with Sonya to prepare herself for raising a child alone. Sonya finds Emily's sessions mostly joyful as they discuss babies and future plans. There are moments of sadness as her patient wrestles with not having a father for her child to actually meet, but mostly she is looking forward to the future. Sonya remembers being terrified about the future when she became a mother; everything suddenly felt hideously precarious. She never thought she would survive divorce and raising her three-year-old essentially alone, but here she is, desperately wishing she could wind back the years and have her little boy stay little for just a while longer.

"Yes, yes, you do. . ." Jessica hesitates.

"Right, so what is it?" says Sonya, irritated at having her hour of peace interrupted already. She hasn't even started on her notes and she needs to book an appointment with Dr. Hillman, her supervising therapist—something she has been avoiding because she is unsure how she will stop herself from telling her that she made the colossal mistake of getting involved with a patient. It's not acceptable practice, not morally or ethically. She can just imagine the way Patty Hillman will look at her, can see the woman's gray eyebrows rising as she taps her pencil against her pad, frowning. Would Patty report her to the Psychology Board of Australia? Maybe. Probably.

But Sonya is not going to say anything and she knows it. She will, in fact, do anything to keep this terrible secret. Anything. Has already done things she would never have believed of herself.

Jessica still hasn't told her what she wants, and Sonya sighs because sometimes the young woman is distracted by her computer or her phone and forgets why she buzzed her in the first place. "Jessica?" she snaps.

"The police are here to speak to you," says Jessica, and she sounds both worried and also a little scared.

Sonya's headache tightens, the thumping in her head louder and stronger than it has been in a long time. On her desk is a can of Diet Coke, which she grabs and takes a deep swallow from, her mouth sticky and dry.

Last night, the wine had sent her into a thick dark sleep, but she woke up three hours later as she knew she would, her mouth dry, her head aching, and wine regret setting in as she replayed her actions from two and a half weeks ago on a loop that spun faster and faster, tormenting her until dawn as she relived one of the greatest mistakes of her life. She blames wine for that as well.

It happened on a Saturday night and Sonya had been alone. Jasper was sleeping at his friend Mika's house, despite her offering her home for the sleepover. Mika's family lived in a large house with a media room and a giant television for gaming, and Jasper loved going over there. Sonya hated being alone and had contemplated calling one of her girlfriends, but even though she knew she would be invited out, the idea of tagging along with her married friends held little appeal. She had treated herself to Thai food, savoring a rich red curry as she enjoyed an expensive glass of dry white wine with the plan of bingeing a Netflix series. But one glass turned into two and her aloneness became so palpable she felt she could touch it, and instead of taking a walk or having a bath, she opened social media and disappeared down the destructive rabbit hole of other people's lives.

She found herself on Marla's Instagram page, scrolling through pictures of Damon and Marla on vacation in Italy and Damon and Marla out to dinner with their children and Marla's beautiful new leather sofa and Marla out with friends, each one of them skinny and polished and Botoxed into plastic perfection, large pink cocktails in front of them, small plates of food untouched. In pictures Marla was glossy perfection, manicured and buffed, smooth and elegant. Jealousy assaulted Sonya as she cursed herself for making the mistake of sleeping with Damon. And then she did something that will haunt her for the rest of her life.

You don't know me but I know your husband and there's something I need to tell you.

A direct message that she should have immediately deleted, that she should have backed away from when Marla responded, that she should never, ever have sent. Sonya blames the wine, she blames her loneliness, she blames Lee for divorcing her, but behind all that blame is the truth that she never wishes to acknowledge. She did it to punish Damon for not remembering her.

"Sonya?" says Jessica and she realizes that her assistant is still waiting for her to allow the police into her office.

"Just coming," she says, trying to keep her voice light. She slides her feet back into her shoes, feeling her toes curl in the tight space, and gets up to open her office door. There are two detectives with their identifications on display for Jessica, and they turn as they see Sonya and show her their badges as well. Sonya nods and steps back. "Is there something I can help you with?" she says as they follow her into her office, the woman closing the door behind them.

"Yes, I'm Detective Sergeant Rahim and this is Detective Constable Stevens and we're with the crash investigation unit. We're looking into a hit-and-run of a pedestrian on Williamsburg Road yesterday and we just wanted to ask you a few questions," says the man, a small smile on his face.

Sonya squares her shoulders. There is no way they would

have found out Damon was a client of hers, and even if they have, there is nothing she can tell them. But they may be able to tell her how he is doing.

"I did hear about that. I mean I read about it and saw it on the news. Is he okay?"

"Serious but stable," says the woman quickly, repeating the same phrase that is in every article about the accident.

"I'm not exactly sure how I can help," says Sonya.

"Well, the thing is," says the female detective, taking her phone out of her pocket and swiping through the screen as though looking for something, "we don't have anything from the traffic cameras at the intersection for various reasons, but we do have some dashcam footage and footage from other cameras in the area. Some of the dashcam came from a car that was going in the opposite direction, so it's pretty clear, and we believe that this," she says, turning the phone around to face Sonya, "is your gold Audi A1 Sportback."

In the picture, the car is moving through a deep puddle, water splaying out in a wave on both sides. The headlights are on because of the gloomy sky, and rain obscures everything except for the bright metallic gold of the car and the license plate... That is very clear.

Sonya knows that whatever she does in the next moments determines how everything plays out now; whatever she says or does will possibly change her life. Outside her office window, a group of cockatoos fly over, filling the air with their squawking calls. Sonya knows it is a nice day outside, the sky blue and the air warm enough that only a light cardigan is needed. In her office, the clock on the wall ticks loudly. The car is a luxury car but the entry model, one that she had been looking at and wanting for years and managed to afford only last year. She will be paying it off for a long time, but she reasoned that it would last a long time too and she loves the color. But she can see now that its distinctive coloring may have been a mistake.

"Can you tell us why you were on the road at that time?" asks the detective.

"I was running late and I was rushing to meet a client here, not rushing as in speeding, just trying to get here as soon as possible. I don't know what that has to do with anything. There are a lot of cars at that intersection." She makes sure to keep her voice firm so that there is not even a hint of what she is feeling.

"Yes, yes, there were and we are eliminating them from our investigation one by one. Can we just take a quick look at your car? Police have been appealing for help from anyone who may have been in the area at the time. Perhaps you were rushing so forgot you were there?" says Detective Stevens, her voice holding an edge of condescension and snark.

There is nothing unusual about the good-cop, bad-cop routine, but Sonya is not familiar with the sarcastic-cop, silent-cop routine. Detective Rahim, who she would assume is the more senior of the two because of his age, just stands silently, the same smile on his face as he had when he first entered the office, as Detective Stevens goads and pushes. Sonya is not as much of a pushover as this woman thinks she is.

"Of course you can. I have nothing to hide. But I do have another client along soon. I'll give you my keys and I would thank you to return them to Jessica when you're done." She sounds irritated and snippy. That's exactly how she wants to sound. "It's parking 2B in the garage. There's only one level and you can get there via the stairs."

Handing the keys to Detective Stevens, she thanks God that Pete, who lives next door with his lovely wife and two children, is a smash repairer.

"That'll come out easy," he said yesterday when she showed him the slight dent. "Just give me a moment and I'll get it done." He took her keys and drove her car over to his workshop, only two streets away. She had waited patiently, watching the street outside, for Pete to return. He could have been too tired to attend to the car or he could have refused to do it immediately because she had shown him the dent only on Thursday afternoon when she noticed it and he was home from work and his day was supposed to be over, or he could have told her he would get to it next week. But she and Pete and his wife, Monica, have a good relationship. Sonya had babysat their two children overnight when Pete and Monica went to a family wedding, leaving them with none of their usual babysitters because everyone was a guest at the wedding as well.

"If you ever need anything at all. . ." Monica told her the next morning and Sonya had nodded and smiled, but she had never called on Pete for help until yesterday afternoon. It was a very slight dent and Sonya knew it would only take him a short time to fix. The paint hadn't even been damaged. It only needed the special suction cup he used for small dents, and he'd returned in half an hour, the car as good as new.

"Looks like something bounced off the front. You're lucky it didn't smash the front light, or that would have been expensive," said Pete. "What happened?"

"No idea," said Sonya, shaking her head. "It could have been a few days ago and I just didn't notice, but it must have happened in a shopping center or when I parked on the street outside work because I was only going to be there for a few hours," she lied easily. Sonya could never have imagined how good a liar she could be, but in the space of a few days she has lied to her neighbor, lied to the police, and, most terrible of all, lied to herself.

"We won't be long," says Detective Stevens, and they leave. As she goes to close her door, Sonya can see Jessica's eyes, magnified behind her glasses, wide and curious. This is the moment to say something, but Sonya doesn't have the energy for it.

Instead, she closes the door quietly and returns to her chair behind her desk. Her shoes come off again, and she takes deep calming breaths to still her racing heart as she neatens the few items on her desk, touching the Newton's cradle to set the small silver balls clicking against each other and squaring the tissue box and the picture of Jasper in a clumsily made blue photo frame from when he was in kindergarten.

Her next appointment is forty minutes away, and she looks down at her pad, where she has made a few notes about her last clients, but she has just written fragments of sentences: *Carol avoiding discussion of Robert—aggression? Holiday?*

She sits back in her chair, realizing that she can't remember much of what was discussed in the session. Hopefully Carol and Robert were so engaged in their own conversation they didn't notice her distinct lack of participation.

It shouldn't take the detectives long to get down to the garage under this building where her car is parked. How long could it take? Five minutes to get down the stairs and two or three minutes to look over the car, maybe another five minutes to return and hand the keys to Jessica. Would they say anything to her assistant? Probably not, but the office is small and sometimes she can hear Jessica answer the phone if she's not concentrating on a client. In fifteen minutes, they should have returned the keys and left. She glances at the digital clock on her desk. Thirteen minutes to go.

Leaning back in her chair, she swivels it around so that the sun coming through the window warms her face and she closes her eyes, concentrating on listening to the sounds outside her office.

The phone rings. "Northwest Psychology," says Jessica, the name an amalgamation of Sonya's surname, North, and Romy's surname, Weston.

Jessica murmurs into the phone, so she can't actually hear what she's saying. Sonya scrunches her closed eyes, cocking her head to one side as though that will make it easier to hear.

But there is nothing to hear aside from the faint tapping

sounds of Jessica's nails against her keyboard. Sonya sighs deeply and relaxes her face. There is nothing she can do except wait. If the police do not knock on her door, it means they have found nothing.

When she sent Marla the message over Instagram, she hadn't expected a reply. Perhaps she had almost hoped that there wouldn't be one, but Marla's reaction was immediate.

Who are you and what do you have to say?

Sonya could have left it there and simply not replied, but she didn't.

How did she get here? Everything she has done over the last nine years has been to make sure that Jasper has a safe, easy life, that they both feel secure.

It's not as if she's never been attracted to a patient before.

A couple of years ago a waiter at a Greek restaurant came to see her. He wasn't just a waiter but the son of the owners and his dark eyes and thick curly black hair coupled with a dazzling white smile had made her stomach dip every time she saw him. He was in his mid-twenties, so way too young for her, but very vulnerable as he struggled to figure out how to tell his parents that he wanted to be an actor instead of take over the restaurant. There had even been a moment when she knew that she could have become intimate with him, when he seemed to be flirting with her, but she quickly pulled herself back and made sure to visualize him as a child, a young man, someone she should want to help, not sleep with. She helped him gather the courage to tell his parents and while they were not exactly supportive, he handled it well, so they agreed to giving him a year off to pursue his dream. He's in a television series now, something made for teenagers, so she hadn't watched it for more than a few minutes when she recognized him. She was happy to have helped, as she always is. She is a good psychologist, but everything that has happened with Damon has turned her into a lesser version of herself. She always hoped that she helped her patients and they were able to move on with their lives. But Damon, Damon was different.

Maybe because he was older or perhaps it was because he looked like the kind of man who appeared in adverts for leather boots and Range Rovers. Or because they already knew each other and he seemed to have completely forgotten her, rendering her an unmemorable notch on his bedpost, forcing her ego to suffer the humiliation of that. Whatever the reason was, she had crossed a very thick line and it was quite possible that her whole career, her whole life was going to be negatively, horribly affected by it.

If it weren't for a dead battery, it would have never happened. That's how strange life was, how filled with coincidence and fate. Well, it wouldn't have happened the second time anyway.

It was a little over a month ago, and Sydney was still mired in the chill of winter. Damon was her last patient for the day, and Sonya had gratefully closed the door behind him when he left and sat down to write some quick notes and to remind herself that she was not meant to be attracted to patients, not meant to let her ego get in the way of helping people.

Twenty minutes later she made her way to her car only to find it wouldn't start. Roadside assistance told her they would be more than an hour in the peak early-evening traffic. Sonya had panicked about Jasper for a moment before remembering that he was at a play rehearsal until 8:00 p.m. Too tired to work anymore, she decided to treat herself to a drink at the bar across the road from her building. It was a Thursday night, and the bar was filled with people from the surrounding buildings, enjoying early dinners or unwinding with drinks after work.

She had pushed through the crowd and was delighted to see an empty spot at the end of the bar with just one stool. Triumphant when she got there, she lifted her hand to signal the bartender when a voice said, "I'll buy," and she turned her head to see Damon on the stool next to the one she had chosen.

"Damon," she said stupidly, and he grinned, making her stomach flip.

"I needed to just sit for a bit and think about everything we discussed," he said.

"My car won't start," she replied, and then she blushed at her silly statement in relation to what he had said.

Briefly she contemplated leaving, but the bartender walked up then and took her drink order for a white wine, which she returned with immediately. The Chardonnay was crisp and tart, deliciously cool in the overheated bar, and Sonya sank onto her stool next to Damon, hoping that he wasn't expecting a continuation of his therapy session. But he wasn't. Instead, he asked her about herself, her son, her work. He was profoundly interested in her and listened to her speak without realizing that he had heard some of it before.

She really should have left. One drink led to two and then when roadside assistance let her know they were nearly there, he insisted on coming to stand with her and wait, and when the car was fixed he suggested dinner, and Jasper texted to say his friend Jake's mother had offered him a ride home. Jasper had a key and was capable of letting himself in the house and warming up the meat pie she had made for both of them. She was free for the evening. "Sure," she replied, when she should have said no.

It was all so tawdry when she thought about it now. They shared a bottle of wine over dinner and then a kiss as they walked back to their cars, and then they were both in her car and somehow...

Instant regret had assailed her as they fixed their clothes. "I need to get home," she said. In her mind, before it happened, she had pictured him touching her and remembering her, admitting that he knew who she was because she had meant so much the first time they were together, as he had assured her over and again on the one night they spent together. "You're so beautiful, you're amazing, my God I can't believe we've just met." But she was a one-night stand. She was nothing to him, and in having sex with him again she had just confirmed how little she meant, how nothing she actually was to Damon Kennedy. The first time he hadn't mentioned he was married, hadn't even been wearing a ring. She hadn't asked him many questions either, assuming that there would be time for that later, not knowing that later would never come.

When he failed to offer her even a hint of recognition the second time they had sex, she was drowned in pathetic humiliation. "Do you do this a lot?" she asked, still waiting, still hoping, for what, she didn't know.

"No, I mean, I've had affairs, we've talked about those, but I've never done this before."

"*Liar, liar, liar,*" she wanted to scream, but all she had been able to do was nod as though she believed him. "I should go," she said.

"Me too," he agreed.

"Look," they both said at the same time.

He was quiet as she said, "I think this was a mistake, and I'll refer you to a new therapist. This was a big mistake."

"It's not your fault. We both got carried away. We can forget it ever happened, we can. I just really want to keep seeing you. I feel like you understand me now and I don't want to start again."

She should have said no. Should have, would have, could have. But didn't.

The next session was awkward, but by the end she understood that the incident had not affected him at all. He had moved on in the way that men are able to move on. She hadn't—she hasn't—and that's a problem.

Outside her closed office door, she hears Jessica say, "Thank you, Officers," quite loudly, as though wanting Sonya to hear her, and she breathes a sigh of pure relief. They have found nothing.

She folds her arms on her desk and drops her head down. How on earth is she going to get through this unscathed? Damon is in a hospital bed because she could not move on. It would be easier if he had died. It really would be.

EIGHTEEN

ATHENA

Friday, 2:00 p.m.

A chorus of tinkling wind chimes tells Athena that someone has come into the store. She immediately gets up from her chair behind the counter and tries to look poised and ready to serve whoever it is. On busy days, Gail says that the endless clinking of wind chimes as the door opens drives her mad, but Athena likes to be alerted to someone walking in if she is in the store alone. She hates the idea of being caught unaware.

Gail has gone for a late lunch, promising to return with some nourishing minestrone soup for Athena. "You look really pale," she told her. "Is the nausea back?"

"Yes," Athena answered because that was an easy answer. She has not discussed the accident with Gail, and even if her assistant has read about it, she has not mentioned it. She and Gail rarely discuss Damon. Gail knows he's married and wants to get divorced, and after Marla came to the store and confronted Athena, Gail was nothing but kind and sympathetic. She has always been one of Athena's greatest supporters.

"What happened to your hand?" Gail asked, looking at the slightly raised red scratches.

Athena had glanced down and only then noticed the sting of the injury. "I. . . I don't know," she said, shrugging her shoulders. "Maybe I did it when I was unpacking the new box of crystals. I need to be more careful. Baby brain, I guess."

"You can go home. I can woman the shop." Gail smiled, making Athena smile too at the joke they had established on day one when the young woman said, "If you need to be out, I can man the shop," to which Athena replied, "Best if you woman it—you'll do a better job."

But Athena had refused because at home she could not stop herself from scrolling through old texts from Damon, texts where he promised that they would be together forever, promised that he loved her, and more recently where he told her of the wonderful future the two of them would have without stating that this future did not include the baby she refused to get rid of.

> Imagine just the two of us on a river cruise around Scandinavia. We can visit the fjords and small fishing towns. I'm sure they have a long history of witchcraft and magic. Imagine what you'll be able to find for your store. It will be wonderful when it's just us finally. Hang in there, babe, nearly there.

He thought those texts were a subtle encouragement to do what he wanted her to do, but they made her angry. Angry that he would dare try to control her body, would dare try to make her do something so contrary to what she wanted, angry that he didn't seem to care at all that the child she carried had been made by both of them. And at the same time, they gave her a kind of hopeful sadness, when she tried to imagine the future he was creating for them but also tried to add in a baby, strapped to her chest, only a fuzz of dark hair showing. Somehow, she could never quite get the picture to work.

Ending things would have been the right thing to do, but she couldn't. Even now, she would go to him if she could. Last night when she walked through the door of her apartment after determinedly taking herself for a walk around her quiet neighborhood so she could breathe in the scented spring gardens, she caught a hint of his honey and leather cologne in the air and her heart flipped, because for just a second she thought he had come over to surprise her. The instant realization that this would probably never happen again drove her to her knees, where she stayed for an hour as she relived everything she had done wrong, every place her anger had led her, and she hated him anew even as she loved him, for turning her into someone she never wanted to be.

Pulling a bright smile from somewhere deep inside herself, she steps out from behind the counter and greets the two people who are looking around her store as though they didn't actually mean to be standing there. They are both dressed in pants suits, a dark-haired man and a large, muscular woman with blond hair pulled back into a tight ponytail. They look. . . Athena feels her stomach roil. They look like they must be from the police. There is something about the way they are looking around, about the way they are dressed that makes this immediately clear to her.

If Gail were here, she would simply bolt out of the back door.

"Can I help you with something?" she asks the woman, praying that even if she is with the police, she happens to be on her lunchbreak and is here to choose a gift for someone. Not for herself. There is a slight smirk on her face that Athena has learned means the person wearing the expression has firm opinions about the things she sells.

"Ah yes," says the woman, turning away from a display of

tarot cards, "I'm Detective Constable Stevens and this is Detective Sergeant Rahim and we'd just like to ask you a few questions about Wednesday."

"Wednesday," repeats Athena, conscious of her flushing cheeks. She runs her hands through her long hair to get it away from her neck, taking comfort in the jangling of the collection of bracelets she wears, one loaded up with tiny silver protective charms like the hamsa hand to keep the evil eye away. She furtively rubs at the charm.

"Yes," says the woman, "it was raining and there was a pedestrian hit on Williamsburg Road. I'm not sure if you've seen the news. Do you watch the news?"

Athena bites down on her lip so that she doesn't rise to the bait. "Yes, I do," she says, "and I did see that a pedestrian was hit. Is he okay?"

It is so strange to her that she is asking the police for an update on the condition of a man that she has been intimate with for months. They have no idea how she is connected to Damon. Few people do. Secrecy was important for their affair, and in the keeping of secrets, she has accepted that her place in his life does not exist at all to the wider world. Only the immediate players in this game know of each other. Her, Marla, Damon. . . only those directly involved, directly responsible for what has happened.

"Stable but critical," says the detective, meeting Athena's gaze with pale blue eyes. Athena has heard those words over and again, in every news report, read them in every article. The detective is repeating the official line.

"The traffic cameras were on the blink," says the detective, and Athena nods because that has also been on the news. She even watched a fifteen-minute discussion between a news presenter and the highway administrator about that issue.

Athena glances at the other detective, who appears to be more interested in a collection of scented candles than he is in the discussion being had. Athena retreats into silence. She's not going to be stupid enough to say anything.

"Yes, broken, but the good thing about modern technology is that cameras are everywhere, so there were dashcams and mobile phones being used and we have quite a lot of footage. Now, while no one actually filmed the moment of impact, we do have a lot of license plates for cars that were there at the time. Do you remember where you were on Wednesday at around eleven-thirty?" The detective's voice is brusque, to the point. Athena wonders how many other people she has spoken to today.

She tries to swallow, but her mouth is desert dry. There is no point in lying. They wouldn't be here if they didn't already know the answer.

"Williamsburg Road," she says softly and the other detective comes to stand next to his colleague. The implication being that this conversation suddenly got interesting.

"Yes, that reflects our records. Your car was caught on dash-cam. Did you see anything, anything at all? There has been an appeal for information."

Athena starts shaking her head before the detective finishes speaking. "Nothing, not at all. I was concentrating on the road. The rain made it almost impossible to see anything, so I was just watching the car in front of me the whole time. I don't like driving in the rain."

The detective waits for her to finish and then studies her for a moment as Athena resists the urge to take her hair away from her neck again, where she is getting hot.

"Would we be able to take a look at your car?" says the other detective as though the thought has just occurred to him. He smiles, white even teeth on display.

Athena can feel her world changing, can feel it collapsing, or if she's honest, collapsing further. The landslide began two weeks ago when she discovered the truth that she did not want to know, that Damon had not told his wife he wanted a divorce and probably never would. All his pretty words were lies meant to keep her subdued and in his bed.

She turns and goes back behind the counter and finds her keys with their four-leaf clover key chain, holding them tightly so that her slightly trembling hands are not obvious. "I can't leave the store," she says, her voice slightly raspy, "but it's parked on the first side street to the left."

"Thanks, we'll be quick," says the male detective, taking her keys from her and offering her another smile. Athena tries to return it, but her face feels stiff.

She could have said no, could have asked them why they wanted to see it, could have demanded they get some kind of search warrant, but she knows there would have been no point in doing that. Let them look, let them see, let them scrutinize her car.

The whole thing is covered in dents anyway.

While she waits for them to return, she tidies a shelf filled with ceramic animals favored by witches, like cats and owls. They get dusty so quickly and need to be cleaned carefully because they are so delicate. With a soft cloth in her hand, she concentrates really hard so that she doesn't break one of the ornaments, but try as she might, she cannot push away what happened two weeks ago, not now, not anymore.

Ten minutes later the detectives return, and the woman silently hands her the keys to her car. "Some of those dents are starting to rust," she says, and Athena nods her head.

"I know," she says. "I am going to get it fixed when I have the money."

"Thank you for letting us take a look," says Detective Rahim, and Athena nods, clutching the cloth tightly as she watches them leave the store.

Once they are gone, she breathes slowly in and out until she can feel her body calm. At least she didn't stay at the hospital to be identified. She should never have gone in the first place, but she also should never have been involved with a man who lies to every single woman in his life.

Two weeks ago, she called him, and Marla answered and she hung up, and that was fine. She knew he still lived at home. But it was not fine for Marla.

When her phone rang an hour later, it didn't cross her mind not to answer a number she didn't immediately recognize. She was starting to order her Christmas stock, and there were a lot of people calling her with estimated delivery times.

"Athena," said a woman's voice, and Athena recognized it instantly. Her cheeks heated up as she contemplated hanging up and blocking the number before she said, "Yes."

"You're still with him?"

"Yes," said Athena, "I'm. . ." What was she going to say? Sorry. She was not sorry or she would not still be with him. And she wanted to feel terrible, to hate herself for being with another woman's husband, but she had her child to think about—her and Damon's child. She wanted Damon in her child's life and in her life, so she refused to feel bad.

"You don't have to say anything. There's no need. I just wanted to check." And she had hung up. Athena had imagined—hopefully, daringly imagined—that it would lead to a confrontation between Damon and his wife and everything would be out in the open. But it hadn't and nothing had changed, until the next time Marla contacted her, and then there was Wednesday and now everything has changed.

The wind chimes tinkle as Gail returns, and Athena catches the smell of the rich herby tomato minestrone soup and she realizes she's starving. She reminds herself that the police found nothing.

Will this be it? Will it be over now, or has it only just begun?

NINETEEN

I return to the hospital on Friday night, my disguise in place, wanting to see him, yearning to see him, and hating myself for my terrible neediness.

It's visiting hours, so I don't wear my nurse's scrubs with my wig and glasses but rather just a large coat, which makes me look heavier. I use colored contact lenses in my eyes as well, making them darker, and I use more shadow under my eyes. Just a woman who is visiting an ill loved one.

If anyone asks, I can say that I am lost.

Once again, I hover near his door waiting for an opportunity. I have to keep moving, to occasionally clasp my phone to my ear and nod as though listening to someone. If one of the nurses comes toward me, I move off and get into the elevator, ride one floor down and then back up again.

It is exhausting, but I need to see him.

When she comes out of his room, I am standing right there, and for a moment our eyes lock and my heart hammers in my chest.

"Sorry, excuse me," she says, not even a glint of recognition in her eyes.

Was I hoping for recognition? But she is too self-centered to really look at me, to see behind the disguise.

She walks toward the elevator, and I am about to go into his room when another nurse appears and moves to his door. I instantly turn away, moving quickly down the corridor and to the elevator.

I bite down on my lip as I enter the elevator, blinking back frustrated tears. I hate being thwarted this way.

I return to the parking lot and sit in my car, waiting to see her again. I don't know why.

I have a good view of the front entrance and I have nothing else to do with my time right now. She will leave through this door. That's what I'm waiting for. I settle in, get comfortable. The minutes to the end of visiting hours tick over and perhaps she will go home then? I would never leave his bedside, but I think she will go home. I resolve to wait until 9:00 p.m. and then leave.

The anger bubbles along inside me for what my life has become, for the choices I made.

Betrayal is such a juicy word, isn't it? Full of spice and heat. It is also the cause of much grief.

You can betray a person or a group of people or a whole country. You can betray yourself. Is that what I did? Did I go against my better nature, against the truth of who I am, and betray myself by doing something that I knew to be entirely wrong, so completely against my moral and ethical code? And what will happen now? Who will pay for that betrayal, because it cannot just be me. Round and round it goes and who is right and who is wrong?

His picture is in all the articles about the accident now. Before, if you googled his name, you would understand that here is a man who has made his life a success. He was in IT magazines in articles on how to prevent hackers, and on the cover of business magazines as an example of someone who had made millions in a difficult industry. Now and again, he was pictured in a lifestyle supplement with his perfect wife and children. But, of course, I knew it was not perfect. Didn't I? Now there is only the accident on the first two pages of Google, only the hideous details of him being struck, of his injuries and of the fact that he remains in a coma, stuck somewhere between this world and the next, in limbo. Only the appeals for information—"Come forward," the public are urged. "Come forward and tell us what happened, so we find the truth." But no one is saying anything. It seems impossible to believe that in this technologically advanced age no one saw or recorded exactly what happened. How is that possible? And is that good or bad?

There are a lot of good-looking men in the world and not all of them flirt and stray and cheat and deceive, but he did, and somehow... somehow that made him even more irresistible. I believed that I would be the woman to finally tie him down, to stop his eyes wandering. I would be the one woman he would not cheat on.

Finally, at eight-thirty, she emerges, exhaustion hanging around her body like a cloak. I want to feel sympathy for her, but I feel only for myself, for what I am being excluded from. I pull out and follow her slowly, as though I am someone looking for a parking space.

When she gets into her car, I follow her home, the need to do something brewing inside me.

She parks in the driveway instead of putting her car in the garage, leaving the black metal gates open. Perhaps she means to return to the hospital or perhaps she is just tired and not thinking straight.

I wait until she has gone inside and then I survey the street, where all is quiet. Lights are on in every home and I can even see the flickering of a television screen in the house I am parked next to. Ordinary people. Well, not ordinary. Privileged people, living their lives without thinking about who might be outside, who might be watching them. She has left her gates open because she lives in a safe neighborhood and nothing can happen in such a place, can it?

Clutching my keys in my hand, I climb out of my car and walk quickly into her driveway, my hands trembling a little with the excitement of it all. And then I move along the side of her car, flinching at the noise I make as a key scrapes the paint of her expensive toy.

When I am done, I dart back to my car and find myself laughing with excited relief as I drive.

She will wonder who has done this, who is watching her, who she should be scared of.

That's exactly how I want her to feel.

TWENTY

MARLA

Saturday, 10:00 a.m.

Marla runs her hands over the selection of chocolates at the hospital café. She picks up a small bar of dark chocolate with almonds in it and examines the sugar content and then she puts it down and picks up a family-sized block of milk chocolate filled with caramel. She will break it into squares and eat them as she sits in Damon's room, one piece every twenty minutes so she has something to look forward to. She's eaten more chocolate and junk food in the last three days than she has in the last three years. Holding on to her chocolate, she looks around for something else to buy and then grabs a can of Coke from the fridge, filled with empty calories and so, so much sugar.

Later today Damon will have his arm operated on so the bone can be realigned and put into place with pins. Damon loves his gym workout, revels in his strength and ability to lift heavy weights. It will be a long time before he can go back to the gym again, if he ever can. Marla thinks about adding a bag of potato chips to her haul but cannot find a flavor she likes. It is impossible to imagine Damon weakened, frail, damaged—but he is.

Last night Damon was given another scan and the decision was made to keep him in his induced coma for only another day or two. "The swelling does seem to be subsiding. We will be able to make a decision soon about bringing him out of the coma," Dr. Sanchez told her.

"Will he recover? Is he going to be okay? When can he come home?" Marla had fired questions at Dr. Sanchez, the same questions she asked him on Wednesday night and Thursday and Friday.

And Dr. Sanchez answered the same way he had since she first met him on Wednesday night. "Time will tell; be patient. We are doing everything we can."

Marla doesn't think she can bear to hear those words again, feels the need to rid her mind of them with her endless consumption of rubbish food.

Her carefully curated life is in chaos.

She is dressed in a black tracksuit because it's comfortable and soft, but it's something she has never worn outside her home before.

Rushing to get here this morning after sleeping through her alarm, she noticed that one side of her car had been keyed. It must have happened in the parking lot of the hospital yesterday and she just didn't see it when she got into her car to drive home. She had stood looking at the gouge for a few seconds, unable to believe it, before she got in and drove to the hospital.

She only just got the car back from Rudy the mechanic as well. He had called her only twenty minutes after the police left her house on Friday in a panic. "Um, Mrs. Kennedy, the police are here. They're here at the workshop and they want to look over the car. They say that you agreed to them doing that?"

Marla had felt her throat tighten and she swallowed

quickly, squeezed her phone in her hand, saying, "It's fine, Rudy... It's just for Damon's accident... It's..." She couldn't explain. "Let them look at it," she said firmly. She had waited to hear from the detectives, is still waiting to hear from them. Rudy brought the car back when she came home from the hospital to eat some dinner, unable to abide the hospital food before going back that night.

He declared the knocking noise a mystery and returned the car with a shrug and sympathy over the accident. "Let me know if the noise comes back," he said as he handed over the keys, and Marla had assured him she would. The sound had completely disappeared, as though it was never there at all.

Whoever damaged her car did it on Friday night. For a moment she wonders whether it happened at home and hopes it did not, because home is her safe space. The idea of someone coming onto her property to damage her car is frightening. The idea that there are people who would want to hurt something that belongs to her...

It is a small thing, but she cannot shake her uneasiness over the damage. Is it someone who just hates that she has an expensive car? Is it someone from the press? Someone who knows her? Someone Damon slept with?

"People are such arseholes," Sean said when she told him about the damage over text, needing to tell someone. Her children will easily dismiss it as some sort of prank, but Marla feels like it means something more. With a shiver she remembers the damaged hedging outside the house. Could that mean something more too? The two things may not be connected at all. But are they?

Sean and Bianca are up there now, sitting with their father, the nurse having relented and allowed them both to be there at the same time. Sean drove his sister in, knowing that Marla would need to stay all day.

When they came on Friday, Bianca had burst into shrieking tears, and her distress had made the nurses aware she needed someone with her. Marla had imagined that Bianca would want her to be in the room when she saw her father again, but instead she had begged her older brother to sit with her. Marla understands. Sean is a quiet, calming presence.

Bianca seemed to be finding it easier this time. She was talking when Marla left the room, just chatting generally to her father, telling him about her day and the novel she is reading for her English class. Sean seems to find it as difficult to speak as she does. He touched his father's hand briefly when he arrived, but when she left, telling them she was going to get something sweet, he was staring out into the beautiful blue spring sky through the window of Damon's room.

Marla takes her chocolate and can of Coke and gets into the line to pay. It's long this morning and each person seems to be sagging under some kind of despair as they all stand silent and patiently wait their turn to pay. Marla knows her shoulders sag too as she stands under the weight of everything that has happened.

The woman in front of her in the line smells of incense and spice, and the smell reminds her of her visit to Athena's store.

She had gone to the store to let the woman know who she was dealing with, to warn her off, to hopefully get her to end her affair with Damon. But that hadn't happened. She understood the attraction when she saw Athena. The woman was not much younger than she was, but there was an ageless quality to her and also a sense of peace. Her beautiful golden curls and her bright blue eyes lent her an ethereal quality, and for a moment as she confronted her, Marla wanted to touch her smooth creamy skin. There were some faint lines on Athena's face and the flowered jumpsuit she had been wearing clung to her curves, emphasizing her small waist and generous breasts.

Marla had felt too thin, plastic and unsexy next to her, but she also knew that it wouldn't matter if Marla looked like Athena and Athena instead looked like her. Damon needed to be with other women to keep his ego fed, the monstrous ego that needed constant adoration and adulation.

Marla had never needed to look very far to see where Damon's compulsion to be feted by all who knew him came from. His mother, Marjorie, called him her golden boy. At every dinner Marla and Damon shared with his parents, Marla would end up speaking mostly to Walter, his father. Marjorie only had eyes for her son, only wanted to hear about his achievements, only wanted to listen to his voice. Damon thought all women should treat him the way his mother did, and women he was with for a short time usually obliged. Perhaps Athena really does adore him completely, perhaps that's the attraction, along with her beauty.

Marla has known for a long time that no matter what she looks like, no matter how often she gets Botox or goes to the hairdressers or buys new clothes, Damon is going to cheat on her, and she had accepted that. But she couldn't accept him falling in love with the woman he chose for his dalliances. She had always done everything she could to make sure that she was the one he came home to whatever happened, and with Athena, she could feel that possibility slipping away.

Marla knows that she should have left when she found out about Athena while looking through a credit card statement. She only looked at the statement for clues as to her husband's activities. Everything started with charges to florists for flowers Marla never received, underwear she was never gifted, restaurants she never ate at. She remembers sighing at the indication of the whole cycle beginning again.

Damon wasn't even trying to hide anything. He could have had a separate card. He had enough money and enough knowledge to hide the affairs if he wanted to, but he never did. He liked getting caught. That fact became clear after the first few times. He enjoyed her anger, her tears of frustration at his betrayal, the long emotional discussions that came, the repledging of his fidelity and the sex. He enjoyed the cycle. She dreaded it, and she knew it was in the same way that a woman being abused dreads the cycle of violence and yet finds herself hopelessly trapped by the love phase of things when her partner is sorry and making up for hurting her. It wasn't the same and yet... and yet it had its rhythms and she knew how it would play out. Damon even liked it when she found out and warned a woman off, liked her fighting for him. *I would just leave him,* she can hear a hundred, a thousand, a million women say, but she would like to ask, *Would you? Would you embrace poverty and loneliness over staying with him?* She still loved him, they still talked, still had great sex. He was everything she wanted in a husband except this, this one thing.

But Athena was different.

It was not the first time she had caught him out, but every other time she had been able to tell it was over. He came home earlier. He bought gifts for her. Damon was easily bored. This time things had gone on for a while and she had needed to see who it was, needed to see what this other woman was offering her husband that she could not, although she was well aware that his cheating had little to do with her. It's why she had managed to not take it personally for such a long time. She lived the life she had been raised to live and Damon had occasional dalliances and they stayed married.

She hadn't even needed to think too hard about how to find the new woman after she put two and two together. Some months previously Damon had come home with a scented candle and some tarot cards for Bianca. An unusual gift and not one that Bianca was impressed with, but she smiled and thanked her father even as Marla laughed. "What made you buy something like that?" she asked.

"Oh, it was a nice store and there was a lovely woman there who was helpful and I was just next door having lunch and wandered in afterward." Damon didn't wander in anywhere. If he shopped, he shopped with purpose. Marla had mentally filed the information away after looking at the sticker on the bottom of the candle that gave her the name of the store, Sacred Energies.

Marla could have walked into the store and accused the blond goddess of cheating with her husband only to be laughed at, and she was prepared for that, but when she told Athena who she was, she saw the woman's physical reaction of horror. She had found the mystery mistress.

It must be terrible to be confronted by your lover's wife and she had even managed some sympathy for Athena, but the woman had still not broken off the affair. And now they were here.

"That'll be six dollars, thanks, love," says the woman behind the counter to the customer in front of her and Marla realizes that she is next. She hands the chocolate to the woman so she can ring it up and taps her card. She doesn't want to go back to the room just yet, so she steps outside into the windy spring air.

Chewing up three blocks of the chocolate quickly, just for an extra treat, she watches other people going in and out, noting a woman in a coat that looks too heavy for the weather, looking around as if unsure about where to go. She looks at Marla and then quickly looks away. Marla puts another block of chocolate into her mouth and remembers thinking that Athena would back off after she went to see her, but she hadn't and the longer it went on the harder it became for Marla to confront Damon about his affair. Perhaps she would have just allowed it to go on forever, or until Damon asked for a divorce, but she did start putting things in place to give herself a bit of a financial buffer, moving money from their joint account into one owned solely by her—small amounts and not enough to really live on, but at least she felt like she was doing something.

It could have gone on forever and none of this would have happened if she had not met Sonya—Damon's therapist and just one more notch on his belt.

And suddenly it was all too much.

Her whole wasted life confronted her, images of everything she could have been if she hadn't believed in marriage as the ultimate achievement, and hanging on to that marriage as her only choice.

She could have ignored the direct message on her Instagram. Ignored it or simply deleted it because it could have been a troll, someone anonymous who hated seeing Marla's perfect Instagram life. But she hated not knowing. That was the difference between the Marla who had been married to Damon for only a few years when she found out about the first affair and the Marla who has been married to Damon for more than twenty years. The Marla of old was heartbroken and devastated, sure that she would have to begin her life again, until Damon assured her that the woman meant nothing, that it was a one-time thing, that he was just stressed about providing for his family because his company had yet to begin making serious money. Now her defensive wall was high and strong and it would not crumble under yet another betrayal by her husband.

But she was not as protected as she thought, and so, when Sonya contacted her, she responded and then there was a discussion that a therapist should never have about a patient. But it wasn't just a therapist discussing her patient. It was a scorned woman talking to the wife of the man she cheated with. And because it was through Instagram it felt safe and distant and almost anonymous. But it couldn't stay that way.

And that's when Marla began to plan how to stop all of it once and forever. She was done and her husband needed to know.

Realizing she has finished the chocolate bar, she swallows down the last square and turns to go back inside to resume her vigil next to the bed of a man she must now stay with until he dies or recovers. She's entirely unsure what she's actually hoping for.

TWENTY-ONE

SONYA

Saturday, 10:00 a.m.

In the garden, Sonya sinks her hands into the soil, feeling the rich earth crumble as she squeezes. Taking deep breaths, she tries to center herself, to simply be in the moment. Jasper is at Mika's house building a robot with Mika's dad—a project he and his best friend have been excitedly discussing for weeks. Jasper has a natural affinity for anything to do with technology, more so than the usual twelve-year-old. He repeatedly tells her that one day he will go into something to do with computers. She has no doubt that Jasper is right.

Taking the small pot of purple daisies from their plastic tub, she carefully adds them to her garden bed, admiring the color and looking forward to seeing them grow over the spring and the summer. Will Damon get to see the summer? Even in the spring warmth she shivers, regret and guilt stealing the peace she usually finds in the garden. Will the police be back to speak to her again? It's a terrifying thought. If they return, her life will change and perhaps that's what she deserves. Everything she was told not to do as a psychologist when she was training—she has done. Last night as she lay in bed, a siren in the distance had caused her heart to race as she wondered if it was the police and they were coming for her. A few deep breaths allowed her to identify the sound as an ambulance, but the worry floats around her all day. She pats the soil around the purple daisies, admiring the color.

Once she had contacted Marla, she had no choice but to keep talking to her. The lid on that particular Pandora's box could not be closed again. They only spoke through private messages on Instagram and later through text.

Sonya hadn't wanted to tell Marla who she was, but she had not counted on the woman's ability to track her through her Instagram, where her handle was just @letstalk.

How do you know him? Marla asked.

It doesn't matter, Sonya replied. A few minutes had passed and Sonya had seen a brief opening to leave the conversation, to just stop replying and let it be.

I see you're a therapist. Is he having therapy? Are you his therapist?

Sonya read the message, her heart racing. She wanted to lie, but the wine, the loneliness, Damon's behavior all stacked up against her desire to just walk away.

Yes.

Damon is having therapy? Bizarre. I've begged him to go with me for years. Why now?

I can't really tell you that.

Look, I have no idea why you've contacted me. What do you want?

I felt like you needed to know. . . Sonya had stopped typing. What was she doing? Was she mad? She could stop this right now. Her hand had hovered over the delete button, and she went to push it even as she could see that Marla was typing.

You've slept with him, haven't you? That's what you need me to know.

She could have backed out, said she'd made a mistake, said she was just worried about Damon. There were a million things she could have done, but instead she typed, *Yes.*

She's deleted everything now. It surprised her that Marla was so composed, so seemingly unaffected. All she really wanted was details of how and where and when.

Has he mentioned any other women? Marla asked after Sonya made her confession.

I can't really discuss that, Sonya had answered her.

Bit late to throw on your therapist's hat, Marla typed.

I can answer any questions about what I did, but I can't talk about anything else.

I know he cheats. I've known for years. I just want to know how many.

Again, I can't answer that. I'm sorry.

Fine, explain how it happened. Don't leave out the details. I can handle it.

Sonya had typed the dead battery story. She had been so intent on being as honest as she possibly could, as a way to soothe her own conscience, that she didn't realize until it was too late that she had slipped up.

Did you want to sleep with him from the moment you met him? Marla asked.

No, but I kind of knew it was coming, I guess. I'm so sorry. She couldn't quite believe she was having this conversation with the wife of the man she had slept with. It felt surreal as she lay in her bed and the bats screeched through the sky outside her window, searching for food.

Stop apologizing, Sonya. You cannot sorry this away.

But I am sorry.

So it was only once and that was it? There wasn't another time?

It had been well after midnight when Marla asked that question and Sonya was tired or she would have lied, but she was so eaten up with guilt that she didn't think through the next words she wrote.

Yes, just once, aside from the first time.

Sonya had hit send before she thought about it, and the message was immediately read. Did she mean to confess the first time? Did she want someone to know, even Damon's wife?

First time??????? Marla had replied, and Sonya had sighed as the clock moved past 2:00 a.m. and her eyes burned as she spilled a secret she had been holding on to for a long time.

The first time she met Damon Kennedy she had just been dumped by her long-term boyfriend, another psychologist who counseled families but had little desire for one of his own. All through their four-year relationship, Sonya felt that she and James were moving toward marriage and children, and he had agreed that they had a future together, until she started pushing for something concrete. Her biological clock was ticking and one night she gave him an ultimatum, telling him, "I want to have a child in the next year, so I need to know you're on board with that."

"I'm not," he said, shaking his head sadly. "I'm sorry."

Weeks of anger and despair had followed, but eventually, Sonya had picked herself up and started investigating sperm donation. The first time she visited a clinic to discuss the process, she emerged hopeful and excited about having a child alone, believing she could do it. She had taken herself out to a steakhouse to celebrate, wanting a steak and a glass of wine before she stopped drinking so she could prepare her body for pregnancy. She sat alone, comfortable with her singleness now that she had a way to move forward. She had caught Damon gazing across at her, more than once, from the other side of the restaurant, where he was having a business dinner. And then he sent over a glass of wine for her.

When the other people in his party left, he came over. Sonya was struck by his physical beauty and his wide smile, and he was so easy to talk to. She stayed longer than she meant to, her bruised ego reveling in the attention.

And then she let him take her to a hotel and the sex was amazing and he left, promising to call her the very next day, but he never did. It was only after three days of silence that she realized he had her number but she didn't have his. She didn't even have his surname, although she knew that he had a scar on his chest from an accident as a child and that he loved his coffee black and dark chocolate desserts. Sonya put the one-night stand behind her, determined to think of it as a last fling and to not allow it to hurt her—but it did hurt her. She felt rejected anew, not good enough for a second date, let alone as the choice for a wife and mother. She nursed her bruised ego for weeks, googled Damon A and Damon B—all through the alphabet— hoping to stumble on his surname, but she never found him. She even went back to the restaurant and asked for his information but was shamed by a waiter who looked at her like she was deranged.

And then he walked into her office and failed to even register who she was. It had only been one night, but it had felt real at the time.

It had felt very real six weeks later too, when she threw up after breakfast three days in a row and visited her doctor, fearful of an ulcer or something worse. She hadn't chosen a sperm donor yet, was still mulling over what kind of a man she wanted to have as a father for her child.

It was thirteen years ago. She didn't get to choose the father of her child. She didn't even get his last name, but she had a permanent reminder of their night together.

He had, however, moved on to another woman. Many, many other women.

Damon had not registered her shock the first time he walked into her office or her alarm as he talked through their first session, as she learned that she'd had a one-night stand with a married man and that pretty much everything he'd told her that night—like his need for new furniture in his apartment, "I've just never gotten around to furnishing it," or about how his friends kept telling him he needed to settle down or about how hard it was to date when you were working all the time—was a lie. Alongside the humiliation at how easily she was deceived and the hurt at how easily she was discarded, Sonya has some admiration for Damon's commitment to his falsehoods. At their first meeting he even told her he was thinking of taking a Vietnamese cookery course since that was his favorite food and he was tired of getting takeout all the time. "But it's hard just cooking for one, you know," he said. With a smile and a dextrous turn of phrase he said everything that would lure a single woman into his arms. He knew exactly what he was doing and she knows now that he has only improved on his early powers of deception. Damon has turned cheating into an art form.

Each time he walked into her office she made up her mind to tell him, to show him pictures of Jasper, to let him know that the child who had been raised by Lee, was loved by Lee and cared for by Lee, was not actually Lee's child. Lee knew the truth. They had met when she was four months pregnant and he believed what she'd told him, that it was a pregnancy from a planned sperm donation. Together she and Lee had agreed that there was never any need for Jasper to know that Lee was not his biological father.

It felt right at the time, but now she knows that she should never have kept things a secret from her son, who may never have the chance to meet his real father. His real father is lying unconscious in a hospital bed.

But she never found the courage to say the words. And then things were made worse by their tawdry encounter in the car. Because how could he not have recognized her then, even if he had never done so before? How could he touch her body and not feel a connection of some sort? His touch had burned her skin with its familiarity.

It should never have happened again. As a psychologist she should have pointed out to Damon that they had met before, had slept together before. He should have been referred to someone else. But wounded pride kept her treating him. "Can't you see me?" she'd wanted to yell on more than one occasion. The mistakes she'd made, the moral and ethical codes she had broken, stacked up higher and higher, a tower of wrongdoing that threatened to topple over and crush her.

A wounded animal will often attack even those trying to help. That's how Sonya has explained it to herself anyway. That's how she has explained the conversation with Marla.

Why have you told me this? Marla finally asked.

I felt you should know. It's not fair that you're treated this way. What she really meant, what she really wanted to say, was that it was not fair that she had been treated this way.

What do you want me to do with this information?

It's up to you, but please keep me out of it—whatever you do, just keep me out of it. When she typed those words, Sonya had begun to sober up as the night moved toward dawn and she began to realize exactly what she had done. She had handed a woman she didn't know a match to light a fire that could destroy her career. A woman whose husband she had slept with, knowing that he was still married.

I'll keep you out of it, Marla said, but Sonya knew enough about human nature to know that she couldn't trust the woman. They exchanged phone numbers anyway. *Wrong, wrong, wrong,* Sonya the therapist repeated in her head.

She wanted Damon confronted. She wanted him to pay for what he'd done.

And now she is paying for that and will probably pay for that desire for the rest of her life.

But there was no way out of this now. She had started this,

and that's why, when Marla called her a week ago and said she wanted to meet, she agreed.

People are not disposable and Damon treated women like they were.

Sonya was not disposable.

But she could never have imagined what her messages would lead to and then the events one meeting would set in motion. She could never have foreseen what has happened and however hard she tries, she cannot see a way out for herself.

TWENTY-TWO

ATHENA

Saturday, 10:00 a.m.

She is in the back office, placing orders for Christmas, scanning wholesalers for something new or different to add to her collection. The month and a half before Christmas is important for her store because it's when she makes at least thirty percent of her whole year's turnover, so she makes sure that she has a lot of choice for her customers. At the beginning of November, she and Gail will decorate the store in golden tinsel with fairy lights everywhere, and a large tree laden with ornaments will stand in the corner. It's her favorite time of the year, not only because it keeps her shop afloat, but also because everyone seems to have a dash of extra kindness in them.

She clicks on a collection of Christmas-themed tarot cards and scrolls through the images before ordering a carton.

The store is quiet right now after a morning rush, so Gail is able to be alone at the front. Athena left her sorting out Christmas lights, untangling them and checking the bulbs so they would be ready to hang when the time comes.

The end of the year is coming quickly, and Athena can't

help imagining what her first Christmas with her child will look like. The baby is due in March so will be reaching for shiny objects by next Christmas. She can see her father holding her dark-haired son, gently removing grasping fingers from the more delicate ornaments, and she sees herself in the kitchen putting the finishing touches on the trifle her father loves.

She cannot see Damon in the picture, no matter how hard she tries, and she doesn't know if that's because he will be with his own family or because he will be... gone.

How is it possible that one meeting with Marla has led to all this?

One week ago, a message came from Marla, the ping arriving on a slow afternoon. Athena had still been hoping that she would have the ultrasound to see her child for the first time with Damon by her side, still hoping that he would realize he loved her more than anything and wanted to be with her and her child, still existing on a steady diet of optimism—despite all evidence that she should get on with her life without Damon.

Glancing down at her phone, she had shivered at the words.

We need to meet. There's a café called the Wooden Spoon, about twenty minutes from your store. Meet me tomorrow at 1 p.m. You need to be there. Marla.

Don't go. Athena had heard her mother's voice in her head and she had felt her there like a physical force—but nothing would keep her away. What would the woman say? Perhaps she was going to tell Athena that she and Damon were divorcing?

The next day, when twelve-thirty came around, Athena's hands trembled as she brushed gloss across her lips. "Are you sure you'll be okay?" she asked Gail for the tenth time.

"I'm fine. Just go, go," her assistant said, waving her hands to shoo Athena away. Gail thought she was meeting with a midwife to see if she could have the baby at home.

The café was easy to spot, a giant wooden spoon on the awning. Athena took a moment in her car to ask the spirit of her mother for help and guidance and then she went inside, allowing herself a smile at the walls adorned with every kind and every color of spoon, from tiny silver teaspoons to chunky timber salad servers and enormous carved metal decorative pieces.

It was just after one, and she quickly spotted Marla, her profile obvious and her dead straight hair perfect. But Marla wasn't alone.

She had not expected the other woman, and her heart sank, fear running through her. The woman was a little older than Athena, obviously in her forties and wearing gray pants and a red sweater, her dark hair pulled away from her face and her pretty green eyes. Was it a friend? Athena did not want to have two women ganging up on her, and she had turned to leave when Marla called to her. "Athena," she said, and the words were not recognition that she was there but a command that she come over. Athena felt her body move to the table and sink into a chair.

"This," said Marla, "is Sonya, Damon's latest one-night stand. Well, for the second time." Marla looked at her, a slight upward tilt of her mouth made it seem as if Marla was actually enjoying this, and perhaps she was. Perhaps she had a right to.

"And I just found out, right this minute, that Sonya is mother to Damon's twelve-year-old son, Jasper," Marla added, saying the words slowly so that Athena heard them clearly. Marla's face shifted, her eyes shone a little, and Athena could see the agony behind the words.

Damon already had a child with a woman who wasn't his wife? Caleb was not the first child of an illicit relationship. Did he know about the child? Did he support him? Was that why he was so angry with her for keeping her baby? She wanted to touch her son but kept her hands away from her stomach.

Damon had another son from another affair. *How could you?* She silently raged at the man she loved.

"Sonya is just one of many, many women Damon has been with. He didn't even remember her from the first time he slept with her. Can you imagine that? He just went right ahead and slept with her a couple of months ago—again. You and Damon were together then, weren't you, Athena?"

Athena wanted to reach across the table and put her hands around Marla's throat. Instead, she rubbed at the charms on her bracelet, certain that she could actually feel evil emanating off Marla.

"I know you think you're the last one and that you're going to be the one to hold on to him, but you're not and you need to know that," Marla said.

Her expression was almost neutral again, but a smirk played around her lips and eyes. As if she was too excited to keep it in.

Damon liked to complain that Marla was cold, frigid—but not just sexually. "Sometimes I wonder if she's actually capable of loving anything except her Instagram profile," he once said. Looking at the wife of the man she was in love with, Athena wondered at what kind of a human being Marla was. She seemed entirely unaffected by a meeting with two women her husband had cheated with, her face a blank mask except for the slight smirk. She was someone who seemed made of steel, her forehead smooth and perfect, her clothes expensive and unwrinkled, her lipstick a slick slash of red. But perhaps she had to be that way. Perhaps that was what loving Damon Kennedy did to a woman, and Athena had felt anger at herself, at Marla, and at Damon burn through her body.

The other woman, Sonya, gazed at Athena with sympathy as she felt her stomach turn, and she put her hand to her mouth, afraid she would be sick.

"Oh my God," said Marla, "please don't tell me you're preg-

THE TRUTH ABOUT THE ACCIDENT

nant." She shook her head and then leaned back in her chair, folding her arms against the truth.

She had not wanted to reveal her pregnancy, had needed to protect her child and keep him secret. Damon didn't want her child. Had he wanted Sonya's child? Had he also promised Sonya the world and then left when he found out she was pregnant? Is this what he did? Was she just another one in a long line of brokenhearted women like Marla said?

But she couldn't deny the baby inside her. "I am," she said, trying to keep her voice steady.

Marla blinked, and Athena, even as she was dealing with the hideous revelation that Damon had cheated on her, saw that truth land on Marla like a hammer blow. Would this remove the smirk from her face. Would this final piece of news cause Marla to run from the café in despair? No. Part of Athena was surprised. But then, she had stayed sitting there in the café as well. All three of them did, trapped by their emotions and their history with Damon.

Dropping her head into her hands, Athena tries to push away the memory of that meeting and everything that came after it.

There is a tinkling of wind chimes outside her office, and Gail says, "Athena, can you come out here a minute?"

Athena stands up, notes that she has been in the back office for an hour and hating that time seems to be getting away from her these days. Damon has been in the hospital for four days and she has no idea how he is and she cannot stop thinking about how he got there.

She stands and walks to the door of the office, but as she goes to open it, her heart skips and she finds herself frozen on the spot. What if the police are back? What if they have some new information? She doesn't want to leave her office, but then Gail calls her again, saying, "I think it's the crystals you ordered and I'm just serving someone," allowing Athena to breathe deeply and open the door.

The conversation in the café keeps coming back to her as she signs a delivery docket and takes the collection of crystals in separate boxes to unpack.

"How far along?" Marla had demanded, sounding as though the words pained her to speak them.

"Eighteen weeks," she had whispered in reply, feeling her skin grow hot as she understood that anything she had hoped for from a meeting with Marla—the news that they were divorcing, perhaps, the news that Damon wanted her, Athena, all to himself—was out of the question.

"Well, you need to know," muttered Marla, and she uncrossed her arms, her mask firmly back in place as she began to speak, "you need to know who the father of that child is and you need to know what's going to happen now."

Marla began to explain why she had invited two of her husband's lovers to coffee. She spoke quickly, detailing what they needed to hear. She told them about the first time Damon cheated and the second and the third. She explained exactly how long his relationships with other women lasted and what he said about them after he was done. *She meant nothing. She wasn't worth anything. I barely even liked her. It was just sex. She was just a fling. She's not important. No one means more than you do.*

Athena had been with Damon for longer than the other women he had cheated with, but she knew herself to be part of the not important, nothing women in Damon's life. And that meant her baby was nothing to him. And that made her furious, anger turning to rage. Had Damon ever told her a single truth? Did he truly find her beautiful? Were the things she loved interesting? Did he actually enjoy her cooking? Was one thing, one single thing true?

She was surrounded by the quicksand of his lies, and she

THE TRUTH ABOUT THE ACCIDENT   163

knew that if she kept hoping, kept believing him, she would be pulled under.

As she listened, Athena realized that Marla was done pretending her life was fine.

And she was done being hurt by Damon.

The wife of her lover was only interested in one thing when it came to her husband. Revenge.

Revenge is a word that Athena always sees in red. It cannot be any other color. She picks up a red agate crystal from her desk, known for cleansing negative energy, and she takes a deep breath. Inside her, Caleb reminds her he is there with a series of fluttering kicks. She is not a person who seeks revenge, not a person who feels strong anger, and yet Damon has turned her into that kind of a woman. Everything he has said and done has led her to this, and logically she understands she should put him out of her mind and get on with her life, but logic cannot change how she feels.

He has broken her heart, and as she sat with Sonya and Marla at a small table in a café on an overcast afternoon, she knew that she was not the only one. And she knew that Marla and Sonya did not need to be named after the goddess of war, like her, to bring down hell upon the head of the man who had betrayed them. They only needed to have loved Damon for however long or short a time they did. Loved and been broken by Damon Kennedy.

But if he walked into her office right now and told her he loved her—she would struggle to tell him to go. If Marla didn't exist and Sonya didn't exist and Damon came to her, she would take him back, and she hates herself for that. Hates him for being the magnet he is, for changing her fundamental nature. Sometimes it seems that he is more than just a man, but he's not.

He is only a man. A man who now lay physically broken in a bed in a hospital. Which was perhaps exactly where he belonged.

TWENTY-THREE

On Sunday morning I wake at dawn and lie in bed and contemplate my future. If he recovers, will he return to me? If he dies, what will I do? If only Marla was not around, if only she would disappear. I smile at this thought. Could I make her disappear? What would it take?

Am I that kind of person? I didn't think I was, but you can become someone you don't recognize. I never thought I was the kind of person to have an affair with a married man until I met him. I never thought I could actively hate another person until I fell in love with him and wanted him in my life forever. Am I now the kind of person who can make someone disappear?

She is a mother and a daughter, but I cannot think of her that way. She's an obstacle, and because she exists I am alone.

Filled with energy and purpose but with no plan in mind, I get out of bed and into my car and drive to her house as the sun climbs higher in the sky. The street is quiet, but then her street is always quiet.

I have paper and pen in my car because you never know when you might need them, and I grab them and write a note to her, a note to let her know I will not give up, I will not let go, that *he should be mine. The paper is plain and white, and I take a vial of scent out of my handbag, something I carry with me all the time, and I spray the earthy spicy smell of patchouli toward the page. Let her think about that.*

I don't read it over. I don't think about what I have written. I slip it into her mailbox, and head back to my car, enjoying the sight of the broken earth where the bushes used to be. And then I drive home.

After coffee and an apple, I climb back into bed and sleep for another two hours, dreaming of a time when he is awake and healed and she is not there. Dreaming of a time when it is only me in his life.

I will return to the hospital tomorrow in my disguise as a visitor and I will carry a large bunch of flowers to further hide my face. This time I will get into his room and see him, if only for a moment, and if questioned, I can stumble through an apology. Who wouldn't believe a woman holding a bunch of flowers? There can be nothing threatening about such a person. Nothing at all.

TWENTY-FOUR

MARLA

Sunday, 10:00 a.m.

Damon has been taken away for another scan, the redheaded nurse wheeling him out with a small sympathetic smile for Marla. If there is not a huge improvement today, they will have to operate. His arm has been operated on and set and is now wrapped in bulky blue plaster.

"He will need a lot of physical therapy to regain the full use of his arm," the orthopedic surgeon told her yesterday afternoon. "He will need your help," she added just in case it wasn't clear to Marla how much her life was about to change.

Marla has already finished one bar of chocolate in the two hours she has been here this morning and she feels slightly sick. Bianca and Sean are coming this afternoon so she can go home and get some rest, and Marla is trying not to let her children know how much she detests being here. The smell of disinfectant and overcooked food clings to her clothes even when she leaves and she can smell it on herself as she gets into her car. Her car that now needs to be repaired so that the hideous scratch is removed. She will wait to get it fixed in case the police return and want to look at it again, a frightening thought that pinches at her every few hours as she sits beside her husband's hospital bed.

She dips into her bag and takes out a tiny vial of sample perfume, rubbing it on her wrists and lifting them to her nose so at least, for a moment, she smells only musk and flowers.

Each time she returns home she cannot wait to tear off her clothes and jump into the shower and wash away the hospital smell, letting scalding water hit her face as she tries to rinse away the image of her husband's bruised face. Some of the bruises are fading to yellow, but his face is still lost in puffiness and damage. Perhaps he will never look the same again.

When she replaces the vial in her bag, her hand touches the note she found in the mailbox this morning. The note that smells exactly like a store she has been into—exactly like that. It's a smell she hates.

She would never normally have checked for post on a Sunday morning, but as she was reversing, a triangle of white paper poking out of the box caught her eye and she realized that she hadn't checked the mailbox since Damon's accident.

She almost left it, almost, but then she stopped, got out of her car, and pulled everything out of the mailbox, throwing advertising catalogs for garden furniture and computers on her seat. There were a couple of cards from people at his work wishing Damon better, but most people have contacted her via email or Facebook. There are so many to reply to that it feels overwhelming and so Marla has just left it. There was nothing else of interest except for the note, written in neat black letters by someone with a steady hand.

You don't deserve what you have. You don't deserve him.

Marla had flipped the paper over, but it was just a single lined sheet of paper, torn from a notebook.

Shocking and simple. Was the note from Athena or Sonya? It smelled of Athena's store, but the words could have come from either of them.

Why would either of them have done this? Why now after everything that has happened?

They had an agreement, all three of them, and yet... she has no real idea who they are, what they both really wanted after they agreed to help her. It is possible she has grossly underestimated the two women her husband was sleeping with. Will whoever wrote the note go to the police? Marla shivers and brings her wrist to her nose, inhaling deeply to keep herself calm. She wonders if the note could be connected to her damaged car and the ripped-out hedging.

The meeting with two of her husband's lovers happened a week ago, and Marla can still see Athena's shocked face as she had registered that there was another woman sitting at the table in the café with her. Athena had turned to try to leave, but Marla couldn't allow that.

She had a plan and she needed the two latest women in Damon's life to help her make it a reality. It was a simple plan to force Damon to confront who he was and what he was doing. That's all she wanted, to force him to acknowledge it, to see what he had done. She found that making this plan, working through it in her head, allowed her to distance herself from the truth of how little her husband cared for her. If she gave in to that feeling, in to that knowledge, she believed she would curl up on the floor and be unable to move, unable to function. Her only hope was to keep planning, to maintain distance, to not feel—because feeling would surely kill her.

Marla could have just left him, asked for a divorce and started over, but she wanted to show him that she knew, wanted him to admit what he had done. Damon was a narcissist, and a person like that can bend the truth in their own minds, bend it so well that they can convince everyone including themselves that they are either innocent of what they are being accused of or that they are the sad victim in the whole situation. Marla knew that if she just told Damon about Athena and Sonya, he would declare them mad, would say that nothing had really happened, that they were lying and, when pushed, he would demote them both to one-night stands who had no value in his life.

Marla needed to put him in a position where he had to look directly at the women he was claiming to feel nothing for.

When Athena covered her mouth, when the shock of Marla's introduction to Sonya hit her, Marla knew the woman was pregnant. She just knew, and then it became even more important that her wayward husband be faced with the consequences of his actions. Her own two children crossed her mind as she wondered how she would protect them from 'a twelve-year-old half-brother and now another sibling on the way. Sonya had never shared the truth with Damon, but Sonya was a one-night stand. Athena was another story entirely.

"Does he know?" she had asked Athena, watching the woman nod slowly and then sniff and look up at the ceiling. Athena wouldn't want to cry in front of her and Sonya.

"I never told him and I don't want to," said Sonya. Sonya's hands were busy holding the ceramic saltshaker shaped like a large spoon, moving it from left to right, letting her fingers touch the grooves and slight chips. "Jasper is twelve." Her voice was matter-of-fact, as though the words had no power to hurt, but Marla knew they did. For a moment, the two women gazed at each other with understanding.

Marla thought about her own children, about what was at risk because her husband couldn't keep it in his pants. Both Jasper and Athena's child would be entitled to support and, one day, inheritance. She tried to imagine having to explain to Sean and Bianca about their father's other children and she could not bear to think of it. Sean would distance himself from his father, would be unable to view him as someone to be trusted, and Bianca would be devastated. All their lives, Marla has carefully kept the secret of their father's affairs to protect them, not wanting them to ever see what he did as a reflection on their family life. And to save herself the humiliation of her children knowing that she was not good enough to keep Damon at home, not interesting enough, not beautiful enough, not enough.

But she did not want to keep the secret any longer. Her children would suffer once they knew, but perhaps they were old enough to understand. A small part of her had felt a touch of malicious glee at the thought of Damon being forced to explain what he had done for years. Marla had no idea how it would all play out, who would be hurt, who would never recover, but she did know, as she stared at the two women in a coffee shop, that she was done being the only one who knew all the secrets. It was time for Damon to be confronted.

"We're three intelligent women," Marla said, "and yet we have allowed this. I have allowed him to remain my husband and. . ."

"Why?" Athena had asked, and it sounded like a genuine question. The woman wanted to know.

Marla looked at her for a moment. "I could ask you the same question," she said. "I came to your store. I told you the truth. Why didn't you leave him?"

Athena had shrugged, her hands busy chipping at her bright green nail polish. Marla had been tempted to tell her to stop as flakes of green landed on the tabletop.

"He thinks he's getting away with it," said Sonya. "He's almost proud of what he does, and we allow him to be because he's so. . ."

"Charming, beautiful, good in bed, magnetic, successful," listed Marla, and both women nodded.

"And when I do confront him—and I'm sure it's the same for you," said Marla, "he's always able to weasel out of it, always able to convince me that the other woman means nothing, that our marriage is sacred and special and the women he sleeps with are meaningless trifles." Marla had meant the words to hurt, liked that both women flushed to hear themselves spoken of as such. She was laying it on as thickly as she could, repeating herself so they understood that Damon had no loyalty to either of them. She needed their help and she needed them ready to hurt Damon for everything he had done.

"So why are we here?" asked Sonya. "Why have you invited the meaningless trifles to sit down with you?" Her words were edged in anger, laced with sarcasm, but Marla didn't care.

"I believe that maybe, maybe if the three of us confront him together, speak to him together so that he cannot deny or dismiss or lie about the other woman in any way, that will force him to confront what he's doing. We will force him to make a choice and then, perhaps, whoever he is left with will have him without the cheating and the lying. It won't be me, but maybe..." She left the sentence unfinished with only a glance at Athena. The woman had gone from pale and seeming to fight nausea to something altogether different. The longer Marla had spoken, the more she had revealed, the more closed off Athena's face seemed to become. Her blue eyes seemed darker and her shoulders drew back as she stopped picking at her nails. Marla could feel Athena's mounting fury at Damon, at her, at the situation.

"That's not going to happen," said Sonya. "And you know that. So why do you really want to confront him?"

Marla had sighed, picked up the plastic menu, and summoned the hovering waitress who was waiting for them to order something. "Can I get an espresso, please? And one of the chocolate biscotti."

"The same for me," said Sonya as the young waitress looked at her.

"I'll just have peppermint tea," said Athena, dropping her gaze to the table.

The waitress nodded and left.

"I want to record it," said Marla, keeping her voice light, not wanting to allow them to understand how vitally important this was for her to do. "I want to record it and use it to get what I need in a divorce."

The words had settled into the air, and silence had fallen as Sonya played with the saltshaker and Athena went back to work on the next polished nail on her hand, chipping away at the color. Marla could see each of the women's minds working as they wondered what Marla would indeed get. Damon was a rich man, a very rich man, and Marla wanted to make sure that after she left him, he was a great deal less rich. It wouldn't make up for what she had endured, not even a little bit, but that didn't matter. Having to give her a lot of his money would infuriate Damon, and that's what she wanted. If she was starting again, then she refused to allow money to be one of her problems.

The waitress arrived with their biscotti and coffee and tea, placing everything in front of them. Marla watched Athena's hands visibly shake as she lifted her cup and took a tiny sip of the tea. She looked like she was battling a storm inside her. Breaking her biscotti in two, she handed Athena a piece. "You should eat," she said and was gratified to watch the woman take a bite and nod her thanks.

It would not have surprised Marla if both women or at least one of them had gone running to Damon to warn him. But that hadn't happened. Things hadn't gone according to plan, of course, but neither of the women had told Damon what was happening. She should never have made both women party to her conversation in the car with Damon, but she had. That was where things had gotten a little off track. The confrontation was supposed to occur with all of them in the same place.

In her mind she had seen the three of them speaking to Damon together and even felt her phone, heavy in her pocket as it recorded the truth. She has no idea why she strayed from the plan made at that coffee shop, but she did.

And now they are here. Her imagined future—a life where she no longer had to worry about Damon's dalliances and still had the financial comfort she is used to—feels very far away now. Unless he dies, but Marla has a feeling that won't happen. It would be too easy, and nothing to do with Damon has ever been easy. Taking quick steps around the hospital room, she swings her arms and twists from left to right, loosening up her muscles. She knows that deep inside her, locked away somewhere, is the love, the true love she feels for Damon, that has kept her with him all these years, but she cannot get to it anymore. Nor does she want to.

The door to the hospital room swings open and Damon is wheeled back in. Marla resumes her place at the window. "The doctor will be here tomorrow morning to let you know what the scans say," the young nurse tells her.

"Thank you," says Marla, and she goes back to staring out of the window, not addressing her silent husband.

Who wrote the note? It must have been either Sonya or Athena, and whoever wrote it, whoever wrote the words laced with bitterness and jealousy, she was dangerous. And what would a person who felt like that be willing to do to prove that Marla did not deserve her husband? How far was either Athena or Sonya willing to go to kick Marla out of her own family picture? Would she tell the police the truth? That's very possible.

Marla stares down into the parking lot, where cars come and go as she experiences the physical sensation of being here in this room, in these clothes at this moment.

What if one of the women reveals a truth that could send her to prison? What if these days are her last days of freedom? What if?

TWENTY-FIVE
SONYA

Sunday, 2:00 p.m.

Sonya slumps onto the sofa and switches on the television, going first, as she has been doing for the last few days, to the news. There is nothing about Damon, which means he is still alive. Her phone is lying on the coffee table, and she finds herself picking it up and putting it down again every hour as she contemplates sending Marla or Athena a message but stops herself. Everything has been deleted now. Why put herself in a position where there is evidence of her contact with the other two women? Her position is so precarious. She cannot risk contact. She just wants this all to go away, to never have happened.

She switches channels, searching for something funny to watch, something that will at least allow her to laugh. She could call Jasper from upstairs, where he is gaming away his afternoon, but she cannot expect her son to cheer her up.

If she went out, she has no idea where she would go. The very air around her feels heavy with despair. Her thoughts race in circles and she has opened her phone onto Dr. Hillman's number more than once today, wishing she could just confess it all so that it was no longer sitting on her chest. But that's not going to happen unless she's willing to consign her career to the scrap heap and she's not.

The meeting in the café keeps coming back to her as she fantasizes that she made a different choice, that she told Marla "no" and got up and walked out. She would merely have been a spectator to the accident. Or it wouldn't have happened at all. Perhaps it would have been easier to walk away if she had not confessed that Jasper was Damon's son. That was something she was never going to share with the woman whose husband she'd slept with thirteen years ago. The first few minutes of their meeting had been beyond awkward. Sonya had spotted Marla quickly and gone to stand next to the table the woman was seated at. "Please sit," she said, as though Sonya needed permission. Placing her bag on her lap, Sonya had held on to the handle, needing something to do with her hands as she felt her cheeks flush. When a text came in on her phone, she had to look at it, and when she saw it was Jasper she said, "Oh, sorry, it's my son." Jasper wanted to know if he could get lunch from the canteen. After she had replied, Marla asked, "How old is he?" and without thinking Sonya told her the truth.

"That's a nice age. . ." Marla said politely, and then Sonya watched her brow furrow and her lips move slightly as though she was counting. "He's Damon's," she said eventually, her voice devoid of emotion. Not a question, just a statement. "He's Damon's."

Sonya wanted to lie, but the look on Marla's face told her she wouldn't believe a lie. "Yes," she said shortly, "but he doesn't know. My ex-husband, Lee, is his father. I don't want him to know."

"You said it was only one night the first time," said Marla, sounding like a journalist just checking the facts. Marla was obviously very good at hiding how she was feeling.

"It was. I assure you it was."

"Dumb luck then," sneered Marla, the first hint she felt anything.

Sonya took a deep breath. "I guess so."

"What's his name?"

"Jasper," breathed Sonya.

And then Marla looked away, at the door, where Athena had arrived.

When Athena was seated, Marla began speaking, and Sonya knew that there was no chance to walk away. The woman knew too much about her life.

Marla wanted to record Damon being confronted, wanted Sonya and Athena to be there when she did it so that he could not deny anything. Sonya knew as a therapist and as a human being that Marla's plan was wrong, but as a woman who had not even been good enough to be recognized by Damon Kennedy the second time he slept with her, she wanted to see him suffer and squirm. Athena's beauty was luminous, and between Marla and Athena, Sonya understood herself to be, as Marla said, "a mere trifle." Marla had a plastic beauty but she was so obviously Instagram perfection, and Athena was completely lovely, if clearly in love with Damon and terribly sad about the situation but changing her feelings even as Marla told her the truth about Damon. Sonya remembers wanting to touch her hand, to express solidarity, but it was not that kind of meeting. Perhaps the other two women had felt a touch of jealousy as they looked at each other and wondered which of them Damon loved best, but Sonya had felt her neck tense as she looked at Marla and Athena. She was nothing compared to them, even though she had been told often enough that she was beautiful. Marla and Athena were the girls who floated through high school being admired, who turned heads, and now still commanded attention. Perhaps Marla and Athena were looking at her and thinking the same thing, but she doubted it.

When Marla looked down at the menu, Sonya had watched how Athena looked at her. Sonya was busy comparing herself to the other two women, but Athena seemed to be feeling something else entirely. She had begun their meeting pale and despairing, but Sonya had caught a look of pure hatred directed at Marla and quickly looked away, not wanting to see what Athena's suffering was doing to her. She loved Damon, but perhaps she also hated him. She absolutely hated his wife, and Sonya was grateful that all she felt when it came to Damon was humiliation. But perhaps that was enough. Can you die of humiliation? Can you kill because of it?

That's why she agreed to the plan, even as she understood that she had nothing to gain from it. Perhaps if Damon was confronted and told about Jasper, he would want to meet their son, but she wasn't sure she actually even wanted that. Jasper had a father in his life. And Damon was no example of how to be a man.

Sighing, she clicks off the television as she acknowledges to herself that all she wanted was to see Damon in pain. And if his wife got herself a large amount of money in her divorce settlement because of that, Sonya didn't care.

Picking up her phone from the coffee table, she contemplates making a call to the detective in charge of the investigation into the accident. What would happen if she just called him and told him what had actually happened? Would she feel better? Was it even her place to try and explain the situation? Dropping her phone back onto the table, she sits forward, folding her arms across her body and looking down at the brown Ugg boots she is wearing.

She should never have agreed to Marla's plan.

She never wanted what actually happened, could never have planned for that. And now he may die. He may die and take everything that happened on Wednesday to his grave.

And perhaps that's the best-case scenario. The very best-case scenario.

TWENTY-SIX

ATHENA

Sunday, 5:00 p.m.

Athena sighs deeply as she shuts and locks the front door of the store. Gail has had to leave early for a family dinner, and so she spent the last hour alone, watching the clock and waiting for closing time. She is exhausted. It is not the pregnancy that is tiring her out but rather her turbulent mind where her thoughts are constantly racing and she can't seem to quiet it. Meditation and deep breathing have not helped at all.

Every time she thinks about the meeting at the café with Marla and Sonya, she wishes she could go back and erase everything that was said there. "You should know cheating is like a hobby for Damon" had been one phrases that keeps going around in her mind.

Marla's words were calculated to hurt, but they were also obviously true. At some point in the middle of a relationship with her, he had slept with Sonya. Marla wasn't enough. Athena wasn't enough. What would be enough for this man? Who would be enough for him?

Sleeping with a patient is surely against some sort of law,

and if Sonya were reported to the Psychology Board of Australia, she would probably lose her license to practice.

Athena has thought about doing that more than once. She has thought about how nice it would be if Sonya were punished and Marla simply disappeared. Her children are almost old enough to take care of themselves.

The fact that her mind has gone to these terrible places is an indication that she is no longer the same person she was.

Damon may not live for any of her questions to be answered anyway.

In her car she grabs a piece of paper and a pen she keeps handy and writes the words *Damon Kennedy is dead*, just so she can figure out how she feels about them.

How terrible would it be for her child to grow up without a father because his father doesn't want to see him, because his father didn't want him to exist? How much easier would it be if his father was not in his life because he was no longer alive? That's a sad story but one that would allow her to reconstruct the truth. She would tell her son that his father loved and wanted him, that he couldn't wait to meet him but died in a car accident. Easier to live with a dead parent than with the knowledge that a parent doesn't want you, doesn't care that you exist.

It's obvious to her which is the better option. Only the part of her that still loves Damon cannot let go, the grasping, desperate part of her that wants him back at all costs.

What would it take for Damon to be with her once this is all over, and what is she willing to do to make that happen?

Athena scrunches up the piece of paper and drops it on the floor.

"What should I do, Caleb?" she asks her unborn son as she starts her car. As she pulls away from the curb, a kick, the strongest she has felt so far, comes from inside her.

"All right, baby," she says, touching her stomach soothingly. "All right.

"Mummy will be the goddess of war for you."

TWENTY-SEVEN

MARLA

Monday, 12:30 p.m.

Every time the door to Damon's room swings open, Marla starts a little. She is waiting for Dr. Sanchez, who has been delayed with an emergency procedure. The scans Damon had yesterday will tell her how her life goes forward. If Damon needs an operation, he may not survive it, but if the swelling has finally gone down enough, it's good news because they will try to wake him up. But if he doesn't wake up. . .? Round and around Marla goes, trying to work out where she will be next week and next month, and who she will be.

There is little to do as she waits except think, and it occurs to her that while she had planned the meeting with Damon and his lovers so that she could confront him and get what she deserved in a divorce, she hadn't totally thought through what that would mean for her children. She had been operating from a place of anger and terrible hurt and she decided that the children were old enough to deal with what happened. She had protected them from their father's behavior for long enough.

But Bianca is in her final year of school, and Marla has

remembered a meeting with the whole year of parents and students sitting side by side as the school psychologist lectured them on how they could best get through the most important year of a student's life. "Don't make any big changes, try to keep everything consistent, understand that they will be moody and difficult sometimes, and be there for them," she had said as she touched her long braid and gazed out at the group listening to her.

If Damon recovers, can she just leave him? According to everyone she has spoken to in this hospital, if he does wake up, he will need months and months of rehab and help. She has tried to imagine Bianca's bewilderment at having her father living away from her or with another woman and trying to recover and it's an impossible picture.

The accident has changed Damon's life forever. Perhaps it is just a temporary derailment, but perhaps he will never be on the same track again. But the truth about the accident is that it has changed everyone's lives forever, not just Damon's. Everyone who loves or loved Damon, everyone who was there, everyone who shares some of the blame. They are all forever altered, and even though Marla would like to think that she could just wait to see if Damon wakes up and then pick up her bag and leave him to the care of others—she knows that's not going to happen.

When she was pregnant with Sean, she suffered debilitating nausea for months, and even though he was at the very beginning of his business and working all the time, Damon would call her every afternoon and ask her what food might tempt her to eat, what she might be able to keep down instead of throw up. And every day, no matter what she chose, he would get it for her.

It hasn't been all bad. The cheating has loomed over everything, but in between she has felt his love for her and their children. Moments of happiness have dominated her life regardless of what she's had to accept from Damon. It hasn't been all bad.

The door swings open again, and again her heart beats just a little faster, but it is not the doctor but the detectives in the suits with their nametags and their cell phones. Marla braces herself, clenches her fists. Do they know? Who has spoken to them? Sonya? Athena? They saw the car last Thursday. If they had found something then, surely they would have contacted her by now? This must be about something new, something they have just found out. Her shoulders drop as resignation weighs her down. They know.

"Is it okay if we come in?" asks Detective Rahim, polite and smiling as always.

Marla nods her assent and then she rubs her hand over her eyes. Taking a moment away from Detective Stevens's gazes. *Stay calm, stay calm. Wait to hear what they say.* She opens her mouth briefly, wondering if she should ask if she needs a lawyer before some tiny spark of self-preservation reminds her to stay quiet until she knows exactly what they are here to say.

Detective Stevens clears her throat and takes out her notebook, pages through it slowly as though looking for something, and for a second Marla believes the woman is going to read her her rights or something equally surreal. But finally, the detective stops on a page and Marla sees a slight flush creep over her face, and it is in that moment that she knows—that she realizes. She's won.

"We wanted to let you know that unfortunately we have not managed to identify the car that hit your husband," says the detective.

Marla hears the words and then she can only hear her heart pounding, the blood thumping in her ears as the detective continues speaking. Relief is warm through her body, and she sags slightly as the stress she has been living with seems to melt away.

"I'm sorry," she finally says, "can you explain it again?" She is standing leaning against the window of Damon's hospital room, actually pushed up against the window, and through the pale blue sweater she is wearing she can feel a chill coming from the glass. The temperature has dropped outside, spring taking a step back for today. Marla is uncomfortable but won't move. The cold against her back keeps her present, keeps her here so she can concentrate. She needs to be sure she's heard what she heard.

"It's not that we won't keep trying to find out what really happened," says Detective Rahim. "It's just that we have looked over all the cars we have been able to identify that were present at the intersection at the time and we can find no evidence of any of them having hit your husband." Marla hears the words *all the cars* and wonders who the police may have missed, whose car might not have been identified.

Neither of her husband's lovers has given her away; neither has communicated with the police. Or perhaps they have and they have simply not told Marla...

But the only thing they have to protect themselves is their silence. That is true for all three of them.

Detective Stevens is staring at her, and Marla realizes that some sort of reaction is required, some sort of indignation, so that her relief is concealed.

Marla lifts her chin a little, prepared to play her part. "I don't understand," she says. "You had cell phone footage and dashcam footage." The detectives seemed so confident last week that they would find the culprit, so sure they would be able to point the finger at someone, but now they are backing off, having failed to find anyone at all.

"Yes," agrees Detective Stevens, "but even though we have identified most of the cars at the intersection, we can't find out which one, if any, hit him. It may be that we have missed some.

The rain was very heavy and so some of the cars that were photographed were unidentifiable."

"Unidentifiable," repeats Marla, and she glances out the window and down into the parking lot where her car is parked.

"The point is, we cannot find the vehicle that hit him," says Detective Rahim. "I just wanted to ask one more time whether you have any idea why he would have run across a crowded intersection like that," and Marla knows that although he seems like he is just checking, what he is actually doing is trying to trip her up, trying, with his confession that they still are no closer to the truth, to relax her enough so that she will say something that incriminates her.

"I imagine the person who did this is living with some guilt," says Detective Stevens. "They may even be grateful if we find them." Marla meets the detective's piercing gaze.

"I'm sure I have no idea about that," she says.

Marla is someone who loves the hottest days of summer. She can't bear the cold and she really hates the rain, but today, right now, she could not be more grateful for the deluge last Wednesday that washed away any chance of the truth coming out. Sometimes the rain is a wonderful thing.

"So there's nothing you can add to what you've told us," says the detective, unable to stop a touch of irritation from creeping into her voice.

"As I said before," says Marla, "we went for a drive, and he asked to get out because he wanted to walk home. He was worried about one of his clients who had their whole system crash. I said he was crazy because it was starting to rain, and he still got out of the car. Walking helped him think. . ."

"Yes, you said, and that's what his colleagues have confirmed," snaps Detective Stevens so that Marla can stop her rehearsed explanation. "But perhaps there is something more you would like to tell us?"

"I can't think of anything else I would like to say to you," says Marla.

"We will keep looking into it," says Detective Rahim, "but for now we just wanted to wish him well. I hope he recovers." Marla nods her head and then drops her gaze to the floor. She is sick of looking at the detectives, of feeling slightly nauseous each time she sees them.

Behind them, the door to Damon's room swings open and Dr. Sanchez walks in with an unfamiliar smile on his face. Marla has only ever seen him look grave as he has prepared her for the worst.

"Good news," he says to Marla and then seems to notice the detectives. "Excuse me, can I have a moment with my patient?" he says, and the detectives nod and go to leave the room.

"If you happen to remember anything else..." begins Detective Stevens.

"Anything at all," adds Detective Rahim, "please get in touch. You have my card."

Marla nods.

The detectives leave, the door swinging closed behind them.

"The news?" asks Marla, her arms around herself. "Good news..." she repeats as though he may have forgotten and will inadvertently tell her bad news.

"The swelling on his brain has gone down, so we're not going to have to operate. We're going to start trying to bring him out of the coma tomorrow, and I have every hope for a full recovery." His smile is wide and confident.

Marla covers her mouth with her hand, an undignified choke-sob bursting from her lips.

"I know, it's an emotional time," says the doctor kindly. "It will be a long recovery, and he is lucky that he will have you by his side to help him."

Marla nods as she gives up trying not to cry. "Thank you," she says to the doctor through her tears, "thank you."

"I'll leave you with your husband," he says, "but I'll be back tomorrow morning to talk you through the next steps."

Marla struggles to control herself but, taking a deep breath, finally calms as the doctor leaves the room.

"Did you hear that, Damon?" she says, going over to the bed and holding his hand. "Did you hear that? You're going to be fine." And in the moment of joy, for herself, for her children, her walls come down, and the love she still feels for him despite everything comes pouring out. "You're going to be fine, sweetheart, just fine," she says as she cries. Dropping her head onto his hand, she feels his familiar skin, and something makes her believe that she and Damon can start again. They can do this properly, and one day she will look back on this time of struggle and trauma and be able to celebrate getting through it unscathed.

She hopes he can hear her. She hopes that he wakes up and they can go on with their lives.

She hopes that he doesn't remember one single thing about what happened last Wednesday.

TWENTY-EIGHT
SONYA

Monday, 1:00 p.m.

I need to speak to you. Please come to his hospital room at
6 p.m. Room 13. It will be the last time we talk.

Sonya stares at the words, calculates how long it will take her
to get to the hospital. What does Marla want? Why would she
request a meeting in a public place? Surely it cannot be good for
them to all be seen together? What if the police are watching
Damon's room?

She shakes her head. An image of the same two detectives
who came to her work to check her car appears as she imagines
them standing next to Marla, notepads open with a list of all the
things she will be charged with. Sleeping with a client will be
first on their list, and it only gets worse from there. Breaking privilege, meeting with the wife of a client, and then. . . Wednesday.
She doesn't want to go. She wants to run. But that will surely
seal her fate as guilty. She doesn't want to go, but she has to go.
There is no real choice.

She has to pick up Jasper from another day of code camp

at four-thirty. She will have to leave him alone for a bit, but she needs to do this. She wants it to be over now, wants to move on with her life and never to have to think about Damon Kennedy again. She checks the news site on her phone again, but there is no update on Damon or the accident, so he is still alive. This could be a trap, some kind of setup so that Marla gets Sonya to say something that may incriminate her.

Or perhaps it is just a last conversation, just final words between them so that they all have their stories straight.

Sonya sighs as she hears her next patient arrive outside her office door, hears Jessica greet Nina. She usually sees Nina on a Thursday, her appointment coming just before Damon's appointment used to be. But now Nina has changed her day and Damon will never return. Their slots remain empty on a Thursday until other patients fill them, and Sonya is dreading when they do. Her energy for helping people seems to have disappeared.

She is not enjoying her work anymore, and she is not achieving what she would like to with her patients. Perhaps it is time to step back, to step away and reevaluate. Maybe she should focus more on children, because at least there, she would not be dealing with ingrained behaviors that were impossible to change. At least then she would not go to sleep and wake up worrying about a call from the board of psychology.

Her intercom buzzes and Sonya gets up to open the door to Nina, and she smiles at the beautiful woman, ready for a difficult session but willing to help.

She has to wait another five hours before the meeting with Marla. What will the woman say? What will she have to tell her?

"How are you, Nina?" she asks as the woman sits down and she picks up her pad, determined to concentrate on her client.

"Well. . ." begins Nina, and Sonya cannot stop her eyes from straying to the clock on her wall, four hours and fifty-five minutes to go.

TWENTY-NINE

ATHENA

Monday, 1:00 p.m.

*I need to speak to you. Please come to his hospital room at
6 p.m. Room 13. It will be the last time we talk.*

Athena touches the words on the screen, wonders what they
mean, what will be said. She will go, of course she will go, and
anything she hears cannot be worse than what she heard on
Wednesday, the terrible rainy Wednesday that changed all their
lives. She has imagined a hundred different ways to get into his
room to see him and yet here is an invitation from his wife. Just
like that.

If he were dead, Marla would just say so, wouldn't she?
After telling them to delete everything, why is Marla contacting
them again? Should she go? Can she stand to hear what Marla
will say?

The wind chimes tinkle as the door to the store opens,
and like it has done every time since the visit from the police,
Athena feels her heart leap into her throat. But it's not the
police, just a customer who makes eagerly for the small collec-

tion of Halloween-themed tarot cards and decorations Athena has on display.

Halloween is at the end of the month, a holiday based on the idea that one day a year the souls of the dead return. People dress up in costumes to disguise themselves and ward off evil spirits.

Athena shivers a little as she thinks of this.

"I'll take these, thanks," says the woman, smiling at Athena as she hands her a delicate glass skeleton and a pumpkin carved out of orange stone. Athena smiles back, trying to remain present, to be here now and nowhere else.

She will go to the hospital tonight with clear quartz in her pocket for protection, citrine for allowing clear communication and boundary setting, and black tourmaline to help repel negative energy. Whatever Marla has to say, she will be prepared.

Maybe Marla is done with her husband and ready to leave him to others. Maybe she will have to accept that there is no fairy-tale ending for her and Damon. Maybe she won't accept that at all. She decides she will hope for the best because the worst has already happened.

What else could possibly go wrong?

THIRTY

All of Monday I think about seeing him, about finally seeing him, and I arrive at the hospital at the right time. The entrance to the hospital is buzzing, grandparents with big grins and exhausted-looking new fathers crossing paths with teary-eyed husbands and wives, coming to visit the ill and the dying. A woman in a wheelchair sits by the doors, oblivious to the early-evening spring wind as she puffs on a cigarette, desperate and quick.

I know, I feel, I understand that everything is about to change. I am nervous as I take the elevator up to the right floor, almost nauseous as I smell the familiar hospital smells, but I am here. I am ready to see him, to look at him and see the damage done by the accident.

Because I have made a decision about her, about "the wife."

She needs to go, and if I cannot make that happen at the hospital, I will make it happen somewhere else. After I have seen him, I will wait for her outside. I know what her car looks like, and I will wait until she comes out and then I will follow her.

I'm not sure how I will do it, but I might just bump her car at a traffic light, might just dent it a little so she has to stop and get out. *I will get out of my car too, and then I will be close enough to her. She won't be afraid at first, not at first. I will pick one of the quiet streets where few people will be late on a Monday night.*

And then, when I am close enough to touch her, I will explain. I will be polite and tell her that she needs to go away, to leave him to me. And if she won't listen, if she won't agree, then I can hardly be blamed for what happens next.

I pack a bag with what I might need. A poison for some, a miracle for others, but it will do what I need.

It may not come to that. Perhaps she will be happy to leave, happy to try a different kind of life, but perhaps not.

THIRTY-ONE

MARLA, SONYA, ATHENA

Monday, 6:00 p.m.

Sonya walks rapidly along the corridor of the hospital. It's dinnertime and there is movement everywhere. Nurses dispensing tablets and an orderly pushing a cart loaded with food trays, a boiled vegetable smell emanating from under plastic domes on each tray. She swallows hard and then she stops outside the room.

Should she go in? Should she text Marla? Are the police in there already? She turns to leave, indecision making her vacillate, and then she turns back to the door. *Screw it,* she thinks, and she knocks and then pushes it open.

The door swings open with a whispered rush of air, and she steps inside, letting it close behind her. The clattering noise of the corridor is drowned out, the smells disappear and are replaced with a crisp disinfectant smell overlaid with the flowery smell of perfume and something else. Something stale and over air-conditioned.

Marla is in the room, but she is not alone. Sonya opens her mouth to say something, and then she sees it's Athena who is standing in a corner, almost trying to hide herself behind a chair. Even though the woman's shoulders are rounded and her head down, her glorious curls and perfect skin make Sonya feel pale and bland by comparison.

"Oh," she says.

"Yes," says Athena, lifting her head as she watches Sonya's face pale a little, "that's about all anyone can say. I didn't think you would come here." She wanted to deal with Marla alone. Athena is aware that her voice is hard, her tone accusing. It's not the way she wants to feel or to act, but she cannot seem to help herself. She has tried to be the kind of person who always forgives others, sure that no one is actively trying to harm anyone else, but she knows that's not the truth now. And now she has her son to protect. Perhaps the mama bear version of Athena is an entirely different version of herself. She is more goddess of war and less angel now than she has ever been. It's just the way it is. She hadn't wanted to be here, but Marla summoned her and Athena felt this was the one thing, the last thing, she could do for the woman whose husband she had slept with. After this, she is done.

Marla is standing by Damon's bed, and Athena watches as the woman stands straighter, pulls her shoulders back as though readying herself for what is to come.

She sees Sonya glance at Damon and then look away again. Athena understands that she doesn't want to see the tubes, the bruises, the arm wrapped in plaster.

After one look, Athena cannot look at the man in the bed either. How can he be the same man who came to her apartment a couple of weeks ago? It doesn't even feel like he's in the room. He could be a complete stranger, but after everything she has learned about him, that's what he is now. She hates that, wants to change that. If she could just have him to herself, everything would be different, wouldn't it? The seesaw of her emotions is driving her mad, making her sick.

Marla watches her husband's lovers react to how he looks. She is used to it now, but she can see the shock of his appearance on their faces. Perhaps that will make it easier for them to accept what she has to say. There is silence in the room, only the slight hiss of the machine breathing for Damon and the beeping of his heart monitor in the air. Tomorrow, they will wean him off the drugs and then he will open his eyes and then he will eventually recover. Bianca and Sean's joy at the news made her cry. Delighted texts from friends and family have been coming in all day. Over and again, Marla has been reminded of her place in Damon's life, what their more than two decades together means for those around them.

Looking at the two other women in his life, she can't believe they have known each other for only such a short time. She feels she has lived a lifetime with these women, a lifetime she should never have had to experience. It is not a good idea to all be here together. But the detectives have left the building, and the nurses are too busy with the dinner run to concentrate on a couple more women walking through the corridors of the busy hospital. Sonya is wrapped up in a long black raincoat against the wind outside, and Athena is wearing one of her tie-dyed dresses, purple and pink swirls of color all over the material. There is no similarity between the three women in Damon's life right now except perhaps that they are all around the same age. And perhaps they are all beautiful in their own ways, Athena most of all. Marla wonders at his choices but immediately lets that thought go. It's time to move on from this, time to try and claw back some kind of a life for herself.

"I wanted to let you both know," she says softly, mindful that anyone at all could be walking past, "that the police told me they can't find the culprit."

She watches as Sonya's shoulders visibly drop, the woman's body loosening with relief, and then she looks at Athena, who has her mouth covered as though she may throw up, her blue eyes wide in her pale face.

"But they had video from phones and dashcams," protests Sonya. "Didn't they?"

"I know," Marla agrees, "but the rain and. . ." She waves her hand. "They've looked at all the cars that were there and they can't find the one that hit Damon. Did they come to you? Did they interview each of you?"

"Yes," says Sonya, and Athena nods her head as well.

"Well, they have no idea who hit him or what he was doing out on the road. I have told them we went for a drive and then he wanted to get out and walk. I did tell them that. They thought my car was at the intersection, but. . . it wasn't."

Sonya raises her eyebrows at Marla, who shrugs.

"So, that means. . ." says Athena.

"It means it's over," says Marla, "and I need for it to be over. I don't know how much he will remember, but hopefully he will have forgotten the argument we had." As she says the words, she realizes how big a roll of the dice this is, how much she is risking with this hope. He could wake up and remember everything and be angry with her anew. He could remember exactly how he came to be lying in this hospital bed and turn on her, but she's betting, hoping, praying that either he doesn't remember or that he is aware of how vulnerable he is now that he needs time to recover. When he wakes up, he will need her more than she needs him, and Damon is a pragmatic man. He will stay silent until he is stronger. "That's what I'm hoping anyway," she tells the two women, who are looking at her with a mixture of skepticism and relief. "He's going to take a long time to recover. He

needs his family around him to do that, so I asked you both here
to. . . I guess, plead with you both to disappear from his life."

"But that's. . ." Athena starts to say.

"I know," says Marla, "I know that you're pregnant and that
Sonya's son is also Damon's son. I know all this, but he's my
husband and I have to stand by him as he recovers. I have to
help him get back on his feet, and I'm hoping that after that—he
might be different."

Sonya sighs. She can hear the desperation in Marla's voice, her
need to put this all behind her and her hope of a future with
her husband and children where he simply comes home to them
every night. The angry, vengeful woman from the café is gone.
Then, Sonya had been able to see the years of hurt and humili-
ations in Marla's pale green eyes. But it is one thing to wish the
man you loved once gone and quite another to actually experience it.

Sonya doesn't think it's possible that Damon will become the
man Marla wants him to be. If Damon recovers fully, chances
are that it will not take long until he is back to his old ways, his
charm on full, his predatory eyes searching for another woman
to dazzle with his beauty. It doesn't matter to her. The man in
a coma who she has barely even looked at is a stranger and he
probably always was, even as he conceived a child with her. She
doesn't care if she never sees or hears from him or his family
again. "It's fine," she says, "I won't contact you again," and Marla
nods. There will be no calls to the board of psychology, no police
charging her with harming someone. She has a chance to walk
away from this, from all the terrible decisions she has made over
the last few months, and she's going to take it. Her son will never
get to meet his real father, but that seems a small price to pay.

. . .

"So I just have to raise my child alone?" asks Athena in a furious whisper as she feels her cheeks heat up and the war goddess rear her head. "I just have to pretend that he had nothing to do with him? How can you expect that?" She will not be pushed to the side like this. She may not get the fairy tale, but she will get something from this man after everything he has taken from her. "My son deserves to know his father, to meet his father and have him be part of his life." Inside Athena is a hissing fury that she is terrified will boil over and then all she will be able to do is scream and shout and then the whole hospital will arrive and the connection between the three women will be revealed. That cannot happen, and yet Athena cannot simply be told to go away.

"Athena, I think—" says Sonya.

"Don't you dare tell me what to think," says Athena, baring her teeth at Sonya, who abruptly closes her mouth.

Sonya thinks that she doesn't need to be here for this, even though as a therapist she should be able to help navigate this conversation. But she no longer has the energy to care about this situation. With some luck, with a lot of luck, she will be able to put this behind her. Unless Marla complains to the board of psychology or Damon does, this whole mess can just go away. It amazes her how close she came to losing everything that she loved. She could have lost her career, and if she had been stupid enough to tell Damon about Jasper, then Jasper would have lost Lee as a father and lost his trust in his mother. So much could have been damaged by one stupid moment in a car and by her unprofessional behavior, and yet it seems she is to remain unscathed. Gratitude and relief flow through her body.

"I'm going," she says. "I wish you well, Marla, and him too. I hope he recovers, and, Athena, good luck with the pregnancy. I hope it all goes smoothly." Her legs cannot move fast enough.

She doesn't wait, but opens the door and leaves quickly, wanting to be out of the sterile-smelling room, out of the artificial warmth as quickly as she can. She nearly bumps into a woman standing outside the room, who turns away quickly, and Sonya doesn't even stop, taking her steps faster and faster. When she gets to the elevator, she is forced to stop for a moment as she waits for it to come, and she turns slightly in the direction of Damon's room. Damon will also get away with his behavior, will go back home to a loving wife and family, who will help him recover. He will be forgiven for his sins—at least by Marla, who wants her family back intact—even though he shouldn't be. Marla should leave him now, just run, and so should Athena, and as a therapist, she should help both women realize that this man will not change for the better. She should go back and try to help.

She has to go back.

In the hospital room, Athena cannot help angry, frustrated tears from falling. "I want my son to know his father," she demands. It is so unfair that Marla has the right to decide. It is not what Damon would want. Athena is sure of that. And how will she survive financially? Gail cannot run the store alone, and Athena will need time to adjust to having a child. How is she going to manage without going to her father, who needs his savings for his retirement?

Marla feels a touch of sympathy for the woman, but it is instantly replaced by steely resolve. Athena knew Damon was married and kept sleeping with him anyway. She should have the decency to walk away now, to just walk away and leave her family in peace. She wants to yell at her but knows that will get her nowhere, so she tries to appeal to Athena's humanity. "Please try to understand that I want to live a different life. I know this is hard and unfair. Perhaps we can put an agreement in place, just the two of us. I will send you money every month to help raise the child. I want to forget this ever happened."

Inside her body, her son gifts her some of his fluttering kicks, and Athena places her hand over her belly. Now that money has been offered, she is humiliated. She feels used and cheap, easily bought off. Her silence and her absence from Damon's life are not things that can be bought. But why force him to acknowledge something he doesn't want to? Caleb kicks out again, and Athena's anger seeps from her pores.

She could fight this, now and into the future, but who will she be if she does? What kind of a person will she become? She slept with a married man. Whatever has happened and however she thinks about this—that is the fundamental truth. She could have walked away when Marla confronted her the first time and she didn't. Perhaps this punishment is deserved. Perhaps it is easier to agree, easier to walk away tonight and calm down before she does anything else.

"Fine," says Athena, knowing she has no power in this situation. What is she going to do? Demand to be part of his life, confront him at home while he recovers from a trauma, barge in when she has been told to stay away? She has no choice, and this makes her more furious than ever. Adrenaline thrums inside her, and she feels the fluttering kicks of her son reminding her of his presence again. "You go back to your big house in your lovely street and pretend that you are married to a good man." She pulls her hair back in frustration and wraps it around to keep it off her neck. She is hot and impatient and she needs the bathroom. But right now, she just wants to be out of here.

"A married man who you slept with," says Marla quietly.

Athena locks eyes with Marla, holds the woman's gaze for a moment, and then she leaves, walking quickly along the corridor to find a bathroom. She's going to throw up; she knows she is. She bumps into a woman just outside Damon's room and doesn't even stop to mutter her apologies, desperate for a bathroom. She makes it just in time and is grateful the bathroom is empty. She vomits her anger into the toilet as the unfairness of it all repeats in her head. When she is done and there is nothing left inside her, she washes her hands slowly, letting the chemical smell of the pink soap wash over her. She should go back and sort this out. He can't be allowed to get away with this. He shouldn't just get to pretend the last months didn't happen as his wife helps him recover.

Marla slumps into a chair by Damon's bedside. She has never been more exhausted than she is now, even after her labors to bring her children into the world. Damon will wake up, but she has no idea how he will be or who he will be. The worst-case scenario is that he is incapable of taking care of himself and she becomes carer forever to a man who cheated on her, a horrifying thought that immediately makes her feel guilty. She loves him, despite everything, and he is the father of her children.

She stares up at the white ceiling of the room and focuses on a small black smudge that could be anything. Will Athena and Sonya just disappear from her life now, from Damon's life? It's what she wants, what she hopes for. It is close to 7:00 p.m., and she is exhausted. Ivan wanted to come by and visit tonight but now he has a late meeting and will come in the morning instead. She can hear the murmurs of visitors and nurses outside the door and she longs to be out there, to be free of this room. There is a long road ahead of her, a long road ahead of Damon as well.

"Will you be a better man after this, Damon? Will you wake up and remember? Will you want to? Will you finally understand what it is to be part of a family? Will you love your wife enough to be the man I married?" she whispers.

Damon doesn't answer her, and she wonders if he will have

the answer to these questions when he wakes up, and if she will have the courage to ask them again.

It's time to go home and have a shower, have a rest, just *be* for a few hours. Leaning forward, she grabs her bag from the chair and takes out her phone. There are a lot of missed calls, a lot of messages, so many people to respond to, but now she just needs silence and air.

She leaves Damon's room, dodging people in the hallway chatting with each other. Visiting hours are nearly over, and soon the hospital will descend into its night-time quiet.

Walking through the hospital without even thinking about where she's going, she is amazed that it's only been a few days. She feels as though she has lived in this hospital for months.

In her car, she drops her head onto her steering wheel, and for a moment allows herself to hate Damon with a whole-body fury for what he has done to her life, to them, to their children. She clenches her fists and bares her teeth and hisses her hate where no one can hear her. She can't leave him. Not now. He went to see Sonya as a therapist first, before anything else. He didn't remember the woman at all. Maybe there was some part of Damon that wanted to change, that wanted to be a better man, and she can help him get there. Perhaps they could try couples' counseling. She still loves him. That's the terrible truth. She still does and he needs her. They need each other. Perhaps she should have told him that, whispered that.

Maybe I should go back, she thinks.

THIRTY-TWO

MARLA

Wednesday of the Accident, 9:00 a.m.

"I think I might work from home today," Damon tells her as he sips coffee and scrolls through his phone.

"You're the boss," she says, a flutter in her chest because sometimes the universe gives you a sign, and she knows this is it—this is the sign from the universe that it's time to put her plan into play. Damon offers her the hint of a smile before returning to his phone.

Marla pours her own cup of coffee and adds her almond milk, her hand reaching for the sweetener but stopping. She picks up a sugar packet instead, picks up two and watches the gold crystals of raw sugar trickle into her coffee as she wonders how many years it has been since she allowed herself sugar in her coffee, how many years since she has eaten something delicious and not felt instant guilt about what she had put in her mouth. Too many years to count.

As her silver teaspoon draws circles in her blue mug, her mind turns over the problem of her cheating husband, her lying cheating husband who fathered a child with one woman and has a baby on the way with another. The story is a comedy, something you see at the movies, but it is Marla's life and there is nothing funny about it. Placing the teaspoon in the dishwasher, she takes a sip of the coffee and savors its deliciousness. This is how she will drink her coffee forever, screw the calories.

"If you're going to be home today, can I ask you to go somewhere with me at eleven?" she says, not looking at him but down at her granite countertop where a few sugar crystals have fallen. Eleven a.m. will mean she has enough time to sort things out.

Damon looks up at her and frowns. "I'm going to be working, Marla. I don't have time for one of your ridiculous shopping trips. Buy a new sofa in whatever color you want." He stands, pushing his cup away from him, dismissing her, dismissing their life together, and she flinches at his tone and clenches her fists, feeling her perfectly painted pale pink nails dig into her palms, kept soft by expensive cream.

Keeping her voice even, she says, "I know about Athena." Her hands loosen as the words hang in the air and she touches a finger to a few dropped sugar crystals, pushing down so they stick and bringing the sweetness to her lips.

She doesn't want to look at him, a little afraid of what she will see. But eventually the silence compels her to look straight at her handsome husband, and she sees the bright red flush creeping up his cheeks from his traitorous heart.

"I don't. . ." he begins.

"If you want to have any chance of still being married by tonight, you'll come. It's only twenty minutes away. I'll meet you in the car."

"Where are we going?" he asks, belligerent at being cornered.

Marla shakes her head. "You don't get to ask that, Damon. You don't get to do anything today except exactly what I ask of you. This has gone on too long."

"Marla, listen. . ." he begins.

"I don't want to hear it," she says, raising a hand to stop him from speaking. "The children are asleep upstairs, and I don't want to hear it. We will talk in the car."

"I have an appointment at one p.m.," he snaps. "I can't cancel it."

She wants to laugh at his assumption that he can get out of this that easily. She doesn't even bother to ask him what he means or how important the appointment is. "This will all be over by one. You'll make your appointment."

And then she turns and leaves the kitchen, leaving him to stew while she locks the bedroom door so she can have peace to plan her next move. He may try to get in, maybe even knock, but he won't make a scene because a scene will wake the children, who are old enough to understand the horror of what their father has done to their mother and to them. He wouldn't want that. She locks the door to the bathroom, just in case, and then she stands under the hot water for a long, long time. Wrapping herself in a towel, she sits on her bed and sends a group text.

> *Wait for me to call you at 11 a.m. Don't say anything, just listen. He needs to confess everything. We will all meet at the café at eleven-thirty, at the Wooden Spoon, and he will have to lie to all of us together if he hasn't confessed in the car. He will not get away with this after today. I want you to hear what I say to him in the car. I will record his confession. And then whatever happens, we need never see each other again.*

Athena and Sonya both have jobs, and it may be that one or both of them will say they are unable to listen to a phone call at 11:00 a.m. and unable to get away for a meeting at the café at 11:30. But since their first meeting, it's like she can almost feel the tension in the air, emanating through the suburbs from each woman's home to her own. She knows they will want this done as much as she does.

The original plan had been for her to pick a day and for them all to meet at the coffee shop, but this morning she understood that Damon needed to be trapped somewhere with her so that he can't deny and walk away, can't throw the words *crazy, delusional, paranoid* into the air and leave.

It needed to be in a space with just the two of them and she needed witnesses, so that when it was time to go to court he could not explain anything away at all. The other women in his life would hear the phone call and the call would be recorded and then Marla would find herself a lawyer. The meeting at the end is just to see his face when he sees them, just to let him know that he is not as good at playing them all as he thinks he is. She is happy with the plan, eager to see it play out, looking forward to getting out of this situation.

At ten-forty-five, she climbs into her car and waits, rubbing sweaty hands up and down her perfectly pressed jeans. At ten-fifty she disables her Bluetooth so that the car won't connect to her phone, and at ten-fifty-one she makes a group call, her heart hammering in her chest as she waits to see if one or both of them will pick up.

"You're on speaker. Can you hear me?"

THIRTY-THREE

SONYA

Wednesday of the Accident, 10:51 a.m.

"Yes," says Sonya.

She wants to tell Marla this is a bad idea, wants to back out and leave Marla and Athena to do this alone, but she can't. She's in this now. Last night he called her, whispering into the phone that he needed to see her today. His desperation was obvious, and even though she said, "I don't work on Wednesdays," his pleading made her give in. Why did he need to see her so urgently? Did he have an inkling of what his wife had planned? It didn't seem possible, and yet she has an appointment with him for just after the organized confrontation. Coincidence or fate or just the universe playing tricks on them all?

Should she cancel the appointment? Should she leave it? He won't turn up, she's sure of it, not after realizing that she has been in contact with Marla.

Her conduct is grossly unprofessional, but Sonya the psychologist is not running the show when it comes to Damon

Kennedy; Sonya the woman is. She won't cancel the appointment because, right now, those two sides of her feel like two entirely different people.

And which one will be left running the show after today, Sonya has no idea.

THIRTY-FOUR

ATHENA

Wednesday of the Accident, 10:51 a.m.

"Yes," says Athena.

"Good," she hears. "I'm waiting for him to get into my car. I will start driving then. We should be on Williamsburg Road about fifteen minutes after we leave home. You can both follow me or you can meet me at the café."

Athena waits for Sonya to protest, to say she doesn't want to be involved, to speak up so Athena can also back out, but she hears Sonya say, "I'm getting into my car now—what do you drive?"

"A black Mercedes, a small SUV."

"I drive a gold Audi," says Sonya.

"I drive a light blue sedan," Athena says.

She picks up her bag, and holding her phone to her ear, she walks out of the store with a wave at Gail, who nods and carries on tidying a shelf of crystals.

As she gets to the street, rain begins, a light drizzle at first but ramping up quickly, forcing her to run to her car, the phone clutched in her hand.

She starts her car as she hears Marla say something to Damon.

And so it begins.

THIRTY-FIVE

MARLA

Wednesday of the Accident, 11:12 a.m.

Outside the garage, Marla hears the pitter-patter of rain hitting the roof. In no time at all, the rain is coming down heavily, the drumming on the roof keeping time with Marla's heart as she waits for Damon. Obviously, he wasn't going to be on time. Obviously, he was going to make her wait. She grabs her phone and carefully turns up the call volume so that nothing will be missed.

Finally, at eleven-ten, he climbs into the car. He has made her wait just so she knows that she doesn't have all the power. But he has no idea exactly how much power she has.

Marla offers her husband a quick smile and then she starts the car and, as the red numbers of the clock on her dashboard click over to 11:12 a.m., she begins to speak as she pulls out of the driveway heading for the café, where he will see all three of them together, where he will finally understand that the lies have to stop.

"For years, I have forgiven, explained away, and basically let you get away with what you've been doing. . ." she begins.

"Where are we going?" he snaps. He is dressed for a morning at home and he hasn't shaved, but he is still wearing cologne, and the scent fills the car, making Marla remember the first time he pulled her close, the first time he kissed her. She had fallen almost instantly in love. She blinks, pushing away those memories. It is memories like those that have kept her here, kept her accepting the way he has treated her.

"We're just driving," she replies.

"Look, Marla," he begins, slightly conciliatory, "just tell me what you think you know." She takes her eyes off the road for a moment and glances at him, seeing his contrite expression but also—a tiny hint of a smile. She returns her eyes to the road. "I feel like this whole thing can be sorted out," he says. "Everything has been difficult for the last few months, as you know. I've been struggling with the new regulations that have come in and getting every single system we've ever worked on upgraded and you have to understand how hard it has been for me. . . and now hackers have bypassed a government system and it's all on me—"

"Let me stop you there, Damon," she says, stopping at a yellow light, something that he hates since he always goes through them. "I think it would be better if you let me talk first." She doesn't want to allow him to keep talking because this is what he always does when they have an argument or she criticizes him. He turns it around so that eventually the conversation is not about the issue but rather about his work, about his feelings, about him. The work that paid for the beautiful house and the private school and her lifestyle. It always came back to that because he was supporting her and therefore his needs were paramount. Only lately has Marla realized that even if she made the money, Damon's needs would still be paramount.

"Okay," he sighs as she pulls off from the light, driving slowly and carefully as the rain intensifies.

Marla risks another quick glance at him. There is a light gray-black stubble across his square jaw and he is wearing the soft gray chambray shirt he likes to wear when he's home. He looks better now than he did the day they got married. He has settled into middle age and wealth with the ease of someone who had always expected to get there.

"Okay," she says, and she takes a deep breath as she hits a stretch of road that goes forever and will eventually lead them down to the beaches. She can handle going straight, and it's easier to say this without looking at him. The café is in this direction as well.

"In the last week I've been contacted by two women," she begins. No need to explain about meeting Athena months ago. Not yet.

"What?" he yells.

"Just listen," she says, raising her voice. "I met Sonya, your therapist."

"You what? That's unacceptable. . ." He blusters. "How did you know I had a therapist?"

"She contacted me, and you had better shut your mouth, Damon, and let me finish," shouts Marla.

In her peripheral vision she sees him hunch in his seat slightly and fold his arms.

"As I said, I met your therapist, Sonya. What you don't know, Damon, or at least what you're pretending not to know, is that she's a woman you slept with thirteen years ago. Thirteen years ago, when we were married. It was a one-night stand, and I remember the exact night it happened because the kids were sleeping at my mother's. We were supposed to have a romantic night, but you told me you had to work. Dinner with clients that you couldn't get out of or at least that's what you said. So, I had a girls' night out and you had your dinner but somehow ended up sleeping with a woman you met there."

"Listen—" he says, but she cuts him off.

Shaking her head, she switches lanes so she is not behind a large truck anymore. "I was worried about the kids that night.

They were only six and four and it was their first time sleeping over at my mum's and I wasn't sure how it would go. They had the best night ever and really the only person I should have been worried about was my husband, who was in someone else's bed."

"I didn't. . . I. . ." he says. She cannot stop herself from looking at him again. He is studying his hands, tapping his fingers on his legs as though he is counting, and then he looks up and his eyes widen. The puzzle pieces fit into place and he remembers. He didn't recognize Sonya, but now he does.

"And before you say anything else, you should know that I found Athena months ago. I know she's pregnant, and I have been waiting and waiting for you to say something, Damon, to tell me the truth, something—but you were never going to do that, were you?"

Marla concentrates on the road as she prays that her phone is recording, that the two other women are hearing this, that she has said things that cannot be disputed. The rain pounds the roof of her car, and her view is obscured by water.

Some part of her hopes for his usual confession, for his pleading with her to let it go, for his restating of how much he loves her and their children. It's a small part of her, but she knows it's there, and as she stops speaking so he can reply, she wonders if she will ever stop loving this traitorous man. And if she can't—what does that say about her?

Damon is silent for a minute and then he takes a breath.

THIRTY-SIX

SONYA

Wednesday of the Accident, 11:20 a.m.

Despite the rain outside, drumming against her windows, Sonya can hear the conversation through her phone perfectly. Marla's car is well-insulated, as is hers. When Marla finishes speaking and there is a beat of silence, she finds herself holding her breath, willing him to say something, anything that could redeem him as a human being. It is horrifying to hear herself spoken about as a one-night stand and she is relieved that Marla never mentioned Jasper. That is a small kindness from Marla and, even though Sonya has nothing in common with the woman who seems to live her life only on the surface, she knows that Marla has kept quiet about Jasper because she is a mother and so she knows the necessity of protecting a child. She will leave it up to Sonya to discuss her son. Marla as a mother is not something she has thought much about, and guilt is thick in her chest at what she has done to this woman, before she reminds herself that she had no idea he was married the first time. But the second time... Sonya focuses on the conversation. There will be time to berate herself later.

If Damon knew about the child and didn't want to meet him, Sonya would want to kill him, and if he did want to meet him, she would have to refuse. It's so complicated and awful, but whatever happens her son must be protected.

"How do you know I slept with someone that night?" asks Damon, and to Sonya, he sounds genuinely curious, like he wants to know what gave him away so he can avoid it in the future.

A thought flits through her mind, *Poor Marla. How terrible to be married to a man like this, to truly love a man like this.*

"She told me," says Marla. "And I smelled it on you when you came home. You'd had a shower and tried to disguise it, but you put your clothes in the laundry basket as though her scent would somehow not cling to your shirt. I remember the scent today: I could never forget the slightly sweet jasmine smell. It was everywhere. I knew, but I kept quiet because the children were so young and I had no idea what else to do, just like all the other times, and sometimes I wonder how many others there have been, others that you have concealed. What's horrifying, from the perspective of a woman, is that you slept with her and then put her out of your mind enough to hire her as a therapist over a decade later."

"Marla," he snaps, and Sonya can hear the anger in his voice, "I let you speak—now you need to let me speak. I never slept with that woman thirteen years ago. I have never slept with her at all. I didn't even know her until I hired her. She is obviously deeply troubled and obsessed with me, and the fact that you would let some lunatic accuse me of something like this and not stand up for me is deeply troubling. What kind of a person are you, Marla, to let your husband, the father of your children, be accused by a madwoman and not stand up for him?"

A car behind Sonya hoots, and she realizes that she has slowed down as she listens to his vile words. Everything that he told her about his moral conundrum over his wife and his mistress is a lie. He was just looking for a way to share what he had done and gotten away with, what he expected to continue to get away with. And after seeing her picture he was also probably seeking a different kind of conquest. It was probably just a game to him, just something to do with his time. Her windshield wipers ramp up in speed as the rain pelts down, and Sonya wishes she were not on the road, not following Marla's car.

"And what about Athena?" says Marla, almost too softly for Sonya to hear.

THIRTY-SEVEN

ATHENA

Wednesday of the Accident, 11:27 a.m.

"Let me tell you about Athena," hisses Damon, and she feels her palms sweaty on her steering wheel. She has to concentrate hard, both to hear, because of the noise the rain is making and to make sure her car stays on the road.

She cocks her head to the side, closer to her phone, when she hears her name. *Please, please,* she thinks because she wants to hear that he loves her. Even after everything he has done, she wants to hear him say the words, and then she thinks she may be able to forgive him. He can come and live with her, and they can raise Caleb together and she will embrace his children. She's seen pictures of them. Bianca could come and work in the shop with her when it's school vacations or something like that. She is so lost in her reverie that she almost misses what Damon says, but then they stop at an intersection where the traffic stretches for miles and Athena can see that the light will change a couple of times before they get through. Driving in such a rainstorm is always a fraught experience for her.

"Athena is also a liar. She says she's pregnant? Well, that's bloody fine. I don't think it's my child at all. She sits in that ridiculous hippie shop of hers all day long, batting her eyes at every man who comes through the door. She's a whore, Marla, and she seduced me. I accept that. I know I did that, but you have no idea what I've been going through at work and at home. Every day is stressful, and I come home to you and you are always unhappy about something, always buying something, and you have no interest in what I'm dealing with. You're selfish, Marla, so, yes, I turned to some little slut for comfort, but there is no way I'm the father of her bastard."

The traffic moves slowly forward and then stops again as the light turns red, but now Athena is at the front. She jams her foot hard on the brake and reaches down for the bag she has taken to carrying with her for when nausea strikes and retches into it. How can he be saying these terrible things? How can this be the same man who said he loved her? What has she done? She will have to raise this child all alone and he will always be denied by his father. A DNA test might prove paternity, but paternity doesn't make you a father. Her baby wouldn't have a father.

There is silence from Marla's car as though Marla and Damon are gathering themselves after what he has said and, as her nausea retreats, Athena looks up and sees that Sonya is next to her, looking at her right now, her green eyes wide with shock, and as Athena turns her head the other way, she sees Marla is on the other side of her. Both Marla and Damon are looking forward, although it's hard to see through the rain. Somehow they have all landed up right next to each other in the traffic, as though it was meant to be.

"And let me tell you," says Damon, his voice strong and sure, "you think you can ambush me like this and force me into this car so you can harangue me about some shit some crazy women have said and everything will be fine."

"Damon—" says Marla.

"No, you don't get to talk anymore. Shut up, Marla, just shut the hell up. You've made a big mistake here, and you're going to pay for it. I want a divorce and I promise you that I will leave you with nothing. Sean is over eighteen and Bianca can come and live with me. There will not be one cent of child support. You were stupid enough to let me borrow against the house to start the company, and when I did that, I transferred everything to my name and you signed your home away, too concerned with your Botox and your diet and with turning yourself into a piece of plastic to pay attention. I own everything, Marla, and you will be left with nothing. You and all those bitches. Screw you, I'm going."

Marla is stunned into silence as Damon opens his door. He owns everything? Was that even possible? It wasn't; she knew that. They had been married for more than two decades, had two children, and she had been with him before he made the money. It would all count and she would get her fair share, but she wanted to avoid having to fight for it. That's what she was trying to avoid with this conversation, with the confrontation that won't happen now. She wanted Damon to agree to them separating as painlessly as possible, but that's impossible now. She will have to fight to get everything she is owed and the process will stretch on for months and years and the people who will benefit the most will be the lawyers. How has she let this happen to her life?

Athena watches as the passenger door to Marla's car opens, despite the pouring rain, and Damon gets out, slamming the door behind him. His hair is instantly plastered to his skull, and then the light turns green and he runs around the front of Marla's car to try to get across the road. But Marla's car moves and it hits him and he moves sideways and stumbles, clutching his hip, but he is still on his feet.

And then he crosses in front of her car as the traffic starts to move and looks up, his jade-green eyes wide and frozen in his face as he recognizes her, and she doesn't even think. She just puts her foot on the accelerator, throwing his body sideways toward Sonya's car, not thinking, not caring. They can have him.

THIRTY-EIGHT
MARLA, SONYA, ATHENA

Wednesday of the Accident, 11:30 a.m.

Marla hears herself shriek as her car hits him. "Oh God," she says, and her foot hovers over the brake even though she is barely moving, but then she touches the accelerator instead and moves through the intersection. She doesn't care. She just wants to be away from here, wants to go home, wants to go to her home, where Rocky will be waiting and her children are sleeping.

"Screw you too," she thinks as she speeds up despite the rain.

Sonya watches his body bounce off Athena's car. Did she just hit him? Did she actually do that? It's hard to tell because all the traffic is moving, but he is suddenly in front of her car, and all the humiliation and anger she has felt over this man not recognizing her, over him treating her as something to screw and forget, over his callous disregard for everyone in his life but himself, rises inside her, and her foot slips off the brake and onto the accelerator. Other cars are hooting. She needs to move too. She feels the bump, sees him reel away to the curb, and she breathes deeply. It's not her problem. He was just her patient.

Athena's shock keeps her foot firmly down on the accelerator. The rain is a wall of water, but she will keep going. She will drive to the beach and watch the ocean in the storm. She will sit with her hands on her body and tell her son about how much she loves him. She will not turn around and she will not stop. She has the appointment to see her child later. Maybe he will come. Probably he won't.

Marla drives through the intersection, picking up more speed until she finds a place to turn right so she can turn around.

On the way back, it is almost impossible to see, her tears obscuring the rain-covered windshield. But she does see that the traffic at the intersection seems to have stopped again.

And as she gets closer to her turn-off, an ambulance screams past her.

She just wants to get home—for however long it is her home—that's where she wants to be.

THIRTY-NINE

I am clutching a large bunch of flowers, pink and white lilies and baby's breath mingled, as I walk into the hospital at five minutes to six on Monday night.

Six days ago, he was in an accident. Maybe it was an accident. Tonight, I will see him again. I have my wig and glasses on and I am holding the flowers up to my chest, trying to look like a benevolent visitor. I smile at everyone I pass.

I am someone visiting a loved one. He is my loved one. He is. And he needs to be all mine now.

I make my way to his room, making sure that no one is looking too hard at me, and then I stop outside and wait, looking down at my phone. I am waiting for the right moment, for the right time. Marla will leave his room and I will go in and tell him how much I love him. I will tell him that I plan to speak to Marla tonight, that I will let her know she needs to go away. Perhaps he will even open his eyes and look at me. Perhaps I will be the princess who wakes the beautiful prince from his sleep.

Nurses move back and forth, but suddenly I am alone in the corridor, outside his room. I push the door open slightly, wanting to check if she's in there. For a moment I think he may be alone, but then I hear Marla's voice and then I hear someone else and someone else again.

I am confused. Who are these other women? They don't sound like nurses. I bite down on my lip, clutching my flowers tightly even as I scan the corridor for nurses, and I listen to what is being said.

The are talking about the accident, about the police, about who is to blame. None of them? All of them? I will never know.

Each word that is said breaks my heart, cracking it open wider and wider until it is a chasm in my chest. There is the wife, the mistress, and the lover, and none of them is me. I thought I was the only one. I accepted the wife—even understood about the wife—but this cannot be borne; it cannot be tolerated. How could he have done this to me?

I feel I am floating, and the bunch of flowers drops to the ground. He was cheating on me. On me. All my beauty could not hold him, could not keep him. I am not beautiful enough for Damon Kennedy, even with my thick black hair and liquid brown eyes. Even with my perfect skin and full lips, even with everything in perfect symmetry—I am not enough.

I could still make Marla go away. I could still explain it to her so she leaves, but even if the wife disappears, there are others, and all at once I know that there always will be. The pain in my chest radiates out to fill my whole being. I bite down on my lip so that I do not scream my devastation into the air.

Marla explains to the other women that he will recover. Perhaps I can wait and see him again and maybe he would choose me. But he will never choose me forever. I cannot get rid of every woman in the world.

I cannot get rid of every woman in the world, and I realize now—that's what Damon wants. The adoration of every woman in the world.

My shoulders round as my body sags with defeat and despair.

He has betrayed me. He has made me into this person who contemplates terrible things, who does terrible things.

Suddenly there is a flurry of movement as the door opens. I step back, stepping on my flowers, and Sonya bumps into me, looks straight at me but doesn't see me. I am ugly and invisible and will remain so. She strides off down the corridor without a second glance.

The door opens a second time and the other woman, the one they called Athena, comes out, and she looks at me but runs off, making for the bathroom, her face pale with nausea. She is beautiful, ethereal, angelic. I can see why he would have chosen her, and now I know she carries his child. I want to call after her, but the words are stuck inside me.

The despair, the devastation, the heartbreak inside me blend together, become a churning mess and harden into fury. Heat rises into my face, my fists clench. This cannot be accepted.

I had a plan to make Marla disappear, but what is the point in that now?

I lean down and lift my flowers, crushed and limp now, into my arms.

I move away from the room, take a few steps down the corridor, glad that I wore my nurse's scrubs under the coat that is making me hot. I drape the coat across a wheelchair sitting in the hallway, placing my withered flowers on top, and I wait. I am a nurse now. I have authority to be here. Another nurse comes toward me and glances at me as I look down at my phone. She moves past me without a word.

I walk away and back up and down the corridor, occasionally darting into the bathroom for a moment when there are too many people around. I can do this all night. I can wait all night as my anger deepens into something hard and black.

I am coming out of the bathroom for the third time when the door to his room swings open. And finally, the wife, Marla, leaves.

With a quick look around the hallway, I move to his room.

The door swishes and I am inside, finally right next to him. In the bed, Damon Kennedy sleeps on, a tube still breathing for him as his body recovers. He will recover. He will wake and then he will one day get up and leave this bed and walk out into the world and possibly, probably, definitely go back to doing what he has always done—stepping over, stepping on the women who love him and the children he has created. A man should not have that much power. Perhaps his physical beauty will be slightly dimmed by his injuries. Perhaps his whole emotional core will change after his near-death experience. But perhaps not.

Perhaps this was always the way this was going to end.

I should have brought the lilies in with me. They are an appropriate flower for him now.

"Hello, Damon," I say.

And then I tell him why I am here.

FORTY

MARLA

Monday, 8:00 p.m.

Marla is in the bath, surrounded by lavender-scented bubbles, with a glass of wine at her side. She can feel the long road ahead of her, helping her husband get back on his feet, but for now she just wants to lie here, mindless, her brain soothed by the berry-flavored wine.

Athena will be a problem, she thinks. It can only be Athena who damaged the bushes outside her house and scratched her car and left her the note. What more will the woman do? Does she still love Damon despite everything he said and did? Marla does and doesn't love him. She is relieved and grateful he will survive. She knows everything he has done now, every terrible misdeed, and still, she will care for him, so she understands that Athena's love for him survives despite everything. But Damon is Marla's husband, and he will come home to her. Marla's life will change and not in a good way.

When her phone rings, she has no desire to answer it, but she picks it up anyway, her damp hand struggling frantically to swipe the screen when she sees it's the hospital.

"Yes," she answers finally.

Ten minutes later she is wrapped in a towel, sitting on the edge of the bath rehearsing what to say to her children.

But before she does that, she sends a text to two numbers, two women who will be inextricably linked with her and her children forever, even though their common link is no longer there.

He's gone.

FORTY-ONE

SONYA

Monday, 8:15 p.m.

When her phone pings, she ignores it, her hands in the sink, covered in soap as she scrapes at the burned sauce at the bottom of the pasta pot. She left it bubbling for too long.

"I guess it's pizza again," Jasper laughed when he saw the mess the tomato sauce had become, and Sonya nodded, experiencing a moment of pure joy for the wonderful child that he is. She had hugged him, holding on until he pulled away. "Don't be sad, Mum. It's just a sauce, and I feel like pizza anyway," he said.

"Me too." She laughed, and she had gone to her phone to place the order. As they sat together on the sofa eating, she had acknowledged that however terrible Damon was, whatever he had done—at least he had given her this child, this perfect child.

After five minutes she gives up on the pot, leaving it to soak in the sink, and she picks up her phone, reads the words from Marla, and then she pours herself a glass of wine and raises a toast to the universe. What is meant to be has happened.

She returns to the living room, where her son is watching television, and sits down next to him.

"What did I miss?" she asks him, thinking of everything she has missed in her life since she has been mired in the problem, the attraction, the charm, the feeling of Damon Kennedy.

"Well. . ." he begins, and she smiles as his words wash over her, determined to never miss anything again.

FORTY-TWO
ATHENA

Monday, 8:00 p.m.

She is deep in sleep, overwhelmed with hormones and grief for the life she thought she would have, taking refuge in nothingness until she can deal with it all, when her phone buzzes insistently on her bedside table. Even through the fog of sleep she makes a decision not to answer it. It won't be him. It will never be him again, and she doesn't want to hear from anyone else. Not now. Her body sinks deeper into sleep, her son twirling inside her as she dreams.

EPILOGUE

Sonya

The morning of the funeral dawns with the promise of a beautiful spring day. Outside her window, Sonya hears a couple of lorikeets, their sweet chirps sounding like a conversation. Sun streams through her partially open blind, catching a small glass orb on her dressing table and forming a rainbow on the hardwood floor of her bedroom.

Today will not be easy, but she needs to attend, to see Marla and Athena, to say her goodbyes and make her peace.

She can hear that Jasper is downstairs already eating breakfast; the tinny sound of something he is watching on his phone carries up the stairs. She has mentioned that she is going to a funeral for an old friend today, but she will never tell him anything more. School has begun again, so he has other things on his mind. He didn't even ask who it was. And now she will never, ever tell him.

Grabbing her phone from her bedside table, she scans the news headlines quickly. The story is not in today's news, and she has to google "Damon Kennedy death" to find it. The press found out two days after he died, and even then, interest was already waning. Perhaps the funeral today will renew interest, but Sonya doubts it. She has read the article more than once already, but she reads it again.

Forty-six-year-old director of Crisis IT, Damon Kennedy, has died from injuries sustained after being hit by a car eight days ago. Mr. Kennedy was initially thought to be recovering from his injuries, but six days ago he succumbed to a heart attack and died. His family have appealed for privacy at this time and asked that people donate to Heart Research in lieu of sending flowers. Police have been unable to identify the vehicle that hit Mr. Kennedy, but Detective Rahim of the serious crash unit stated that the case would remain open.

So, it was over. The case would remain open forever hopefully, and they could all move on. Something that would be hard for Damon's children with Marla, and perhaps hard for Marla as well. Damon should have survived. He was in good shape, and there had been no indication of a heart problem. But he had died. Sonya wants to feel something for his loss, but she is numb after everything that has happened, numb and desperate to get today over with. She and Marla and Athena will never see each other again after this. And that's fine.

Marla has told her that she will give her and Athena one hundred thousand dollars each from Damon's estate. She called two days ago and Sonya had answered, shocked to see the woman's number again.

"That's not necessary," said Sonya after Marla explained.

"It is," replied Marla. "It really is."

Sonya is not sure how Marla will handle the lawyers and probate and having to explain that she is giving away two hundred thousand dollars to two strangers, but Sonya has a feeling she'll find a way. Marla is perhaps the strongest of the three of them, used to pretending everything is just fine and tough enough to make that pretense work.

The money is a generous offer and one that both Sonya and Athena have accepted. Sonya supposes that she and Athena could fight in court for more. DNA tests would quickly prove the truth, but while she cannot speak for Athena, she has no desire for a fight. She will keep the money for Jasper's future. And if money is the only thing her son inherits from Damon, it's enough. Even with a degree in psychology she has no idea how the man became the narcissist he was. He had a childhood where everything he desired was given to him. Perhaps it was that coupled with his good looks that made him grow up to treat people like things that could be discarded.

"Mum, I'm going to school now," shouts Jasper from downstairs. It's unusual for her to still be in bed at this time, but Jasper is more than capable of getting himself out the door and down the road to school.

"Okay, got your lunch?" she calls.

"Yep, love you, bye," he says, and she starts to say it back but hears the front door slam as her son leaves.

He is more independent every day. Sonya has resolved to start dating again, to put herself out there in the hope of finding someone to share the rest of her life with.

It shames her to admit to herself that somewhere inside her, she carried a fantasy of Damon finally recognizing her and then leaving his wife for her. A ridiculous, silly fantasy. She will never admit such a thing to anyone and feels physically uncomfortable when she allows it to cross her mind. In bed now she shifts and sighs. All she has to do is get through today.

She is not glad that he's dead, but she can say for certain that she's not sorry either.

Athena

The funeral is being held at the graveside on a beautiful spring morning, the sky painted in ice blue. Athena stands quietly at the back of the large crowd, her hand on her belly, where little bubbles of movement comfort her with their energy. If anyone asks, she will say that he was an acquaintance who sometimes came into her store, but she doesn't think anyone will ask. There are a lot of people here, all murmuring quietly as the priest gets ready to speak. When someone Damon's age dies, there are always more people at the funeral. It's the shock, Athena supposes. There are groups of people standing together, the men looking a little uncomfortable in their suits because of the warmth in the air. Athena can see a group that look like work colleagues and another that seem to be catching up on each other's lives as light laughter sometimes carries across the graveyard. Old school or university friends probably. No one has even thrown her a second glance. She has tied her hair back in a low bun and is wearing the only black dress she owns. She feels unfamiliar to herself, as though the real Athena is not really here today. The real Athena is planning more Christmas stock and looking forward to spending time with her father. The real Athena is back, and the avenging goddess has retreated.

She will raise her child alone, but she's made peace with that. Her father had been delighted to learn that the baby is a boy. "I thought I missed my chance to be a grandad, and a boy, Caleb. How wonderful," he said.

"There's no father in the picture. I know I told you there was, but not anymore," she explained on the call.

"Ah well," he replied, philosophical as always, "all he will need is love, and the two of us have plenty of that to give."

She had fantasized about a meeting between Damon and her father, had seen them chatting over dinner. Taking a deep breath, she lets the fantasy go again. She will have to keep letting go every day and every hour until one day she will no longer think about Damon as anything except a sperm donor. That's her hope anyway.

The money that Marla has offered will help. Athena wanted to refuse, but when Marla called to make the offer, she said, "I know your pride will make you want to say no, but don't. Your son deserves something, and it's not that I'm trying to stop you from taking me to court, but I need to make this gesture, so please take it. A baby needs so much."

Athena has agreed to take the money, and there is no way she will go to court for more. All that negative energy would be too much for her to handle. She is thinking of a move to the Blue Mountains, where she will probably be able to afford a small house. Her store will work well in a town that is always filled with tourists. Gail will finish her course next year and thinks the Blue Mountains would be the perfect place to be. So far, Athena is only considering it, but the space and the peace appeal to her. It will be a lovely place to raise her child.

The priest begins speaking, but when he talks about Damon as a loving husband and father, she tunes out. After this she will take a walk by the beach and get some hot chips, something she's been craving lately.

Looking around the large group of people, she spots Sonya, severe in a straight black dress. Marla is standing right next to the gravesite, her two children by her side. She is wearing a slimline blue fitted dress, and she looks perfect, with her dead-straight blond hair and immaculate makeup. She has a tissue in her hand in case of tears, but it's not being used.

If Damon could see this, would he regret the things he has done, or would he look at all the people who have come to pay their respects and congratulate himself on a life well lived?

Athena just wants this to be over so she can walk by the sea and catch the salty smell of chips in the air.

A movement in the crowd behind Marla catches her eye,

and she stares at a woman she thinks she recognizes. She's about Athena's age with black hair pulled up into a tight high ponytail, her slim body encased in a wraparound silver-gray dress. Her beauty makes her a standout, and Athena focuses on her, wondering why she is so familiar. Has she seen her before?

"And so, we lay Damon Michael Kennedy to rest," says the priest, and Athena forgets about the woman and watches as the casket is lowered into the grave.

She shivers a little in the sunshine. Marla texted to say that Damon had a heart attack soon after their meeting on Monday night. She texted to let Athena know that it was all over, although Athena hadn't felt it was done until she read the news two days later and saw that the police are no closer to finding the car that hit Damon. There was a lot of rain. It could have been anyone at all.

Damon's son steps forward and drops a white rose into the grave and then he wipes his eyes and turns to hug his mother, holding tight. Marla will be comforted by her children, as will Sonya and Athena. Whatever this man took from them, at least he left them with his children.

"And that's enough," she whispers to her child as the bubbles come again. It's enough.

Marla

Marla walks away a little from the crowd and bows her head so that she will be granted a moment of peace. If you are not actively grieving, overwhelmed with sadness and despair, all that's left of the business of death is tedium. She doesn't want to hear one more person tell her how wonderful Damon was, and there is still the wake to get through, which promises to stretch on for hours.

Does she miss her husband? Perhaps, but perhaps she only misses the facade of her husband. Not who he really was.

When despair at his loss catches her, she reminds herself of the
man who appeared in the car on that road in the rain, the spit-
ting angry vicious man. Perhaps that's the real Damon and she
is better off without him.

The sun warms the back of her neck, and she takes a breath,
inhaling the scent of lilies, too sweet sometimes but fine out here
in the open with the scent of freshly cut grass as well.

She should be standing with her children, but they are
adults and able to handle things.

A sound behind her makes her turn, and she sees a beautiful woman coming toward her. In this context, for a moment she
doesn't recognize her and then suddenly she does. It is the nurse
who administers her Botox. It's Nina.

"I just wanted to tell you how sorry I am," says Nina.

"Thank you," says Marla, amazed that someone who knows
her only slightly would come to Damon's funeral. But then she
supposes it has become part of the news cycle. "It was kind
of you to come," she adds, hoping that will be the end of the
conversation.

Nina nods her head but she doesn't move, and Marla begins
to feel uncomfortable. She probably won't see Nina again. She
will give up the Botox, the dieting, the social circle she and
Damon have been part of for decades. She may even decide to
sell the house once Bianca is done with school. She would like
an apartment by the ocean, where she and Rocky could take
walks on the beach every day. Mostly she will try to find out
who she is now, who is behind Instagram Marla.

"Thanks again," she says as she pushes her shoulders back,
readying herself to return to the fray.

"I heard you, you know," says Nina.

"Heard me?" asks Marla, her heart pounding a little faster,
unsure where the conversation is going.

"I was outside the room when the three of you were talking,
you and Sonya and Athena. They're both here. I've seen them. I

was outside the door and I pushed it open a little, but then I heard voices and I waited. I heard what you said."

"I'm sorry, I don't..." says Marla, looking around, hoping for the attention of a family member or even the priest. What on earth is she talking about?

Nina steps closer to her, lowers her voice. "You know what I mean, Marla. If you think for a moment, you will know exactly what I'm talking about. I heard the three of you discuss the accident, and then you walked past me as you left the room."

"Oh," whispers Marla, unable to find any words, as the nurse standing outside the room returns, the nurse who she saw a few times when she was at the hospital. But that nurse had mousey brown hair and glasses...

Marla feels her stomach twist. Is this happening? Is Nina going to tell everyone the truth? Does she even have any proof—could they deny everything? In the sunshine she feels pools of sweat form under arms, and she hates the dress she is wearing with a vengeance. She would like to walk away, but she cannot go anywhere. Why was Nina there?

"Don't worry," says Nina, and she smiles, her beauty quite dazzling. "I knew what he was like. I mean I knew about his wife, but the other mistress and Sonya surprised me a little. I have no idea how he found the time for all of us and still ran his company." She shrugs. "But none of that concerns me. It wasn't our job to make sure he behaved in a moral and ethical way, and yet I am sure that we would be blamed. The truth is, he wasn't a good person. I met him three months ago, and he told me we would be together forever. But he lied to me, just like he lied to all of you. It's best he's gone, isn't it?"

The woman smiles again as Marla stares at her open mouthed. Where would Damon have even met Nina? Was it chance? Was it planned? How could there be yet another woman he was sleeping with?

And why was Nina at the hospital? Marla feels overwhelmed,

exhausted, detached. She could lose everything. She can't go through this again. She just can't.

"What did you. . . What will you do?" asks Marla.

"Nothing," says Nina. "I did nothing and I will do nothing. You did nothing and Sonya and Athena didn't do anything either. We are all just women Damon used and discarded and we are too weak to take our revenge. Isn't that the truth, Marla?" Her voice is low and menacing.

"What do you want?" She is as good as admitting that Nina is right, admitting to the conversation she heard. But it's too late now. Nina did hear, Nina may not have any proof of what really happened the day of the accident but she knows the truth, and Marla needs to know what she intends to do with that truth. Does she intend to keep it to herself, or does she have entirely different plans that involve the police?

"Nothing," says the woman. "I want nothing," and she turns and walks away.

Marla watches her as she pushes past the crowd and walks away across the green lawn, past the headstones and toward the gates of the cemetery. The damaged bushes outside her house, the scratch on her car, and the note telling her she didn't deserve Damon crowd into her mind. She thought it was Athena, but maybe it wasn't; maybe it was Nina. Nina who poisoned her face every few months and who is trained as a nurse.

Damon shouldn't have died. His heart was healthy and he was strong, so he shouldn't have died. But he did.

If she adds up all the *shouldn't haves* that her husband did anyway, the list would go on forever. It's only stopped now because he is gone. Marla keeps watching Nina as she moves through the cemetery, knowing that she will never return to the clinic, or any other cosmetic clinic for that matter.

Marla watches her until she disappears.

Nina

Naughty Nina, he called me, the words turning my stomach slightly even as I blushed and giggled.

We met by chance at the entrance to the building where Sonya has her office. I was coming in as he was going out, and he held the door for me, offered me his glorious smile. Sonya and I had already been working together for months as I tried to accept that despite everything I had to offer the world, I was still single and I had lost my chance to ever have a child. "You can do it alone," Sonya kept telling me, but I am not a woman of half measures. I am a woman of extremes, and if I was going to have my happy ending, I wanted it all or I would accept nothing. Still, I had the discussion with my therapist, even began to think about it. Would it be so bad to have a baby on my own?

"It's a lovely day, isn't it?" he said as I brushed past him to get into the building and caught the scent of honey and leather wrapped up in his aftershave.

"Yes," I agreed and smiled.

"You have a beautiful smile," he said, and I blushed because his physical beauty was so arresting, the combination of thick black curls and jade-green eyes, and a perfectly sculpted jaw.

"Thank you," I said, and I turned and went on my way to sit with my therapist and discuss how I could find peace and acceptance as a single, childless woman at the age of forty.

A cheetah will stalk its prey for seconds or hours, however long it needs to until it is close enough to pounce at speed. Damon only needed an hour because my session only lasted an hour. The building where Sonya works is small and only houses a physiotherapist, a chiropractor, Sonya's psychology practice, and a suite of GPs. Damon took a chance waiting for me, but it was not that great a chance. I wonder now how long he would have waited until he gave up.

He was there when I came out of my session, waiting just

outside the door to the building, standing in a pool of afternoon winter sunshine.

"Oh," I said as I came out, startled to see him there.

"I'm sorry," he said. "Please don't find this creepy and weird, but I couldn't . . . I just had to know . . . Shit, I'm really messing this up, but you're the most beautiful woman I've ever seen and I couldn't just leave and never see you again. It's weird, I know it's weird, but maybe we could go for a cup of coffee . . ." I can't remember the rest of what he said, but I do remember he mentioned that our meeting was fate, was a message from the universe. His physical beauty somehow made him seem more trustworthy. His obvious wealth meant I was flattered rather than freaked out. People are pathetic. If he had been old or ugly, dressed in cheap clothing and less sure of himself, I would have run and been afraid. I should have been afraid.

Of course I went for coffee. Of course I met him for dinner and I fell for his constant texts and lovely gifts and words of affirmation. He wanted to have a child with me. "We would make a beautiful baby," he said, telling me what I wanted to hear. He knew exactly what to say. Perhaps he told Sonya she was clever and Athena that he believed in astrology or that he wanted to learn about what she did. I've googled everyone now—I know everything about the other women who were in his life. Everything they allow out into the world and everything they are hoping to conceal forever.

I don't know exactly what he would have said to each of them, but I am sure that, at first, he said what they needed to hear.

I saw the accident on television after a day of missed texts and unanswered calls. Really, it's a wonder the man had the energy.

I thought I knew everything about him. I thought I would love him for the rest of my life.

I certainly knew more about him than he did about me.

As I walk away from the funeral, warmed by the spring sunshine, I reflect on the things that he did not know about me. He knew that I worked in a cosmetic clinic, poisoning into perfection the faces of those who could afford it. His wife is my client. She comes in every few months. I knew as soon as I googled him, and then of course I looked through her Instagram, where her pictures are perfection. I do good work. She will never know how close I came to adding just a little too much to her face when she came in after I started sleeping with her husband.

She will never know about the vial filled with Botox that I was going to force into her heart on the last Monday of Damon's life.

Damon knew what I did, even seemed interested in how it all happened, and mentioned his wife got it done often although he hated the way it made her look. "Too plastic," he said, "too unemotional."

I agreed without mentioning that I am partial to some help myself. I'm no longer twenty and holding on to beauty can become a kind of addiction.

What Damon didn't know was that in order to do what I do, I needed to be a nurse, and that I am a nurse who used to work in hospitals tending the sick for little money and less appreciation.

In the hospital, even as I swallowed the bile rising in my throat, the conversation ringing in my ears, I knew what I was going to do.

Air bubbles in an IV are not usually a problem, as they dissolve quickly enough, but when you inject a syringe full of air into an IV, that is a problem. And it's completely undetectable without an autopsy, and even then it would be very difficult to prove. And I knew no one was going to give Damon an autopsy. It was a wonder he survived the accident in the first place. He was very lucky, but luck, the kind of luck that lets you get away with the things he had been doing for years, has a tendency to run out.

I was in and out in seconds, and I didn't care what the result was, only that I had done something. Only that I hadn't let him get away with what he had done to me. I left his room with my heart in pieces, but I left with my dignity intact.

Lifting my eyes to the sun, I breathe in the rich, sweet smell of the grass and let Damon Kennedy go, and then I continue to my car and climb in, driving away. I will take myself for a late lunch, fill my body up with something delicious and healthy. I won't be able to let him go entirely, not entirely, but he will simply become someone I met in the past, someone of no significance other than his biological contribution. At the traffic light I briefly rest my hand on my flat stomach. Inside my womb, cells are rapidly dividing every day.

It's early days, very early days, but I think it will be a boy.

And I know he will be beautiful.

A LETTER FROM NICOLE

Hello,

I would like to thank you for taking the time to read *The Truth About the Accident*.

When I was writing this novel, the famous line "Oh what a tangled web we weave/When first we practice to deceive," written by Sir Walter Scott, kept coming to mind.

What a tangled web these three women wove, and even as they were planning and plotting, they had no idea that someone else was doing the same thing.

It's hard to have sympathy for Damon, who was given everything he ever wanted in life and instead of being grateful allowed it to make him a weak and shallow man, only concerned with his own gratification. But I hope you will feel some sympathy for Marla, Athena, and Sonya.

As Damon's wife, Marla is one person I felt terribly sorry for. She was raised to be an adjunct to a man instead of a person in her own right. The decision to leave was very difficult for Marla, especially when her children were young. She feared being on her own and making her way in the world without Damon's support. I'm sure she'll get her apartment by the sea and a new life.

Perhaps all three women deserve to be punished for the accident, but none of them had murderous intent. Only Nina had that and it's fair to say that her heart was broken as well.

I really enjoyed writing these women, and I wish them all

the best in the future—even Nina—as they all raise Damon's children.

As always, I will be so grateful if you leave a review for the novel.

I love hearing from my readers—you can get in touch on my Facebook page, through Twitter or Goodreads. I try to reply to each message I receive.

Thanks again for reading,

Nicole x

facebook.com/NicoleTrope
twitter.com/nicoletrope
instagram.com/nicoletropeauthor

ACKNOWLEDGMENTS

My first thank-you goes to Christina Demosthenous for bringing me into the Bookouture family. I would never have believed I could find an editor like you and you, will be very much missed. I wish you all the very best as you start your new adventure.

My next thank-you goes to my lovely new editor Ellen Gleeson, who has taken over from Christina and done such a wonderful job. I had no idea what to expect from the first edit we did together, but it has honestly been a joy, and I look forward to working with you on many more novels.

Thanks to Victoria Blunden for the first edit and for editing me for the last time with Bookouture. I wish you luck as you too begin a new adventure, and I hope our paths cross again one day.

I would also like to thank Jess Readett for all her work, enthusiasm, and patience in answering my emails and helping me with whatever I need.

Thanks to Ian Hodder for the copyedit and Liz Hatherell for the meticulous proofread.

Thanks to the whole team at Bookouture, including Jenny Geras, Peta Nightingale, Richard King, Alba Proko, Ruth Tross, and everyone else involved in producing my audiobooks and selling rights. A big thank you to Kirsiah Depp for her help with the paperback edit for Grand Central. I would also like to thank Lauren Sum, Leena Oropez, Liz Connor, and Tareth Mitch for their work on this version of the novel. It's lovely to see it going into stores.

Thanks to my mother, Hilary, who is always ready for a new novel.

Thanks also to David, Mikhayla, Isabella, and Jacob and Jax.

And once again thank you to those who read, review, and blog about my work and contact me on Facebook or Twitter to let me know you loved the book. I love hearing your stories and reasons why you have connected with a novel.

Every review is appreciated, and I do read them all.